GUARDED SECRETS

Payback Mountain– Book Four

Diane Benefiel

PRAISE FOR USA TODAY BESTSELLING AUTHOR DIANE BENEFIEL

Solitary Man

NATIONAL READERS' CHOICE AWARD WINNING NOVEL

"I am in love with this story. I devoured this book and didn't want it to end. The chemistry between the characters and the plot kept me wanting to read late into the night. This is my first read from Diane Benefiel but definitely not my last. I can't wait to read more from this amazing author. Thank you Diane Benefiel for getting me hooked on your books!" ~ CJ's Book Corner

PAYBACK MOUNTAIN SERIES

Dangerous Secrets
"I couldn't resist this compelling tale of a wrongly convicted man and the woman who never stopped loving him." ~ Sue's Reviews

Honest Secrets
"I really enjoyed this book and the chemistry between Emory and Shane is phenomenal. Would love to see more of these books, to bring the other couples in Sister's together." ~Kathy Bateman

Secret Lies
"The book was excellent. Just the right amount of suspense and angst between the two characters. I loved the book and while it was the first time I've read this author, I am now sold on her books. I'll read all of her books." ~PR

THE JAMESONS U.S. MARSHALS SERIES

Hidden Betrayal

"An exciting, romantic read with a sexy hero and a determined heroine who is hell-bent on doing things her own way. The romance heats up as the plot thickens. Linc and Mikayla need to work together to survive, but along the way, the sparks start flying. You need to read this!" ~danube eichinger

Hidden Judgment

"Don't buy this book if you want to get anything done!! I couldn't put it down! I laughed, I cried, I felt all the emotions that a brilliantly written romance novel brings. I am anxiously awaiting the third novel in the series!" ~Sandy Morris

Hidden Loyalty

"5 EXPLOSIVE STARS!! This book was explosive and had me flipping pages. I love law enforcement and this one was perfect... Seth was hot and bossy, Bella kept him on his toes. This was my first book by this author and it will not be my last." ~Rhonda

HIGH SIERRAS SERIES

Flash Point

"Diane Benefiel takes us on a story filled with mystery, suspense, and action as we try to solve what is going on in the small town of Hangman's Loss. Flash Point is a story that will have you flipping the pages and wondering who is the behind the attacks against Hangman's newest resident and why." ~ Sarah Reads

Dead Giveaway

*"I loved this second book in the High Sierras series. This is a story of two people who are attracted to each other, but reconnecting under the worst of circumstances. I discovered Ms. Benefiel's books and have loved the careful way she draws you in to the story with characters that make you feel as if you are reading about friends. I am really looking forward to the next High Sierras book, **Already Gone**."* ~paytonpuppy

Already Gone

"This series has only gotten better and better! Seriously, there's something that really speaks to my heart about Maddy and Logan, and Hangman's Loss FEELS like a small California town tucked away in the Sierras. They're such a power couple! I read this book in just a couple of days--totally sucked me in. It's that perfect blend of fun, sizzle, and suspense! I just want to live in Maddy's life forever but since I can't--I can't wait for the next book!"
~Katharine Montgomery

Burnover in Rescued Anthology

"Sweet, Sexy stories featuring furbabies and helping to save lives, it's a win win for all." ~Kara's Books

Deadly Purpose

"This book took me by surprise. I didn't expect to get so caught up in this book that my whole day was spent captured in its pages. It has been a long time since I couldn't put a book down but Deadly Purpose did this to me. I loved every page." ~WildfireJane

Clear Intent

"I'd been waiting on this one awhile!! I truly loved the story! I laughed, cried and got so frustrated I couldn't see straight! I'm now hoping there will be more from Hangman's Loss, I don't want to see this series end! Thank you for a very wonderful getaway!! I highly

recommend this complete series!!!! Wow! Just Wow!!" ~Linda
Helms

Break Away

"Oh man did I love this book. It was well written and has a great storyline. It's emotional and has a nice amount of suspense. I really need to go back and read the first six books in the series. Now saying that, this book definitely reads as a standalone. I haven't read the first six books, but I never felt lost or like I am missing anything with this story. You will obviously have some small spoilers since the books are all connected. ~CrazyBookLover

www.BOROUGHSPUBLISHINGGROUP.com

PUBLISHER'S NOTE: This is a work of fiction. Names, characters, places and incidents either are the product of the author's imagination or are used fictitiously. Any resemblance to actual events, locales, business establishments or persons, living or dead, is coincidental. Boroughs Publishing Group does not have any control over and does not assume responsibility for author or third-party websites, blogs or critiques or their content.

GUARDED SECRETS
Copyright © 2024 Diane Benefiel

ISBN 978-1-957295-74-9

GUARDED SECRETS

8

CHAPTER ONE

Keeley steered through the curve in the mountain road. The low western sky reflected in her side mirrors showed sullen clouds against the faintest lavender remnants of the sunset. Spring had made a tantalizing showing earlier in the month, only to be followed by snow last weekend. And more was predicted by morning. She was plenty tired of winter.

The big curve up ahead led to a straightaway where the road became steep before going through a series of switchbacks, and then another straightaway that went into Sisters, the cutest of all the historic gold mining towns in the Sierra Nevada mountains of California.

Okay, she might be a little biased, but she loved her hometown, and it was, hands down, the best place to raise a family in California. Which she'd been thinking about a lot lately.

Turning thirty had been no big deal, but thirty-two? Definitely a big deal. A disastrous relationship after college had made her wary of trusting anyone with her heart. But she needed to get past that. She wanted a husband and kids, and the mental image of her ovaries shriveling with every passing year wasn't helping.

With the window cracked open to enjoy the piney mountain air, and the heater cranked because it was *cold* out there, like a true Swiftie, she sang along with Taylor about unrequited love, steering through the next curve, and then onto the straightaway.

Click, click, click. Uh-oh. Not a good sound.

The rapid metallic clicking continued and she sat up straight, tightening her fingers on the steering wheel. She muted the music and listened intently. Lifting her foot off the accelerator slowed the clicking as the car decelerated. The steering wheel gave a weird shudder and the tire pressure warning light flashed on like the dark omen of doom it was.

"Oh, good lord." Nothing obliterated a good mood like car trouble.

Maybe it was nothing. Or if it was something, maybe it wasn't serious enough that she couldn't make it home. She'd take it nice and slow and get the tires checked first thing in the morning. The delusional thinking lasted about fifteen seconds before the clicking morphed into a squishy sound that could only mean a flat tire.

Damn it. Weren't new tires on her summer to-do list? The current set weren't in bad shape, they still had tread, but they needed replacing. She'd kept up on the maintenance and had checked the tire pressures only a week ago.

Despite comments from a certain cranky bar owner who said she shouldn't be commuting down the mountain in her "tin can," Keeley was a responsible car owner.

Owen Hardesty had a way of getting her back up as no one else could, and she'd defended her "tin can."

With good maintenance, a Honda CRV could run for a couple hundred thousand miles. Thank goodness because hers was nearing the two-hundred-thousand milestone.

Faithfully, she'd followed the monthly maintenance checklist her dad had made for her when she'd first moved away from home. But she had the unhappy feeling the clicking sound meant she'd picked up a nail, and it had punctured a tire.

No amount of maintenance could prevent a nail puncture.

Resigned, she pulled to the side of the road along a stretch that in the spring would be a wide meadow bursting with wildflowers, but currently held the snowy remnants of the storm that had swept through the previous weekend.

Mountain spring was different from calendar spring. It was a time of year that teased with hints of warmth and color, only to dump six inches of slushy snow to remind you that Mother Nature could do whatever the hell she wanted.

The dirt shoulder was wide with plenty of room so she should be safe.

Putting on her hazards, Keeley got out of her car, sighing fatalistically when her cute suede Uggs sank into the mud. The dark seemed to be closing in, the clouds from the west swallowing the stars.

Vehicles sped by, headlights lighting up the road in front of them. Using the light from her cell phone, she found the front tire on the passenger side with rubber pooled like a pancake beneath the rim. "Terrific."

First things first, she needed to call for roadside service. Back in the car, she tapped the screen of her phone and uttered a low groan. No service. A fact of life living in the mountains: cell service was spotty. But darn, she wished she could call for help.

Leaning back onto the headrest, she closed her eyes and thought the word she never allowed herself to say out loud. *Fuck.*

Pulling the zipper up on her light cotton jacket—because who wanted to wear their heavy winter coat in April?—she considered her situation. She could deal with this. Her dad had taught her how to change a tire, plus he'd put together a safety kit for her car that included a reflective vest and a battery-powered light.

"This sucks. But I can do it." If she said it loud enough, maybe it would be true.

Getting out of the car again, she opened the back and gave another mental curse. She'd forgotten that everything necessary to change the tire, including the spare, was beneath the CRV's cargo floor, currently buried under crates and boxes of books, papers, and school supplies, all tightly packed around her desk chair and bookcase.

Why had she thought it was a good idea to bring her own desk chair and bookcase to what had been another teacher's classroom? Thankfully, her genius pal Yousef had mad Tetris skills and had banned her from packing her car herself. He'd done his magic and fit everything together in a way she knew she could never replicate. He'd folded the back seats forward to make more room, and it was needed. Even the front passenger area was jampacked.

No way would she be able to get all that stuff unloaded, change the tire, and then reload and fit it all again. To cap it off, the cotton jacket and jeans she wore had been great for the we're-sad-you're-going-away drinks and tacos at the cantina, but the temperature was dropping and she was already cold.

Somewhere in one of the carefully packed boxes was her down coat, plus the fuzzy blanket she'd kept in her classroom for emergencies.

Her home in Sisters was only six miles away, but it might as well have been six hundred. A coyote howled, not quite far enough away for comfort.

Pushing the back door closed, she checked her phone again. A single bar appeared like a beacon of hope. *Yes!* She texted a quick note to her mom. "Flat tire. Pulled over on highway to Sisters. Calling AAA now."

Staying glued to the spot because moving could mean losing the signal, she spent a futile ten minutes trying to get the Auto Club app to work while the lonely service bar appeared and disappeared in the corner of her screen. Maybe calling would be better.

She returned to her seat in the car, the window all the way up to keep out the cold, and sorted through the cards in her wallet. Not finding it there, she looked through the pockets of her purse. Finally finding the card, she dialed the roadside assistance number. The chirpy voice answering barely got through "How can I help you?" before the call dropped.

Tears threatened. She was a wimp with tears, but there was no one to see. Spending the night in her car was beginning to look like a real possibility.

Vehicles zipped past, more going up the mountain than coming down as commuters who lived in the mountains sped home to start their weekends. This time on a Friday night, traffic was light. Should she try flagging someone down, see if they'd give her a ride to Sisters? That would break every commonsense safety rule ever drummed into her head.

Maybe she should hike down the road a bit to see if she could get better cell service. Using the flashlight on her phone and keeping to the edge of the snowy meadow so she didn't get hit by a careless driver, she started walking, her boots making squelching sounds in the mud. She'd hiked all the way down the straightaway without any improvement in reception. Continuing around the curve in the highway where the only place to walk would be the side of the road seemed too dangerous, so she turned around.

Wet was seeping into her boots around her toes. Apparently her Uggs weren't waterproof. Shivering, discouraged, and seriously unhappy, she retraced her steps.

She was almost back to her car when a vehicle on the highway braked and slowed, then pulled a U-turn.

There was that moment of worry: what if the driver was a predator and a stranded woman alone was too tempting to pass up?

Even as she had the thought, the vehicle stopped behind her CRV, the driver's door opening at the same moment she recognized the charcoal gray Bronco. She closed her eyes briefly and breathed deep, relief making her lightheaded. She had absolute faith in girl power, but she desperately needed help, and as much as Owen Hardesty didn't bother to hide his dislike for her, he was here, and he'd never leave her stranded on the side of the road.

CHAPTER TWO

He rounded the hood of his Bronco, all six feet plus of long, lean gorgeousness. If she had the recipe for the perfect man, Owen Hardesty, a.k.a. Hunky McHunk, would be the result. (Torture on the rack wouldn't make her divulge her nickname for him.) Physically, for sure, because he was that gorgeously delicious in a rough-hewn sort of way. Personality-wise, he could work on losing the grump. He was perfectly fine with other people, not particularly chatty, but he had friends and people seemed to like him. But with her? He was surly, rude, and had made a bad habit of bossing her around.

Gratitude loosened her tongue. "Owen, oh my god. I'm so glad to see you. Thank you so, so much for stopping." He'd shown up when she was in desperate need of help. He probably hadn't realized it was her, but still. She'd hug him if she didn't think he'd recoil in horror.

His scowl, the habitual frown he wore whenever he had to deal with her, was clearly visible in the wash of the Bronco's headlights.

He might treat her like she was an Ebola carrier, but that hadn't stopped her stupid heart from developing the tiniest of crushes on him. For the past several months she'd been trying to squelch that crush, to stomp out the feelings until they died. She didn't need the blow to her self-confidence by the man she had a thing for actively disliking her.

She'd even posted a profile on a popular dating app and gone on several dates with the idea that finding a romantic partner would help her kill the crush. And, if she was lucky, one of those dates would result in a relationship that would lead somewhere.

Good on him though for pulling over for a person in need on the side of the road.

He strode toward her, taking her hand to pull her in front of the Bronco where the headlights shone brightly.

Dark brows lowered over his sharp eyes as he glared at her, but his gravelly voice lacked its usual bossiness. "You okay, princess?"

"Um, yeah." His gentleness combined with her skyrocketing pulse was disconcerting. "Except for being stranded on the side of the road with a flat tire, I'm okay. I walked all the way to the curve trying to get cell service. I had one measly bar for about a minute, but it wasn't enough to call for roadside service."

"What the hell? You walked along the road in the dark? Are you trying to get yourself run over? Or kidnapped?"

Annnd he was back.

That. Exactly that was why Owen could light a match to her temper like no one else. Sure, the tiny crush was a true thing, but so was the fact he managed to put her back up with apparently no effort at all.

It also didn't help that he'd never touched her before, and now that he was holding her hand, she was experiencing Owen overload.

She might've been able to reestablish her equilibrium except for that one thing.

His calloused hand enveloped hers with a warmth that sent a surge of heat over her skin like a shield against the cold wind blowing ahead of the storm. Very nice indeed, until he suddenly seemed aware they were touching and dropped her hand, shoving his into the slit pockets of his jacket.

Right. Ebola carrier.

If she knew where in her car her hand sanitizer had been stowed, she'd offer him a squirt. He angled his head and she realized his rant had held a question.

He'd asked if she was trying to get herself run over. Of course, she was devoid of intelligence and common sense and couldn't keep herself safe.

Self-preservation had her tone coming out sharper than she intended. "Listen up, pal." She stepped back and his scowl deepened. Yet, with all that, she missed his warmth. "First off? I had my phone flashlight on and was walking along the turnout as far from the road as I could precisely because I didn't want to get run over.

"Second? I can't deal with this tire myself, and need to call a tow truck, otherwise I'll have to spend the night in my car and it's cold and I really don't want to spend the night in my car. Calling a tow truck requires cell service, so yeah, I walked along the turnout.

"And third? I'm not an idiot, and maybe you should remember that."

"Got it. Give me your keys."

Got it. Give me your keys? That's it?

No wonder the man was single. At least she thought he was single, but what did she know? Maybe he had a grumpy girlfriend to complement his grumpy self.

"Keeley, would you *please* give me your keys?" she muttered as she fished her keys from the back pocket of her jeans and handed them over. She shivered as the wind picked up, flakes of snow beginning to swirl in the wash of the headlights.

"Why aren't you wearing a coat?" Of course, he wore one of those heavy wool Pendletons that made him look like he could fell tall trees with a few strokes of an axe.

"I have a coat. It's in my car, but I'm not sure where. I'm fine." He made her feel like she'd failed an IQ test.

Shaking his head, he rounded the hood of his Bronco to open the front passenger door. Reaching in, he pulled out a heavyweight hoodie and thrust it at her. "Wear this." He motioned to the seat. "Stay here while I change the tire."

"Umm—" He was already stalking toward the CRV.

Keeley pulled the sweatshirt over her head and tried to ignore the intoxicating scent of him. She wondered if the sweatshirt had been in front of a heater vent because it felt fabulously warm. The weight and thickness made her feel safe and secure, which was dumb. It was only a freakin' sweatshirt.

Telling herself to suck it up buttercup, she scrambled after him, catching up as he crouched to examine the tire.

"I told you to stay in the Bronco. The keys are in the center console. Push the start button to turn it on to run the heater."

He rose to his feet and she had to step back. Usually when she saw him, he was behind the bar at his place, Easy Money. This close up he seemed taller.

She cleared her throat. "You won't be able to change the tire."

He sent her a look that made her roll her eyes and moved around her to open the back hatch. She couldn't blame him for the stunned expression. "What the hell, princess?"

"Keeley, Owen. My name is *Keeley*."

"Princess works for me."

"I'm hardly a princess," she muttered. It irritated her that he thought of her as spoiled and snobby, but he'd come to her rescue so she'd be nice, even if it killed her. "I'd have changed the tire myself if my car wasn't packed as tightly as a can of biscuits."

"A can of biscuits?"

"Yeah, a can of biscuits." Was he laughing at her? There was a quality to his voice that made her suspicious. She waved her hand at the bins and boxes. "All this is from my classroom. If we unpack it to get to the spare, we'll never get it back in because we're not Yousef."

He stared at her like he was trying to make sense of a foreign language. "Okay, I'll ask. What the hell does that mean?"

"It means that I had to clear out what had been my classroom because the regular teacher is coming back after spring break from her two-year maternity leave." She glanced at the back of the car. It really was a lot of stuff.

"Not that, the other thing."

She replayed what she'd said in her head. "That we're not Yousef?"

He nodded.

"Yousef is one of my best friends. He teaches, actually it's now past tense, he *taught* sixth graders in the classroom next to mine. Well, I taught in the classroom next to his because he was there first and he's still there. He's a wizard with packing and got everything to fit, but if we pull stuff out, we'll never get it back in like Yousef did.

"We, as in me and Yousef, also went out tonight with friends. To our favorite cantina for adult beverages and tacos. It was kind of a going away party. For me. But I only had one small margarita and that was at least two hours before I got behind the wheel, in case you were wondering, because I don't drink and drive."

Owen looking at her like she was an alien from another planet had her snapping her mouth shut. He made her nervous, and when she was nervous she talked. A lot.

"He your boyfriend?"

"Who? Yousef?" At his slow nod, she said, "No. Of course not. I don't have a boyfriend. At least, at the moment. Things could change."

She thought his interest sharpened, like he'd been listening before but had shifted suddenly to hyper-focus. But he didn't say anything more so she asked, "Is there space in the back of your Bronco to put some of my things? Dividing the load is the only way I can see to get to the spare tire."

He was already shaking his head. "I've got equipment back there. We'll leave your car here tonight. Come back for it in the morning." He must've caught her look because he added, "It'll be fine."

A thought struck. "You were on your way down the mountain so you must've been going somewhere. I'm sorry." As much as she loathed the idea, she felt compelled to make the suggestion. "If you want to take off to where you were going, you could make the call to request roadside service for me. I'll wait with my car until they get here." She flashed him a smile. "That is if I can keep the sweatshirt you loaned me so I don't freeze."

She'd seen Owen pissed off plenty of times; he got especially pissed at the bar when guys were jerks to women. But that was nothing compared to the fire that ignited his eyes now. "What do you take me for? You think I'd leave you alone at night on the side of a mountain with a storm coming in? That's not who I am."

His vehemence surprised her. "We don't really know each other, and I thought you might've been on your way to a date or something, and stopping to help me messed that up. Though it's a little late for a date. But not for a hookup. I'm so sorry if that's the case. Maybe she's, or he's, still waiting."

"Jesus Christ, the way your brain works. It's like you've got a squirrel up there going off in a dozen directions." He did the guy chin lift thing. "You like ticking things off in order, so let's do that. One, I'm not gay. Got nothing against gays or anyone else, love is love and all that, but I'm not gay. If you think I'm gay, then you haven't been paying attention." She'd barely had a second to wonder what he meant before he went on, ticking his points off on long fingers. "Two, I was *not* going to meet a woman for a date or a hookup. And three, your mom called me after you texted her and asked if I'd look for you. That's why I was driving down the mountain."

"She didn't." Keeley closed her eyes and breathed through her nose, which she'd read was a calming technique. It didn't work. She opened her eyes. "I'm sorry. Mom loves you like a long-lost son, but that doesn't give her the right to bother you, especially on what has to be a busy night at Easy Money."

"Your mom can call me for anything, any time she wants. It's not a problem. What is a problem is us standing here in the cold. I want to get on the road and there's not a chance I'm leaving you here alone."

Over the years, Owen had avoided her, she knew he had, which limited their interactions. Keeley thought over the past few minutes he'd broken the record for the number of words spoken to her at one time.

With the current situation, he'd come to help her and he was right about the cold, so she'd cut him a break for being bossy. "Understood," she said primly. "I don't really want to be here by myself, but I'm still sorry to be a bother to you."

He shook his head. "Get whatever you need from your car."

She retrieved her purse and turned off the hazards. Owen handed over her keys. She locked her car and followed him to the Bronco. He turned the heater up and once she had her seatbelt secured, he steered it onto the highway.

She was safe. She leaned back in her seat and screwed her eyes shut against the sudden onslaught of emotion. *Stupid, stupid, stupid. She was an idiot to cry when she was safe.* She hated that she cried so easily.

In with a deep breath, slowly exhale. She repeated the process, hoping to beat back the tears.

"There a problem?"

He was too perceptive. He'd come to her rescue as a favor to her mom, but still he'd dropped everything to drive down the mountain. He'd saved her from a scary and uncomfortable night sleeping in her car, he'd given her his sweatshirt to wear, and he'd turned up the heater. She'd been feeling scared and alone, and now she felt safe and protected.

Altogether not what she needed to diminish the crush threatening to grow past the tiny stage.

She angled her head to surreptitiously wipe at her eyes and swallowed against the tightness in her throat. "No, no problem."

Once she had herself under control, she stared into the darkness. Swirling snowflakes danced in the cone of light from the Bronco's headlights. Owen turned on the windshield wipers.

"Thank you for coming to find me. I didn't want to spend the night in my car. I could've done it, but I'm a wimp, and I'd have been scared."

"Shit."

She gave a startled laugh. "That's not the usual response when someone says thank you."

"It's my response. You're not a wimp. Most people would've been scared. Don't beat yourself up about it."

"I'm not beating myself up." His strong profile was silhouetted against the light from a gas station as they passed the outskirts of Sisters. "*You* wouldn't have been scared."

"I wouldn't have been happy, but no, I wouldn't have been scared. Women are more vulnerable than men. You have more reason to be scared."

"I'll accept that. Regardless, you saved me from that and I'm grateful."

"Don't want your gratitude." The words were a surly grumble.

"Well, you have it." She gave his response some thought. "Do you like pie?"

He gave her another one of those all-encompassing looks that warmed her as much as the heated air pumping from the vents. "I like pie."

"Then I'll bake you a pie."

"I told you I don't want your gratitude."

"And I said you have it anyway. The pie isn't like a payment that diminishes the gratitude, it's simply a way to say thank you."

He tapped his fingers on the steering wheel. "Apple. I'm partial to apple pie."

"Good, then I'll make you an apple pie."

In minutes they were pulling into the long driveway that led past her parents' house to the little cottage in the back where she lived.

In years past there'd been tall pines in the courtyard between the two structures, but those had been cleared so the trees ringing the property were far enough back that there was a defensible space in case of a wildfire.

Keeley'd moved into the cottage the year before so she could help with her dad. Since then, she'd been making the commute up and down the mountain to Sacramento. Moving home meant she could be part of her dad's care team, and of real help to her mom, instead of the few hours she'd been able to spare on weekends.

Alzheimer's sucked, and early-onset Alzheimer's sucked even more. She and her mom were giving Bruce Montaigne the best life they could, given his diagnosis, but there were days that were simply exhausting. Knowing her dad's condition would only worsen was like having a dark cloud forever looming overhead.

Her parents had built the cottage when Keeley was a teenager when her grandmother had been widowed. Now Keeley was living there. With its little kitchen, living room, and beautiful bedroom/bathroom suite, she had her own space while still being close enough to help with her dad.

Owen parked in front of her single-car garage. The back door of the main house opened as Keeley stepped out of the Bronco, Owen exiting on his side. Even wearing a long parka thrown over slim-fitting sweats, Abigail Montaigne always looked put together and beautiful.

"Oh, Keeley, I'm so glad you're safe." She pulled her daughter into a tight hug.

"I wasn't in any danger, Mom. But I'm glad to be home. Thanks for sending Owen."

Abby turned to Owen. Keeley felt a pang when Mister *I'm grumpy and love my solitude* Hardesty not only returned the embrace, he went so far as to lay his cheek on Abby's head and hold on as snowflakes swirled around them. Who'd have thought the guy could give such good hugs?

Owen had become friends with Keeley's parents when she'd been living in Sacramento. During the early stage of her dad's disease, he would often spend afternoons at Easy Money, drinking the one glass of beer he allowed himself while hanging out with his buddy, Ted Alvarez, and a couple other guys. They'd called themselves the Devil Dogs, given they'd all been in the Marine Corps, including Owen.

"Thank you for taking care of my girl, Owen."

"Always."

Always? Right. No point forgetting her mom's request was what had sent Owen down the mountain looking for her.

The flicker of hope that his relief in finding her might've been some sort of reflection of romantic feelings were smothered by a heavy dose of reality.

See? Another step closer toward beating her tiny crush into submission.

***

Bzzzzz. Keeley groped on her nightstand, knocking her phone to the floor with a thud. It could stay there. She snuggled into her pillow. She loved her pillow. Nice, soft, fluffy. She started to drift again.

Bzzzzz. The *Hey, you didn't read your text* reminder buzz. Yawning, she felt around on the floor until she found her phone, then dropped it again when the plugged-in charger cord pulled it out of her hand.

Picking it up, she managed to pull out the charger while simultaneously rolling out of bed onto the floor. Deciding she needed to open her eyes, she pushed herself up to a sitting position and squinted at the screen. "Unknown number." Tapping and swiping, because apparently she couldn't remember how to use her phone—god she needed coffee—she finally opened the message app.

Unknown Number: It's Owen. Dealing with your car.

The events of the night before came crashing back, images of the wheel with its puddle of deflated rubber, desperately trying to get cell service, then Owen in all his broody gorgeousness stepping out of his Bronco, bringing with him the feeling that she was absolutely safe.

She rubbed her eyes. Her phone read seven a.m. Didn't the man sleep? Trying to wake up, she tapped back a response.

Keeley: Oh! You don't have to do that. I was going to call AAA and get a ride to meet the driver and have it towed to town.

She reread the text for grammar, considered adding a car emoji, but figured it would be wasted on Owen, then hit send. She added him to her contacts list.

McHunk: Got keys from Abby. I'll deal with it.

Keeley: Okay, sure. That's great. Thank you. Can you tell the tow truck driver to take it to Lou's Tires and to let me know when it gets there?

She pulled her purse off her nightstand, located her card to take a picture of it, and added it to the text.

Keeley: Here's my AAA information. Thank you, again. I was planning on taking care of it, but now I don't have to. Thanks.

She'd waited for the three dots to show he was responding. Nada. Owen's conversational brevity apparently carried over to texting.

CHAPTER THREE

Keeley turned up the driveway to the big house, tires crunching over the thin layer of snow from the night before that had mostly melted, and parked her mother's car. The "big house" was how everyone referred to the two-story farmhouse that was the heart of Cider Mill Farm. It was barely nine o'clock, but apparently everyone was up and around.

After breakfast, she'd texted Delaney, her bff since fifth grade, a brief message.

Keeley: I had a flat coming up the mountain last night and Owen came and got me.

She figured when they actually talked, she'd fill in Delaney with the details. Which hadn't accounted for the whole bff thing because her simple text set off a whole flurry of excited texts.

BFF: WHAT!!! Owen finally made his move?

Keeley: Umm, what move? Nvm. I need to make him thank-you pie.

BFF: Pie? This is more serious than I thought. Give me a minute.

Shortly after, in a group text that included Delaney's sisters, Emery and Cam, Delaney called an emergency brunch meeting at the cabin she shared with her husband, Walker, at Cider Mill Farm.

Cam had responded, suggesting everyone come to the big house where she lived with her husband, Sawyer, telling Keeley she was welcome to use the larger kitchen to make Owen's pie.

Keeley bit back a sigh. Without a doubt, she would be facing an inquisition.

So much had changed for Delaney in the past couple years. Her one-time love, the wild and broody Walker McGrath, had returned to Sisters at about the same time a predator from their past had resurfaced. The whole thing had been scary, but had also pushed them together.

Then there was the story of Delaney's grandmother, Clara, searching for her lost granddaughters, Delaney's half-sisters they'd never known existed.

That quest had resulted in Emery and Cam's addition to the family.

Delaney's family owned the rustic and charming Cider Mill Farm, which had been the perfect venue for a whole slew of recent weddings.

First had been Delaney and Walker's. Walker had been so handsome in his suit, but still with a not-at-all-tamed look. Keeley'd had to choke back big, fat tears when her friend, escorted by her grandmother, had come down the aisle wearing a gorgeous off-shoulder dress.

Then last fall Emery married her hot cowboy, Shane Keller, from the nearby Lone Pine Ranch. That had been so much fun, especially with Emery's twin brothers, the flaxen-haired teenagers who'd set up a treasure hunt on the farm for the younger guests.

Most recently Sawyer, Walker's brother, had tied the knot with Cameron, having fallen fast and hard for her even when Cam had been living at the farm using a fake identity. Their wedding had been smaller and more intimate. Keeley thought Sawyer'd been close to ditching the wedding entirely in lieu of whisking his bride off to his camper for their honeymoon trip to visit national parks in the West.

Her friends getting their happily-ever-afters had been the kick in the pants Keeley'd needed to make a dating profile and get herself out there. Her ovaries weren't getting any younger, and her own HEA wasn't gonna happen if she didn't do something to find that special someone.

She wound her scarf around her neck and lugged her full grocery bags across the wide wraparound porch. She so wanted to be able to box up her winter clothes and put them in the garage.

The door opened before she could knock.

Cam, looking shabby chic in baggy pants and an oversize sweater, her blonde hair loose over her shoulders, held her tiny Morkie, Willa, under one arm and hooked one of the bags with the other. "Here, let me get that for you." She looked inside and she gave a quick smile. "Seems strange to bring apples to the apple farm."

"If apples were in season, I wouldn't have dreamed of it."

They put the bags on the island as Delaney, curly black hair in a messy bun on top of her head, rose from her stool to give Keeley a hug.

Keeley squeezed back. "Hey, I'm sorry about Callie." The old pointer had died quietly in her sleep the previous week. "It's strange for her not to be at the door."

"I know. Walker and Sawyer buried her out back. There's a little area surrounded by stones where family pets are buried. Callie lived a good life, and she's resting in a good spot." Delaney stepped back and sniffed back the tears. "Okay." She cleared her throat and forced a smile. "I'm under Emery's strict orders not to let you say anything until she gets here."

Keeley unpacked her bags, leaning her recipe card against a mason jar holding sprigs of dried lavender, then she organized the ingredients on the island. "I don't get it. Why is a flat tire such a big deal?"

"It's not the flat tire that's a big deal. It's Owen." Delaney mimed zipping her lips. "But we can't talk about it even though I'm dying of curiosity. I promised."

Cam set Willa in her little bed with a chew ring. She put up her hands when Keeley turned to her. "Don't look at me. I just live here." She picked up the recipe card, then set it back against the jar. "Solid recipe, my friend. Want me to make the crust?"

"Oh, thank goodness. Yes, please. My pie filling is superb, but pie crusts are not my forte." With Cam being the baker for the Cider Mill Farm café and bakery, Owen's pie was now guaranteed to be the best.

Keeley pulled a band from her wrist to put her hair back in a ponytail and opened drawers until she found a paring knife. "If you want to do that, I'll get started peeling and slicing the apples."

"Hang on, I've got something better. It'll be a lot less work than using a knife." Cam went to the walk-in pantry and returned with a contraption she clamped to the edge of the countertop. She took an apple, forced it onto the prongs, and turned the crank.

"Ooh, that's clever." While the apple turned, an angled blade peeled the skin while another sliced the apple into a long spiral.

"Isn't it?" Cam nodded. "I got this at Antonia's store so it's vintage. All you'll need to do is chop the apple spirals into pieces."

Keeley noticed Delaney standing at the window to the backyard, a faraway look in her eyes. In fact, Cam also seemed a little distracted.

The front door opened and a moment later, Emery rushed into the kitchen, her face glowing. "Sorry it took me so long! Did I miss any of the good stuff?"

"You didn't miss anything," Cam assured her.

Delaney pointed a finger at Emery. "Your cheeks are flushed."

"I had the heater on in the car."

"Uh-uh. That's not what's given you that look. I'm thinking you're late because you and the hot cowboy were engaging in a little morning nookie."

Emery's cheeks flushed even redder. "I couldn't help it. Shane came back from taking care of the livestock and he's so damn sexy. And the kitchen counter was right there." She fanned her cheeks with her hands. "Besides, you can't tell me you two," she did her own finger pointing, wagging it between Cam and Delaney, "couldn't have all the morning nookie you want any day you want it."

Since Cam and Delaney both wore expressions that said yes, indeed, they'd both gotten morning nookie, Keeley ground out a frustrated breath. "Y'all need to keep reports of morning nookie to yourselves, because there's someone here who's mighty jealous."

"I bet Owen would be happy to help you with that." Delaney waggled her eyebrows.

Keeley felt her own cheeks flush. "I don't know where this sudden Owen obsession of yours is coming from."

"Just connecting the dots. I've witnessed plenty of hot looks between you two," Delaney claimed, "but always when the other isn't looking."

Keeley tried for a nonchalant shrug. "He's a handsome guy. Who wouldn't look?" After gathering peeling scraps and putting them in the bin for compost, she put another apple onto the prongs and turned the crank.

"I want to know what's brought us all here this morning," Emery said as she took a mug from a cupboard. "It better be good if I left my sexy husband when we could've gone for nookie round two."

"Now you're bragging." Cam grinned at her sister as she used a pastry cutter to cut shortening into the flour.

"All right." Delaney held up her hand like a kid in school. "Here's what I have from multiple sources. Well, two sources anyway. Owen got a call last night that our pal Keeley was stranded on the highway halfway up the mountain and flat-out raced to her rescue with a whole 'my woman's in danger' vibe."

"Oh no." Emery turned to Keeley. "What happened? Shane said Owen is coming to the ranch this morning to borrow a trailer. Does that have anything to do with you being stranded?" She filled a kettle with water and set it over a burner on the cooktop.

"I'll get to that in a moment because first I need to say Delaney is way overstating Owen's motivation and actions. Last night he was intense, but he's always intense. And sure, he rescued me, but he was doing it because he's a decent man, and because my mom asked."

She went on. "About the trailer, maybe Owen decided getting to the spare is too big a project and using Shane's flatbed makes better sense than calling for a tow truck."

At the questioning look from Emery, Keeley clarified, "I had a flat at an inopportune time." She proceeded to tell her friends how her belongings were Tetris-fitted into her CRV. "I would've changed the tire myself if I could have gotten to the spare."

"Those are the basics of the story, but let's focus on what's important," Delaney ordered. "Jen, who's now assistant manager by the way, says how Owen is working the stick at Easy Money. It's Friday night, busiest time of the week, and a call comes in and he's instantly alert. You know how growly sexy he gets. He signs off and shoves his phone in his pocket, points at Jen to tell her she's in charge and not to burn the place down, and he's out the door in under a minute."

"Ooh, that's hot. *Very* hot," Cam said as she added cold water to the flour mixture.

"Got that right. Jen said he went from the 'Friday night chill' zone to the 'alpha protector' vibe in less than two seconds."

"What about your other source?" Cam asked.

"The other source is Mateo, who saw him leaving the parking lot and flooring the Bronco to speed down Main Street. Owen's always a cautious driver, but last night with Keeley alone on the side of a mountain road, he wasn't wasting any time getting to her."

"This is all nonsense, you know that, right?" Keeley stared at her friends. "I wasn't in danger, and my *mom* called Owen.

"Owen and my parents are friends. He and Dad bonded over their Marine Corps experiences, and Owen's been a good guy and helped them out a few times.

"He went looking for me because Mom asked. Before last night he hardly ever talked to me, and if he did, he was always growly and bossy. He was better last night. I'll give him that. I wouldn't say he was *nice,* he was still Owen-intense, which is his default, but he didn't make me feel like a pain in the butt because he'd had to come get me."

She gave herself a mental finger-scolding to stop rambling. "Anyway, last night was an anomaly because normally I annoy him more than anything else. Me breathing annoys him. There's no way he thinks of me as 'his woman.' That's ridiculous."

She stopped talking and her friends looked at each other, then at her, wide grins breaking out on their faces. Keeley crossed her arms over her chest. "What?"

"You're flustered," Emery observed.

"*I am not.*" She was. Damn it. "Okay, maybe I am. A little bit. And maybe I have a tiny little crush on Owen. A super small, tiny little crush. But I've pretty much killed it, and since it's a one-way kind of thing, it has no bearing on Owen doing a favor for my mom."

"I knew it," Delaney crowed. "I knew you had a crush on Owen. You'd check him out every time we went to Easy Money. Just like he checked you out," she added with a smirk.

Cam had wiped down a section of the quartz countertop and was now sprinkling it with flour. "I agree. I think he's into you. But setting that aside, what happened last night when he got there and didn't make you feel like a pain in his exceptionally fine butt?"

Keeley kept her attention on working the apple peeler-slicer gadget with more focus than was probably necessary. "Nothing happened. I'll admit he was a bit, um, forceful when he first got there because I'd walked a bit trying to get cell service.

"Apparently in Owen's world, that was risky." She didn't mention he'd held her hand because it hadn't meant anything. Or that he'd loaned her his wonderful Owen-scented sweatshirt. As to him being forceful, that was probably more irritation at having his evening disrupted than anything else.

She cleared her throat. "I told him he wouldn't be able to change the flat tire either, and he gave me this look like 'Don't you worry, little lady,' but then he saw how my car was Tetris fitted and said it could wait until today."

"Hmm, I'm with my sisters on this," Emery chimed in. "Evidence supports Owen having a thing for you."

"He was doing a favor for my mom," Keeley repeated, working to keep the whine out of her voice. "Anyway, he texted this morning to tell me he was taking care of the car. I told him I could do it, because it's my problem, you know? But he overruled me, and my mom had already given him the spare set of keys. It's hard to text argue with someone when they respond with like four words. It's annoying."

"You're nervous. You talk too much when you're nervous." Delaney grinned as she poured water into mugs for tea for her and Emery.

"I'm not." She totally was.

"Plus," Emery bobbed her tea bag in the hot water, "I don't know Owen very well, but I think what he did last night? That's his love language."

"Doing my mom a favor is his love language?"

"No, dropping everything to get to you when he thought you might be in danger is. Dealing with your car this morning is."

Keeley dumped sliced apples into a big yellow mixing bowl and sprinkled carefully measured sugar, cinnamon, and nutmeg over them. It wasn't that she discounted her friends' assessment, but they hadn't witnessed Owen's surliness toward her over the past year or so.

Cam draped the rolled crust over a pie tin and used a sharp knife to trim the excess dough around the edges. "I can verify Owen tracks you whenever our gang has a barbecue or hangs out at Easy Money. As long as you're not looking at him, he's got his eyes on you and knows where you are. Then for him to drop everything when you needed rescuing? That's telling." She bumped Keeley's shoulder and shot her a grin. "Since you have that tiny crush, having his attention is a good thing, right?"

"If he has a thing for me, why doesn't he ask me out? Instead, he acts like he's the boss of me, and that's so not going to fly." She and Cam worked in tandem. Keeley poured in the apple mixture and Cam carefully placed the top crust over the pie, then used a knife to cut slits. Keeley crimped the edges and slid the pie into the hot oven.

Cam wiped down the countertop while Keeley squirted dish soap and ran hot water into a basin.

"Thanks for the use of your kitchen, friend," she said as she set the mixing bowl onto the drainer.

"Anytime," Cam murmured.

When the kitchen was back in order, she and Cam sat on stools across the island from Delaney and Emery.

Delaney sipped her hot tea and looked like she was trying not to grimace. Keeley narrowed her eyes, her gaze traveling to each of the women in turn as Delaney raised her mug again, the tag from the tea bag hanging over the side. "You're drinking tea. You hate tea." She turned to skewer Emery with a laser-sharp look. "And you, you drink Earl Gray in the morning, but now you're drinking herbal. In fact," Keeley turned to Cam to confirm the absence of a coffee cup, "not one of you is drinking anything with caffeine. Are you all pregnant or something?"

CHAPTER FOUR

The three sisters stared at each other wide-eyed, then at Keeley.

"Oh my god," Keeley said. "I'm right?"

"I peed on a stick yesterday morning." Delaney spoke in a hushed voice, her hands crossing over her chest like she was trying to contain her heart. "It came back positive. Walker and I are dazed. We're elated, a little scared, and still processing. We weren't going to say anything for a couple weeks in case, you know, something goes wrong."

Keeley ignored the brief sting of sorrow as Delaney's words brought up a memory that made her heart ache. She jumped from her seat and rounded the island to grab her friend in a fierce hug. "You're going to be a mom. Oh my gosh, this is so exciting."

"I know this might be hard for you," Delaney whispered.

Keeley took her friend's face in her hands, shaking her head. "It's wonderful and beautiful, and I'm so happy for you."

"We totally didn't expect for it to happen this quick."

Keeley beamed at her. "You know how babies are made, right?"

"But we just started trying." Delaney gave a flustered laugh. "And I know that's silly because it only takes one time, but we really didn't think it would happen this fast."

"How was Walker with the news?" Cam asked.

"Oh my god, he's so happy. You'd think he was the first man to be a baby daddy."

Delaney turned to the other women. "Are you both pregnant too?"

"I'm three days late for my period so yesterday I bought a test kit." Emery's smile lit up her face. "I peed on a stick this morning too, and it came up with two little lines. But the second one is kind of faint." She dug into her purse. "I brought it with me to get a second opinion. Is this gross? I don't want it to be gross."

"It's not gross. Let's see."

Emery removed the test stick from the box. She showed the picture printed on the side. "See their lines? Now look at my test."

"Friend, those are two red lines. The second one is fainter, but it's still there." Keeley gave Emery an arm-across-the-shoulder hug. "You're pregnant."

"That's what Shane said." She wore a secret smile. "He was over the roof."

"I bet that's what led to morning nookie," Cam teased.

"You wouldn't be wrong. Shane was especially, um, reverent." Emery beamed again. "He'll be such a good dad," she said dreamily.

"What about you?" Delaney asked Cam.

"I don't know if I'm pregnant. I mean, I could be since Sawyer and I decided we wanted to try to start a family. I'm late too, but I've never been super regular. I'm going to the drugstore to pick up a test as soon as we're done with our emergency meeting."

"Oh my god, we're baking pie and you don't know if you're pregnant?"

Cam had Keeley's recipe card and was turning it over and over in her hands. "I was going to go tomorrow to buy a test thinking I'd give it another day, but I don't want to wait any longer. It's all I can think about, so I decided to go buy one today. Or have Sawyer pick one up on his way home from work. But now I'm nervous because I don't want to be disappointed." She put the card down and began tapping the countertop.

"This kit came with two tests." Emery pulled the extra foil-wrapped test from the box. "Use it. Go pee on the stick."

"I don't know." Cam took the test and box, worrying her bottom lip with her teeth as she frowned over the directions. "Don't you have to do this first thing in the morning?"

"The hormone it detects is stronger in the morning, but you're more likely to get a false negative than a false positive." Emery patted Cam's shoulders. "We're not pressuring you. You can keep the test if you like and use it later so you can have Sawyer with you."

She picked up her phone. "Let me call Sawyer and see if he wants to be with me when I do the test."

She walked into the living room, returning minutes later with a tentative smile on her face. "Sawyer says he's on his way home anyway, and he's fine if I don't wait for him to do the test." She took a deep breath. "Okay, okay. I'm fine too," she said the words like she was trying to build up her nerve. "I'm going to do it."

Cam disappeared down the hall, and Keeley had to force herself not to bounce on her toes. "I can hardly stand the suspense. How long does it take?"

"Three minutes."

Cam returned from the bathroom and placed the test on the counter. The women gathered around. All of them were focused on the tiny window.

Cam put her hands over her eyes. "I can't look."

Delaney and Emery each gripped one of Cam's shoulders.

"We'll look for you. The first line is showing," Emery reported.

"What about the second line? Is the second line showing?" Cam pulled down her hands. "I can't not look."

The faintest second line appeared, a collective gasp sounding as it darkened.

She held the test stick up to the example, studying the comparison image on the box like it held the secrets to the universe. "I think I'm pregnant," Cam whispered.

She stepped back, her expression stunned as she looked from sister to sister. "All three of us are pregnant." They each nodded slowly, seemingly unable do anything but stare at one another.

Keeley remembered finding out she was pregnant as being so monumental it was like the earth shifting on its axis.

"How is this possible?" Cam asked.

Delaney looked at her sisters, who gazed back with wide eyes. "I don't know. What are the odds of us all being pregnant at the same time?"

"I think that would be really long odds." Emery gave a shaky laugh. "Life is about to get very interesting."

Delaney linked arms with Keeley. "We're all going to be aunties. This will be so much fun." This was why Keeley loved these women. Even though the three of them were sisters, she never felt like an outsider.

Delaney's comment broke open the floodgates. With loud whoops of happiness, they met in a tangle of arms in a group hug. They broke apart when the kitchen door opened. The room suddenly felt overly crowded as four tall, gorgeous men trooped in, taking up most of the space.

"What the hell's going on here?" Walker dropped his scowl when he stood in front of his wife, reaching out to run a finger down the side of her face. "Hey, babe."

Delaney leaned into him. "Hey yourself."

Sawyer looked handsome in his uniform, the deputy star shiny on his chest. Cam grabbed his hand and pulled him back out the door. "Come on, lieutenant. I've got something to tell you."

Shane dipped his head to nuzzle Emery's neck.

Keeley scooped up Willa so she wouldn't get trampled, dropping a kiss on the little dog's head. Despite the pang of longing, she was absolutely, one hundred percent happy for her friends.

Three babies? That was the best kind of happiness, surpassing all others.

She wiped happy tears with her sleeve.

Owen planted himself beside her, his sharp blue gaze locked on her. "Why are you crying?"

"I'm not," she said as she wiped her cheeks again. At his look, she said, "Okay, maybe a little. But these are happy tears."

A shout sounded from outside. Keeley peeked out the window to see Sawyer lifting Cam off her feet, his face buried in her neck. When he let her down, she gestured to the house, talking fast.

Walker bracketed Delaney's face with his hands. "I repeat, Laney, what the hell's going on?"

"We're pregnant. We're all pregnant."

Owen jerked like he'd received an electrical shock, and his brows slammed down in a scowl.

"What?" Shane growled, dropping an arm over Emery's shoulders. "That's not possible."

Sawyer and Cam trooped back in, hand in hand, both with happy grins on their faces.

"You too, brother?" Walker asked.

At Sawyer's dazed nod, he, Shane, and Walker shared a moment of stunned silence much like the women had, then let loose in an exchange of bro hugs and back slapping that could've toppled tall buildings.

"What the hell, princess?"

Owen's fierce look had Keeley's brows arching. "What?"

"You pregnant too?"

She gave a disbelieving snort. "Not *me*." She flicked her hand toward the room at large. "Them. They've all peed on a stick and each one came back with two lines."

He stared hard, then shook his head. "No idea what that means. Explain."

"Pregnancy tests. They all took pregnancy tests, and they all came back positive."

"You're not pregnant?"

"No! No. Good grief, Owen. I'd need to have sex to get pregnant, and that's not been happening."

"Good."

"Good that I'm not pregnant or good that I'm not having sex?" Willa licked her chin.

He paused a beat, then shook his head. "I'm not answering that question."

He turned to everyone else, glowering at the men. "What'd you all do, coordinate sex so you'd knock up your women at the same time?"

"Didn't coordinate with anyone." This from Sawyer. "Cam and I decided we're ready to start a family, and that was a couple months ago."

Sawyer and Cam stood, shoulders touching, their fingers tangled together.

God, Keeley wanted that. The "I've got you, you've got me, and we're crazy in love forever" kind of love.

She wanted someone she could love, depend on, build a life with. Someone who adored her in return. Her friends had hit gold with men who cherished them. All of which should be a strong incentive for Keeley to go through the notifications from her dating app. There'd been three that morning.

"Nobody coordinated, but damn, it's fucking crazy all three are pregnant." Walker stuck his hands in his pockets and shook his head. Keeley didn't think she'd ever seen him look uncertain. "How the hell are we going to deal with three babies?"

Sawyer, who could handle anything, still looked shellshocked and hadn't let go of Cam since they'd come back into the kitchen. "I'll admit to being scared shitless, but we'll figure it out."

"Seems like you'll have time to do the figuring out part. Congratulations." Owen said the right words. but there was something about his tone that caught Keeley's attention. He didn't reveal much, ever, but something was there.

"It's still sinking in," Emery sighed, leaning back against her hot cowboy. Shane rested his chin on her head, arms wrapped snugly around her waist.

"We need to tell Gran. We're early in our pregnancies, but this is too big not to tell her." Delaney looked at her sisters. "Are you both okay with that?"

They nodded in agreement.

"Let's call when she stops for the night," Emery suggested.

Owen cocked his head. "Where's Clara?"

"Gran and her friend DeeDee are on a bus tour of Canada. I think they're in Alberta today with a stop scheduled at Banff." Delaney turned to her sisters. "You all up to doing a group video chat this evening?"

"Yep," Cam said as Emery nodded.

Sniffing the air, Sawyer turned to Cam. "You baking something, darlin'?"

"Keeley's baking an apple pie for Owen."

Walker flashed his lightning grin. "It's like that, Keels?"

All eyes turned on her and Keeley could feel warmth flooding her cheeks, especially since Owen had parked himself at her elbow.

Why was it that she wore every emotion on her face? She cleared her throat and soldiered on. "When I had a flat tire last night, Owen was kind enough to help me as a favor to my mom." She could feel his gaze boring into her but kept her attention determinedly on everyone else. "I'm baking him a thank-you pie."

"Bro, you sharing?" Shane asked. "I can go for thank-you pie."

"Hell no. Keep your hands off my pie." The words may have been growled, but Keeley saw the humor in his eyes.

"Not that I don't appreciate four handsome men in the kitchen, but what brought you all here?" Emery tipped up her head back to look at her husband.

"Owen's borrowing my flatbed trailer to get Keeley's car," Shane answered.

"And since Shane needs his truck today, Owen and I will take my pickup," Walker added. "It has a V8 and can tow the flatbed."

Keeley turned to Owen. "I texted you my auto club membership number so you could call a tow truck." Willa squirmed so she passed her off to Cam.

"That's the other reason we're here. I called Triple A and drove down to meet the driver. He couldn't tow it because all four tires are flat."

"All four tires aren't flat."

"They are." Owen's expression hardened. "Your car's been vandalized, princess. Looks like someone gouged the tires with a screwdriver. Several times."

Keeley sucked in a sharp breath. "Gouged my tires? Why would anyone do that?"

"Don't know. Pisses me off."

"I'm on duty," Sawyer said. "I'll follow Owen to the car and do a report."

Now she needed to deal with not one, but four flat tires. The thought that someone had maliciously punctured her tires was unsettling. "If you can wait until the pie is out of the oven, I'll go with you."

"You don't need to go."

She speared Owen with her teacher look that every one of her students knew meant they were on thin ice. "It's not on you to deal with my car problems."

Owen rubbed a hand over his stubble. "No disrespect, princess, but have you ever loaded a vehicle with four flat tires onto a flatbed?"

"No. But possessing a Y chromosome doesn't mean you know how to do that either."

"It's got nothing to do with being male and everything to do with skill sets. I couldn't teach a kid with a learning disability strategies for reading. That's your skill set so that's what you do. Since I've loaded M1 Abrams tanks stalled with sand ingestion onto flatbeds, that's what I can do. I'll deal with your Honda."

She processed his comment and decided he wasn't exactly praising her, more like stating a fact. She sighed glumly, elation at her friends' baby news supplanted by the disturbing thought someone had purposefully damaged her tires. "Point taken."

She turned to the others who seemed to be watching the back and forth between her and Owen like a tennis match. "I'm sorry for taking up your Saturday. I appreciate you all. I need to bake more thank-you pies."

Sawyer tugged on her ponytail as he moved to the door. "No pies necessary, Keels. You're one of us. This is what we do for our people."

CHAPTER FIVE

A biting wind howled up the mountain as Owen knelt with Sawyer to examine the damaged tire. He pulled his beanie low over his forehead. Spring weather needed to hurry the hell up.

Walker had situated his truck and the trailer in front of Keeley's CRV and was busy readying the chains they'd need to pull it onto the flatbed.

Owen pointed to the metallic head of a screw lodged in the tread of the front passenger tire, the one that had initially gone flat.

"That's what put Keeley on the side of the road last night." He tapped his finger next to puncture marks in the sidewall and pushed back on the anger that made him want to punch something. "This was done after we left. Three gouges here, two here." He bit out the words. "That's five, and the other tires have more than that. Ten alone on the rear passenger tire. This is more than petty vandalism." It fucking infuriated him.

"Agreed." The men rose to their feet. Owen stepped back, shoving his hands in the pockets of his heavy coat to keep them from freezing while Sawyer circled the car taking photos.

"Effort like this indicates someone was pissed. Interesting that they focused on the tires and didn't key the paint or bust windows," Sawyer stated. "Question is whether this was an impulsive crime, someone driving by who took the opportunity to be an asshole, or if Keeley was specifically targeted."

The thought of Keeley being targeted was exactly what had Owen's temper boiling. Her car being vandalized? Truly fucked, but a price of living in the modern world.

But if she'd been specifically targeted? He'd do whatever needed to keep her safe, and God help the perpetrator when Owen found him.

"I'll have the door handles and the fenders around the wheels, areas where the asshole might have touched, dusted for prints. We'll see if anything pops." Sawyer grabbed his tablet from his sheriff's department SUV.

Owen nodded. He'd been a cop and knew petty vandalism didn't usually rate serious investigation. He appreciated not having to convince Sawyer that's what needed to be done.

Walker joined them. Sawyer looked up from tapping information into the tablet, gaze skewering Owen. "You'll keep an eye on our girl while I work this?"

"Got that right."

Sawyer flashed him a grin. "Have fun with that. Keels has that sunny disposition, and she's hands down the sweetest person I know, but she's got a backbone of solid steel along with a stubborn streak of independence. If you want to keep an eye on her, you'll have to convince her that it's what she wants. Otherwise, she'll freeze you out and you won't stand a chance."

"Doesn't matter what she wants. Her safety is the highest priority, so she'll have to listen to me."

Walker gave a bark of laughter. "Man, you've got a lot to learn about women. Better get up the curve quick or you'll have your ass handed to you."

Owen was still thinking how he'd go about protecting Keeley when Walker backed the trailer into the parking lot at Lou's Tires. They offloaded the CRV and helped Lou's crew get it to a lift. He went into the office to talk with the man himself.

Lou sat behind a metal desk with a dent in the front, a torque wrench holding down a stack of papers. A space heater buzzed in a corner, and the room smelled of stale coffee and motor oil. Lou took a pull from a chipped coffee cup, studying Owen over the rim. White hair stuck out from under the fielder's cap with "Lou's Tires" stitched inside a big tire.

"Hey there, boy. Bar business keepin' you busy?"

Owen had lived in Sisters long enough to know doing business was never about just doing business. He was more inclined to get in and get out, but people liked to shoot the shit—talk about the weather, town gossip, fire danger—whatever the hell was on their minds. He'd gotten good at giving them enough that he didn't come off like a jerk, but he also didn't spend half the day yapping.

"Bar business is steady for this time of year. It'll pick up more when it warms up and then it'll be the summer tourist season. Got a good band Friday night and your wife likes to dance. Bring Jimena by and hang out."

"Might just do that. You bring in little Keeley's CRV?"

Little Keeley? That's what you got when you lived in a small town all your life. He nodded. "She'll need four all-weather tires."

"Got off the phone with her a minute ago. We worked it all out. I recommended the all-weathers but she went with a line of less expensive tires we carry. She gave me her card number and I only need to process the purchase and we'll be all set."

"She needs the all-weathers."

Lou pulled at his lower lip. "Those cheaper ones aren't bad tires. Not what I'd recommend, but I don't carry bad tires."

Owen was already shaking his head. "Put on the all-weathers. I'll pay the difference." With her new position come fall at the local high school in Sisters, at least she wouldn't be commuting up and down the mountain anymore, but that didn't mean she wouldn't be better off with the all-weather tires.

Lou considered him from under the bill of his cap. "Well now, that girl was mighty clear she wanted the less expensive tires."

"I'll work that out with her. Like I said, I'll pay the difference. I want her safe."

Lou's face broke into a gap-toothed smile. "That the way it is? Congratulations, young man. You've got a winner there. We'll get those all-weathers on for you, and your girl will be safer for it. Give me a couple hours to get her done."

Owen didn't bother correcting Lou's assumption that he and Keeley were together. "Thanks, Lou."

***

Two hours later, Owen stood in front of the bathroom mirror rubbing a towel over his hair, another tucked around his waist. Jen had opened Easy Money and he'd scheduled himself from four until close. He'd been developing his crew, had trained Jen behind the bar, then promoted her to assistant manager. Plan was for him to cut back his sixty hours a week to something that would give him time to have some semblance of a normal life and work on his house project.

That was the theory anyway. He strapped his watch to his wrist, then rubbed a hand over his beard. He needed to run the rake over it. He was reaching in the drawer for his razor when his phone buzzed.

Jen: Bad news, boss. Ariana broke her leg skiing. Won't be able to work for months. We're screwed.

He shoved the razor back in the drawer. He'd just about finished training Ariana, gotten her so she didn't have her phone in her hand every damn minute. Now that investment was a waste. Sure, he was sorry for the girl, a broken leg sucked. But damn, this was shit news, seeing as it put him back at square one trying to fill out his crew for the coming summer tourist season.

Hiring and firing were the worst parts of owning his own place.

He tapped to open the text that'd come from Lou while he'd been in the shower. The tires were mounted and Keeley'd already picked up her car. Lou had said Owen's *girlfriend* had picked up her car. Fuck.

A sharp rapping at his front door had him muttering another curse. He finger-combed his wet hair, pulled on briefs, then Levi's, buttoning the fly as he crossed the room. He pulled open the door and his breath jammed in his throat.

Seeing Keeley unexpectedly when he didn't have time to brace for impact always had the effect of making his breath back up in his lungs. There were millions of women in the world, but not one of them could stop his heart like the woman standing at his door holding a pie.

Keeley Montaigne likely had that impact on any man she came across. Some women were like that. Golden brown hair, hazel eyes that gleamed with hints of gold, green, and gray, and a smile so bright when it beamed his way, it made a guy feel like the luckiest bastard on the planet.

Not that she beamed at him a whole lot. Everyone else got the sunshine, but with him she covered that sunshine with a thick layer of fog.

His apartment was located upstairs from Easy Money, accessed from the back parking lot by an outside flight of stairs. She stood on the narrow landing, and instead of her default sunshine she was one hundred percent pissed-off female.

She held a plastic carrier by its handle. "You're a deceitful, lying bastard."

"Not usually. Got a problem, princess?"

"Yes, I've got a problem."

Even as she spoke, her gaze ran over his chest. She caught her bottom lip in her teeth, the gold in her eyes glowing. It didn't hurt his feelings that she seemed to like what she saw, but it also made him wary. Then her attention snagged and she went still, her cheeks going pale. He knew what had caught her eye: a small round circle of uneven skin the size of a bullet right where his arm met his shoulder. She raised a hand and he froze.

He knew he should back up. Get far enough away so she couldn't touch him. But he remained standing there like an idiot as she reached a finger to lightly brush the puckered scar. The first time she'd voluntarily touched him, and he felt it like a bolt of lightning.

She raised her face, expression stricken. "You were shot. Someone shot you."

"Yeah. Vest caught the first one." He thumped a fist on his chest, right side, keeping his voice even. "Right here. Almost knocked me on my ass. Second one got past the vest, messed me up some."

"Did it happen when you were in the military or when you were a cop?"

It figured that Abby or Bruce had shared his background.

"Cop."

She waited like she expected him to explain. When he didn't, she said, "I'm so sorry you were shot. It must have been agonizing."

She was so empathetic her eyes reflected his pain. It took every ounce of control not to take the hand resting on his chest and...do what? Something stupid like pressing his lips to her palm? Like kissing her knuckles?

Where the hell did those ideas come from? He wasn't a romantic, and he certainly wasn't the right man to act like one with her. He shook his head to clear it. "My partner got it worse."

Which was more than he wanted to say. He never talked about what happened. Ever.

Because he liked her touching him too much, and was afraid his control would break and he'd do some touching of his own, he stepped back to snag the rest of his clothes from where he'd left them hanging over the back of a chair.

She seemed to take his movement away from the door as an invitation because she stepped over the threshold into his apartment, closing the door against the cold wind. Shit.

"Look, princess, we're short-staffed tonight and I need to get downstairs. You can be pissed at me later."

"I'm not a princess, and I can be pissed at you now." She held out the carrier in her hand. "Here's your thank-you pie."

"Thanks." He took it across the room to the kitchen counter. Good move because it put more space between them. Facing her again, he noticed her watching as he buttoned his shirt.

He wished she wouldn't do that. Self-preservation dictated he stay away from her. But if she was attracted to him, his self-control would erode away to nothing and he'd be screwed.

"Not-annoyed me wants to say I really do appreciate you coming to get me last night. I didn't want to spend the night in the car. And you arranged for it to be towed to Lou's. I know you were doing it as a favor to my mom, but thank you."

He opened his mouth to contradict her assumption, then snapped it shut. Some things were better left unsaid. He pulled on a navy t-shirt, followed by a long-sleeved polo with the Easy Money logo. "Spit it out, Miz Montaigne. Tell me what I've done to annoy you so I can get to work."

She gave him a narrow-eyed glare and turned her back on him. She wandered to the bookcase and picked up his baseball mitt from a shelf and fit her hand into the glove. He never should've let her in.

Now he wouldn't be able to get the image out of his head. Her in his space, touching his things. She tilted her head to study the titles on his bookshelf, loose golden-brown hair hanging down in a shimmering curtain of color.

"*Angela's Ashes*," she murmured. "That one's gut-wrenching."

She smacked her fist in the pocket of the glove that was way too big for her. Not that she was small. She was probably medium height for a woman, and he liked her sturdy build. Waif-like women made him feel ham-handed and clumsy.

Keeley looked tough enough to take wild sex and want more. He scowled. That was *not* what he should be thinking about. He'd worked damn hard to keep any ideas of Keeley and sex out of his head, and it irritated him that his brain went there.

"You gonna explain the deceitful, lying bastard comment or are we done here?"

She set the mitt back on the shelf and faced him, crossing her arms in front of her. He'd irritated her more than a few times in the past, but he didn't think he'd ever gotten her mad enough her hazel eyes sparked green. Which was a stupid thing to notice.

"You lied to Lou and told him we're together."

"No. Lou came to that conclusion by himself. I didn't correct him."

"You should have because Lou's a gossip and he's already spread that tidbit around. When I went to get my car, one of the guys who works there, Jimmy Drummond, acted offended I was going out with you."

"He must want to be the guy to go out with you."

"Maybe he does. We'd been chatting on this dating app, and today he accused me of being dishonest since, according to Lou, I already have a boyfriend."

"What the hell are you doing on a dating app?"

She held his gaze even though her cheeks were reddening. "Lots of people find good matches on dating apps. It's not like I'm selling myself."

"If he found you on a dating app, he wants in your pants. You outclass him in every aspect. You should be thanking me."

"Maybe I want him in my pants, as you so crudely put it. Jimmy's a nice guy, so no, I'm not thanking you."

"He's not the guy for you. You'd run circles around him."

"You don't know that, and you don't know what kind of guy is for me. I'd like to find someone, but you acting like we're together isn't conducive to me achieving that goal."

"Those are some big words you've got there, Miz Montaigne."

She narrowed her eyes. "Don't make fun of me. I'm thirty-two years old and I want to find someone to spend my life with. I'd like to get married and have a family, and suitable men aren't exactly knocking down my door." She glared at him. "Don't you dare judge me."

"Jesus, princess. I'm not judging you." He stabbed his fingers through his hair. He was coming perilously close to saying things he had absolutely no business saying. He needed her to leave before he did something stupid.

"I'll straighten Lou out if it's important to you. That all?"

"It is important to me, and no, that's not all. I told Lou what tires I wanted, what tires I could *afford,* and you convinced him the little lady didn't have a clue what she needed and had him put on different tires."

"The all-weathers are better tires."

"I didn't want the all-weathers. I wanted the ones I ordered."

"Which weren't the best for driving in the mountains. It fucking snowed overnight. The roads were icy this morning. Your car isn't even all-wheel drive. The tires I ordered are safer. I told him I'd pay the difference."

She stalked toward him, as predatory as a mountain lion. "Listen to me, mister. I chose the tires I did for a reason. I'm selling my CRV once I start my new teaching position and get my first paycheck. Then I can buy a new car better suited to mountain driving. A new-to-me car, anyway, because it's likely to be a used car. I didn't want to put expensive tires on the CRV given we're almost done with winter weather *and* I'll be selling it. Now I either have to go to Lou and explain that you're *not* my boyfriend and have no authority to override my decision, and then get him to put on the tires I ordered, or I'll have to pay you the difference for tires I didn't want in the first place."

"Or take the third option and keep the tires and keep your money. I don't want you to pay me back."

"That's not how I operate, relying on a man to take care of me. I pay my own way, and now I owe you money when I'm without a paycheck for the next four months unless I can get seasonal work for the summer." Briefly, she closed her eyes. "And it's dawned on me since I drove over here, the tires Lou put on have road dirt on them. It's not fair to him to return used tires."

"Keep the tires, and keep your money," he repeated. He raised a hand and when he realized he was going to jam his fingers through his hair again, he dropped it. He hated having a tell. "Pay me back in a different way."

She narrowed her eyes. "Exactly what are you suggesting?"

"What do you think I'm suggesting?" He couldn't help messing with her.

"I don't trade anything for sex, Owen."

"Get your mind out of the gutter, Miz Montaigne. Come work for me."

"You mean at Easy Money?"

"Yeah. You've waited tables, right?"

"Only all through college. I waited tables at a place near Sac State, and once I turned twenty-one, I worked the bar side."

"Good. You start tonight."

Her eyes widened. "Tonight? I still have to unload all my things from my car, and to do that I have to move things around in the garage to make space." She tapped her chin. "Maybe if I offer to feed him, Yousef would drive up the mountain and help me."

"Work for me tonight and I'll help you unpack tomorrow."

She cocked her head, and he could see her considering his offer. "How long will I need to work to pay off my tire debt?"

"You'll work for an hourly wage plus tips. Your tire debt is paid by saving me the hassle of having to look for someone and going through the interview process. I hate that shit. I need someone reliable, which you are. As you're fussy about honesty and punctuality, I won't have to worry about that. Added bonus, you turn that sunshine smile of yours on the customers and you'll be raking in the tips."

"I'm fussy because I'm trustworthy and on time?"

He caught her look. "Maybe not fussy. Fussy's the wrong word. I meant particular. In a good way."

"You make positive character traits sound boring as heck."

"Not at all. They're all good qualities in an employee." The more he thought about hiring her, the more the idea appealed. "Added benefit? I'll be able to keep an eye on you."

She tossed her head back and he got the clue the ice he was skating on was getting thinner. "Keep an eye on me? What makes you think you need to do that?"

"Some asshole stabbed your tires multiple times, princess."

"My car being vandalized doesn't mean you need to keep an eye on me."

"Look, someone messed with your car. Could be an asshole was being an asshole. But it could also be someone who recognized that CRV as yours. I don't like the idea of you being targeted, so I'm keeping an eye on you."

"Is that so?"

"Yeah, that's so." He wasn't oblivious, he recognized that snooty tone for what it was, a way of trying to freeze him out. It wasn't going to work, but he figured talking about it any further would give her too much time to dig in her heels. "You in? You want to spend your summer serving drinks at Easy Money?"

She chewed her bottom lip, seeming to be considering all the angles. "I'm thinking about it. Not because of your silly notion I need a babysitter, but because I need income this summer." She tapped her fingers. "I'd have to work out a schedule with Mom so someone is always with Dad."

"Of course. Your family is a priority."

He waited for her answer with more anticipation than he wanted to admit.

"Yeah, okay. But I'm holding you to your promise to help me unpack my car."

He let out a breath he hadn't been aware of holding. "Not a problem." He lifted his chin in the direction of the door. "Let's go downstairs and get the paperwork filled out."

CHAPTER SIX

On her break, Keeley sat on a stool at the end of the bar, arching her back to stretch tired muscles. Owen held a glass under the tap, filling it with the clear amber of Cider Mill Hard. There was no denying the air of competence Owen exuded as he moved around the bar. He worked one side while Jen did the other. He must know exactly how long it took to fill glasses from the tap because he didn't even watch what he was doing. Instead, his gaze was constantly scanning his bar and the floor before returning to the tap at the right moment to cut the flow.

She hoped he saw that people were having a good time. Easy Money was a popular establishment, and Owen had set it up to be comfortable and welcoming. She'd spent many enjoyable hours there. It was a vital part of the Sisters' community, especially since he sourced much of his food and beverages locally.

An Eagles cover band from the nearby town of Nevada City was performing on the stage and Keeley hummed along with "Peaceful Easy Feeling" while watching dancers out on the small dance floor.

Owen set the trio of glasses filled with cider in front of three middle-age women who looked like they were having a girls' night out. Keeley didn't think it was an accident they'd chosen Owen's end of the bar. Why not enjoy the view? In this case the hot guy working the taps, while having that girls' night.

Another server moved up to the bar. Josie'd been in the same year as Keeley and Delaney at Sierra High. Keeley had no idea how much time it took Josie to apply her makeup, but it looked flawless. Her skin was radiant and her eyes were an artistic masterpiece. Keeley's own makeup was nonexistent. Add to that, Owen hadn't had size medium so the Easy Money polo shirt she was wearing was a large. Keeley figured the combination made her look about twelve years old.

"How are you holding up, prom queen? This job isn't for sissies."

Ah, there it was. Josie had been unhappy ever since Keeley'd shown up, and she'd learned her high school rival was her new coworker.

Back in the day, Josie'd tried bullying her, but Keeley'd had a tight friend group who'd stuck up for her. She recalled overhearing teachers talking and Josie being described as rough around the edges. The assessment seemed right.

Keeley could get along with pretty much anybody, but Josie'd made that a challenge. She saw everything as a competition, whether for swim team captain (which had gone to Josie), GPA (an easy victory for Keeley), or, during their senior year, prom queen.

Josie had not taken it well when Keeley'd been chosen by the student body and earned the prom queen crown, and she had no doubt Josie and her coven of mean girls were responsible for the Montaigne house being TP'ed, eggs thrown against the windows, and a crude chalk drawing of an erect penis with the word "slut" showing up on the garage door the following night.

So here they were, both working at Easy Money, where right off the bat Josie'd telegraphed the message loud and clear that Owen was hers and Keeley better not even think about looking in that direction.

"It's Keeley, and I'm holding up fine."

Josie had gone the opposite direction on the Easy Money polo and was wearing a shirt a size too small. She'd left the buttons undone, and the material pulled tight across her chest showcased her impressive boobs. Points for Owen that he kept his gaze well above the danger zone when he took the check holders with credit cards from Josie.

Cyndi Lomeli, who'd been a couple years ahead of them in school, sat at a stool two seats away. She leaned toward Keeley to whisper conspiratorially, "Let me know if you need any pointers, sweetie. I come in here so often I bet I could run the place myself. Or if Owen doesn't treat you right. He can be a grump sometimes, but he's really a big teddy bear."

Owen was a big teddy bear? She'd seen him moody, growly, and intense. But not once had she thought he acted like a big, cuddly teddy bear. She smiled. "Thanks, Cyndi."

"Owen, honey," Josie cooed as she leaned over the bar, cleavage on full display. "My car is acting up so I had to walk here today. You think you could give me a ride home after we close?" She gave an obvious wink. "I could make it worth your while."

Owen set drinks on Dion's tray then took the check holders to Josie. Dion, a college student with beautiful brown eyes and a Don Juan vibe, was the other server for the evening.

Owen nodded to Josie. "I'll get you home."

When Owen moved down the bar to mix a drink, Josie turned to Keeley and Cyndi, a smirk on her lips. "And that, ladies, is how it's done. See the big hands and big feet on that man? You know what that means, right? I'm gonna get me some of that tonight."

Barf. That kind of predatory pursuit had never appealed to Keeley, but she wondered if it might appeal to Owen. What did she know? Maybe he was a man-whore and was into it.

Ignoring the unsettled feeling, and unwilling to attribute it to jealousy, she stretched her legs. She needed to build up her stamina if she was going to be on her feet and on the move for long stretches of time.

Owen had started her bussing tables, taking the empties through the swinging door. Three cooks worked at the grill and prep station at the far end of the kitchen. Closer to the door was the stainless sink and a heavy-duty dishwasher. She'd already pushed through four loads, mostly glasses.

Wrangling middle schoolers was exhausting, but waitressing was exhaustion on a whole different level. Her mind was still spinning over what had transpired over the past two days.

Was it only yesterday that she'd packed her teacher things into her car, ending up stranded on the mountain until rescue came in the form of the grumpy, sexy bar owner?

And this morning she'd been there when her friends learned they were all pregnant. That was mind-blowing in itself.

And now, only hours later, she was working in a bar for the grumpy, sexy bar owner who thought she might be in danger. Unreal.

In the last hour, Owen had relented and given her two tables. She'd been to Easy Money often enough as a customer she was already familiar with the menu.

In addition to beer and hard cider, the bar served hard liquor and basic cocktails. So far, taking orders had gone pretty well. She'd messed up only once, delivering a gin martini because she'd neglected to specify the customer had ordered one with vodka.

Owen set a glass of ice water in front of her with a scowl. "Drink it."

"Bossy much, boss-man?" That earned her another scowl.

She felt like she'd been moving nonstop, carrying trays heavy with drinks and clearing the empties. At a guess, she'd walked back and forth across the floor to the bar at least a hundred times. She arched her back again. Maybe two hundred.

She spun on the stool to take in the ambiance. Easy Money was a popular hangout for both regulars and tourists who visited the mountain towns of California's gold country where fortunes had been made as often as dreams dashed in the gold rush following the discovery of gold in 1848.

A glass-block three-quarter wall separated the dining area for those who preferred a quieter atmosphere.

Keeley thought Easy Money looked charming with its open beams and the long mahogany bar gleaming in the warm light. The place had been in operation since before the turn of the twentieth century, and she liked how Owen respected its history. He'd made large prints from black-and-white photos showing the early days of the town and hung them in tasteful groupings along the walls.

She also liked how Owen supported local producers, including Walker's Cider Mill Hard line of hard ciders: apple, apple cinnamon, and pear. The glass Owen was filling was for a customer sitting on Cyndi's other side, who'd ordered a hard cider for the first time. Sometimes converts were made one sale at a time.

The kitchen at Easy Money had closed at ten and the band that had kept the crowd dancing and singing along was packing it in.

A few customers were having their last drinks before the bar's last call at midnight. Big city bars might stay open later, but in Sisters, midnight was late enough. Thank god.

Teaching middle schoolers kept her mentally on her toes, but taking orders and serving beers kept her *literally* on her toes.

The other thing that kept her on her toes? Time and time again she'd look up to find Owen's sharp blue gaze zeroed in on her. He was keeping an eye on his new employee, but the result was she'd become hyperaware of him.

Of the way he moved. The low timbre of his voice. His competence as he filled drink orders.

She'd had the fleeting thought that killing her tiny crush might be more successful as she got to know Owen better. Like maybe the attraction would sour the more time she spent with him. The opposite was proving to be true, and she realized she was in deep, deep trouble.

The other revelation of the evening? Turned out she was special, and not in a good way because Owen wasn't grumpy with everyone the way he was with her. He wasn't what could be described as affable or effusive in his interactions with people. In fact, she'd say he was reserved. But he paid attention and had conversations, real conversations, with the people sitting on stools at the bar.

Keeley knew good and well Ted Alvarez drank only Coke, and most nights occupied the last stool at the bar for a couple hours, but Owen never tried to move him along so a higher ticket customer could have the spot.

On a completely different level was Owen's habit of bracing his arms against the bar and leaning in. If he was wearing his shirtsleeves pushed up to his elbows, as he often did, the tendons in his arms rippled.

Why she found that ridiculously sexy, she had no idea. He was currently talking with Ted like he was the only person in the room. That was a singularly unique skill, being surrounded by people, but able to tune them out and attend to the individual.

Ted said something and Owen threw back his head and laughed. Sweet baby Jesus, she felt that laugh like an electric current glowed red hot in her belly.

If he kept on being so dang appealing, she wouldn't last the week, much less the summer, without propositioning her boss for sex.

***

Keeley groaned when a pounding sound breached her consciousness. She didn't bother opening her eyes. Any o'clock on a Sunday was too early for someone to be outside making a racket. The pounding stopped, as it should. She snuggled farther under the covers and let herself slide back into sleep.

"Out of bed, princess."

"Shh. Sleeping."

Dream Owen should let her sleep. In the darkest hours of the night, Dream Owen had been outrageously sexy, leaving her all wet and wanting, and wishing she'd invested in a vibrator. If he was going to be like that in the middle of the night, he could leave her alone in the morning. Dream Owen had lost his chance and now she only wanted sleep.

The quilt and bedding she'd pulled up around her ears was rudely yanked down. "Last chance, sweetheart. Out of bed."

"Thought I was princess."

"Got that right."

That didn't even make sense. She tried to tug the blanket back up, but gave in. "If you're gonna leave me all hot and bothered again, you can just go away," she mumbled.

The mattress dipped and she managed to open one eye. A sharp gaze burning with the bluest part of the flame bored into her.

"You're not Dream Owen, you're Real-Life Owen."

"Real-Life Owen is interested in what Dream Owen was up to."

Braced with his hands planted in her pillow on either side of her head, and, yep, arm tendons rippling, he leaned over her. His gaze traveled from the top of her head down, heating her skin like a physical touch. She really hoped her oversize sleep shirt hadn't slipped down to reveal boob.

Her jaw cracked with a yawn. Yeah, that was sexy. "What are you doing here?"

He closed his eyes, the muscle in his jaw tightening. "Trying my damnedest not to swallow you whole."

"Too bad you're not Dream Owen."

If he were Dream Owen, she'd tug him down next to her to cuddle while they both drifted back to sleep. Or maybe they'd have sexy times, and then go off to dream land.

But nope, Real-Life Owen wasn't interested. At least she didn't think so, but maybe swallowing her whole was a sexy innuendo?

She'd have to think about it after caffeine had been consumed.

He straightened with a sigh as weary as any eighty-year-old's. "Goddamn it."

He scrubbed a hand over his face, his whiskers making a nice crinkly sound that gave her goose bumps.

Everything about him, from the way he filled out his faded Levi's, to the outline of his pecs on his navy knit shirt, gave her goose bumps.

Feeling slightly more clear-headed, she studied him. He looked to be waging an internal war with an uncertain outcome.

He wanted her, that much was evident given the substantial bulge in his jeans. A new development, but his behavior said he didn't want to want her.

She sat up, pulling the bedding around her shoulders like a shroud. "What are you doing here? Why are you in my bedroom?"

"I'm here because I promised to help you get your shit unpacked and stowed in the garage. I'm in your bedroom because your fucking door was unlocked."

She rubbed a fist across her forehead. Sex dreams featuring the man standing in front of her followed by said man in the flesh—no, *flesh* wasn't a word she should be thinking if she didn't want to combust on the spot—was making her feel more than a little like she'd been sucked up by a tornado and then spit out a mile down the road.

"I didn't leave my door unlocked. Did you bring coffee?" She had more to say, but it'd have to wait because, again, caffeine. The struggle was real.

"Me standing here is evidence the door was unlocked." Real-Life Owen gave a head shake. "You got a coffeemaker?"

She nodded.

"I'll put the coffee on, you get your ass out of bed. I'll meet you in the kitchen in five minutes."

It was closer to ten minutes before Keeley shuffled into the kitchen.

"Bunny slippers?" He leaned back against the counter holding one of her white crockery mugs. His face might appear to be perfectly expressionless, but she'd been paying attention and was learning the silent language of Owen Hardesty.

It was subtle, but there was something around his eyes that suggested a hint of humor.

"Shut up." She got creamer from the fridge and saw him wince when she poured a generous amount into her mug. "You judging me?"

He wisely shook his head. "Hell no. Why—"

Finger raised to forestall his question, she sipped the ambrosia of the gods. "Too many words." She pointed to the halfway mark on her mug. "About here. No more words until coffee has been consumed to this point."

He frowned, which was actually helpful for her equilibrium because it was normal and helped banish her sexy Owen dreams.

She shuffled to the fridge and took out a bag of whole grain English muffins. She held them up with raised brows. He nodded. Communication with no words. Perfect.

Within minutes toasted English muffins on pretty plates, a bowl of sliced bananas, peanut butter, and a jar of the boysenberry jam she'd made the previous summer were all on the little dining table with its cheerful tablecloth.

Owen took the seat opposite her. He spread peanut butter and jam on a half muffin, eating a good portion of it in one bite.

Peanut butter, banana slices, jam. Yum, she bit into the goodness. Breakfast was her favorite meal of the day. It was twenty minutes where she could savor the simple pleasures of toast and coffee before tackling whatever the rest of the day had in store. And somehow this morning she had the moody and hunky gorgeousness that was Owen Hardesty sitting across from her.

He glanced at her mug. "We safe to talk now?"

She gave him a sunny smile and nodded "Yep. It's all good."

He paused, seemingly snagged by her smile. That was a nice boost to the ego.

"All good," she went on, "except for you coming in my house and in my bedroom without an invitation. Why is that?"

"You weren't answering your door. I was concerned, so I tried the knob. It wasn't locked."

He said it like that explained everything. "Still not seeing it, big guy. I'm pretty sure I locked my door, but even if I hadn't, that doesn't somehow imply permission for you to wander in."

"I was making sure you were safe. Someone vandalized your car, remember? Maybe you were targeted. That means you could be in danger. You can't fucking leave your house open."

"Okay."

"Okay? That's all you have to say?" He was back with the scowls and growls.

"About that? Yes. I should have double-checked that I'd locked up last night. It was late, I was tired, and I must've forgotten. I'll do better." She took another sip of coffee. "That still doesn't explain you being in my bedroom."

"That's where you were, so that's where I went." His expression shifted, and she had zero trouble reading exactly where his thoughts had gone because his eyes smoldered. Yes, smoldered.

Like they'd done when he'd leaned over her, caging her in with his hands fisted in her pillow. She'd open a window to let in the bracing mountain air if it wouldn't give away that he'd gotten her hot with merely a look. "You have a sex dream about me, princess?"

Holy smokin' moly. His already low voice had lowered to bedroom voice, the type of bedroom voice that whispered dirty, seductive words in the darkness.

He quirked a brow and she opened her mouth to reply. Reply what? She had no idea. The front door swung open and she was saved from having to answer.

Wearing a Van Morrison t-shirt and flannel pants, Bruce Montaigne walked slowly into the cottage. His hair was mostly gray and curled around his head in a halo. He'd lost the erect posture that'd always made him seem so tall when Keeley was a child.

"Hey, Dad. Where are your shoes?"

Bruce looked down at his feet, seemingly surprised to find them bare. "Breakfast?"

Keeley had noticed her dad not tracking conversations and using shorter sentences, another symptom of his disease. God, she wished she could stop time.

Bruce sat at the table. Before Keeley could push her plate in front of him, Owen was handing him the half of his English muffin he hadn't eaten.

"Have some breakfast, Bruce."

"Oorah, Marine."

"Oorah, brother," Owen responded.

Keeley grabbed her phone. "I'll get you some socks." She rushed to her bedroom. Sometimes her father's condition hit her harder than others. This was one of those times.

She screwed her eyes tightly closed against the tears, leaning with her back against the wall while drawing in deep, shaky breaths. Wiping her eyes, she texted Abby to let her know Bruce was with her.

Socks in hand, she returned to the table. Owen gave her a searching look. He took the socks and held them up to her dad. "You do these yourself or you need help?"

Bruce raised his bare foot, chewing thoughtfully while Owen pulled the socks on for him, first one foot, then the other.

Damn it. Why did he have to be kind? Why couldn't he stay grouchy and surly and be generally disagreeable so she could make progress on killing the crush? She needed grumpy Owen back, stat.

"You got back too late, young lady."

Keeley raised a brow. She hadn't heard that tone since she was a teenager.

"I'm working at Easy Money now, Dad. It closes at midnight, so I get home late."

He shook his head. "Clock said two forty-two. I heard the car out front. Had my window open a crack. I like the air. I heard you walking around."

"I was already home and asleep by two. I wasn't walking around."

"I heard you walking around." Bruce's tone turned bellicose. "I may be losing my mind, but I know what I heard."

"It doesn't matter, Dad." There were so many things she hated about Alzheimer's, but Bruce becoming combative was one she hated more than others.

"Bruce, you and I can look around. See if we find any footprints. If Keeley wasn't walking around, it could've been someone else."

"I'll get his shoes."

CHAPTER SEVEN

Owen glanced at his watch. It wasn't like he was worried about her. Keeley could take care of herself. She was competent, smart, and as much as he gave her a hard time, she didn't take unnecessary risks.

But his time in the military, and then as a cop, had taught him to respect his gut. It'd saved his life more than once, and he'd learned not to dismiss the instinct. And right now it was telling him something was going on with Keeley.

He and Bruce had walked the property. There were footprints here and there, but it was impossible to say they weren't from the family or people who'd visited in the recent past.

Same with the fresh tread marks in front of Abby and Bruce's home. The couple's cars were parked in the garage, and Keeley's was in the spot to the right of her cottage.

Maybe the tire tracks were from a delivery van or the postal carrier, or the paint guy Abby'd called to get a quote for painting the exterior. Or maybe they'd been made in the middle of the night by someone scoping out where Keeley Montaigne lived.

Another glance at his watch. Five minutes until she was due to start her shift so it wasn't like she was late. He picked up the remote and turned the channel on the TV over the bar to distract himself with the Kings basketball game. The effort at distraction didn't work because spending the day together meant his head was filled with images of her.

Her cottage had a small one-car garage with no room for a car because Keeley was storing furniture and boxes from the apartment in Sacramento she'd moved out of months ago. They'd worked together to make room and then unloaded the contents of the CRV.

He'd known helping her was a bad idea. Like hiring her to work at Easy Money was a bad idea. Sure, he needed staff, but being in her orbit messed with him.

Case in point, she sang under her breath while she'd worked unloading shit from her car. He didn't think she was even aware of it. It was fucking adorable.

Then she'd found this huge envelope made from pink construction paper and sealed with a smiling heart sticker. Her students had made going away cards liberally decorated with glitter and crap, and her guy friend Yousef had stashed them in her car for her to find.

She'd sat right down on the garage floor and read every one of those cards. And cried. Sure, he realized now she happy cried, but it still gutted him to see her with tears on her face.

It made him think he had to do something, fix something, make it all better. Anything to stop the tears.

Did he need to know she sang while she worked or had a soft heart? Hell no, because it was one more thing that made her too damn appealing.

The other thing that made her too damn appealing? Finding her asleep in her bed that morning, soft, warm, and desirable as hell.

But finding out she'd had a sex dream? Featuring him? Holy fucking shit. He'd never in his life wanted something as badly as he'd wanted her. He'd managed only a shaky hold on his sense of self-preservation, which had kept him from climbing into that bed and giving them both what they wanted.

And now he was getting worked up all over again. He needed to get his shit together.

He pulled the tap to fill tall glasses with Cider Mill Hard and set them on a tray for Dion to deliver to the trio of college-age bros at a high-top table in the corner. They were barely old enough to drink. He knew that because he'd checked their IDs.

He resisted looking at his watch again and restocked the well, then checked the contents of the underbar refrigerator: pickled onions, maraschino cherries, juices, and syrups. All good.

Another minute and she'd be late. A movement in the hall had him jerking up his head, and he saw it was Josie. She gave him a cool look before heading through the swinging door to the hall with the employee lockers.

She could be pissed at him all she wanted because he was damn pissed at her. She'd asked for a ride home. He'd given her a ride home. No big deal. But he sure as hell hadn't expected her to reach across the center console to grab his crotch before they were even out of the parking lot. He'd removed her hand, and she'd followed up with an offer of a blow job. He'd made it clear if she tried something like that again he'd fire her ass. She could deal with the rejection if she wanted to remain employed.

The memory put him in a sour mood all over again. He'd give Keeley one more minute and then he was calling her. She'd think he was overstepping, but that was too bad. His watch showed exactly four o'clock. He was reaching for his phone when she walked in. He immediately felt that something coiled tight in his gut relax.

She was with him and she was safe.

He sighed in resignation. He was truly fucked.

Business was good for a Sunday night, mostly couples having an early dinner with a few solo drinkers sprinkled in. Once he realized Keeley didn't need to work up to waiting tables, he'd scheduled her as waitstaff. He listened to her patter. She knew drinks and wasn't shy about pushing the Cider Mill Farm line.

As he'd expected, she charmed customers with her sunny smile and talent for chatting with sincere interest even when keeping an eye on her other tables.

It was because he was paying attention that he noticed her freezing mid-stride. Owen followed her line of sight to the man who'd come in through the front door.

"Keeley, baby." A guy with a waxed handlebar mustache and a stupid man-bun rushed across the floor. Were man-buns still a thing? Were handlebar mustaches ever a thing?

Keeley had a tray tucked under her arm and was backing up when he grabbed her shoulders and brought her in for a hug. "Long time, no see, sweet thing. I can't believe you're working at a bar. It's cool, but not what I'd have chosen for you."

Keeley pushed back from the embrace, turning her face away so the kiss the asshole aimed for her lips ended up on her cheek instead.

Oh hell no.

Owen rounded the end of the bar, only stopping when Keeley flashed him a warning look.

"Jaxon, what are you doing here?"

"Why, I'm visiting you, of course. I couldn't believe it when I heard you'd moved back to your little hometown. I've looked around a bit. I'll give you that it's quaint but, honey, you'll be bored out of your gourd in weeks. There's nothing to do here." He spoke in an overly loud voice, glancing around like he was checking that he had an audience. Man-bun's scan of the room checked when he caught sight of Owen, eyes narrowed and with his arms crossed over his chest.

"Hands off, pal." The guy jumped at the growled words.

"No worries, dude." He gave a nervous laugh. "Keeley's my girl."

Owen stepped forward. "The hell she is. Get your hands off her."

"Owen, it's fine. I'll take care of it." She looked pointedly at the guy's hand still on her arm and he had the sense to release her. "You're my *ex*-boyfriend, Jaxon, and hardly even that. We casually dated, and only for a couple months."

"They were a good couple months though, right, sweet thing? Take a break and have a drink with me. I'll pay if you can get us a discount." He winked. Owen had a hard-and-fast rule never to trust a dude who winked, and when this douche did it, he had to fight the urge to mess up his mustache with a punch in the face.

Keeley must've sensed Owen was close to violence because she gave him a narrow-eyed look. "I'm taking my break." She pointed to a table in a quiet corner and told man-bun, "Go sit down. I'll be there in a minute."

The asshole had the temerity to give Owen a two-finger salute as he sauntered off.

"I don't like assholes in my place," Owen growled.

"Kind of hard to filter out all the assholes." She circled the bar and grabbed a couple glasses and filled them with ice, water, and lemon slices. It made him feel marginally better she wasn't drinking with the guy.

Owen returned behind the bar and began filling orders to get caught up. He also paid attention to the two in the corner.

Keeley appeared to be giving it to him with both barrels, talking emphatically and gesturing, while man-bun's body language went from cocky and open to insolent and surly, his movements jerky as he emphasized whatever he was saying.

Finally, he shoved up from the table, bending to say something in Keeley's ear. What she said back had him whirling around to stare daggers at Owen. He was all attitude as he sauntered toward the door, flipping Owen the bird over his shoulder before pushing through.

Keeley took their glasses through to the kitchen. Owen caught up with her as she stood at the sink, eyes closed, breathing through her nose like it would somehow settle her. "Take your break. Go sit in my office."

Her eyes flared open. "I already had my break. I'm fine. I need to get back to work."

"You're not fine, princess. You had a run-in with an asshole with a fucking stupid man-bun. My office is quiet. Go sit in there." When it didn't look like she was moving, he added, "That's an order."

She scowled, and he thought she'd blast him. But then her shoulders sagged and she gave a terse nod and crossed to his office, shutting the door firmly behind her.

He gave her five minutes before checking on her.

She looked better, sitting tilted back in his chair, though he'd caught her rubbing her forehead. He closed the door behind him, using his foot to roll her chair over so he had room to lean back against the edge of his desk. His office was claustrophobic to begin with, and with both of them in the space it was damned cramped.

"What'd he want?"

She crossed her arms over her chest. He kept his eyes determinedly on hers when the move pushed up her breasts.

"First, you can't give me orders. Even as my boss, you can ask, but you can't order."

He rubbed a hand over his face. "Here's the thing, princess. Sometimes I'll give you an order and you'll have to obey it. I was a Marine, I was a cop. That's how I operate. If it's important, I'll give an order and you'll follow it."

"Baloney. It's not like me taking a break in your office was a life-or-death situation. If you want me to do something, ask nicely."

"It was for your own good."

"I'll decide what's for my own good."

He shook his head. "We'll come back to this later. What'd he want?"

"Nothing. I took care of it."

"If you took care of it, then he didn't want nothing."

"It's none of your business." She stared up at the ceiling for a second then back at him. He had the feeling she was weighing how much to tell him. "At least it wasn't your business until he said something stupid, and I said something stupid back. I shouldn't have said it but I did and now I'm regretting it."

"Sounds interesting."

She gave him a withering glare.

"What'd you say that's got you upset?"

This time she looked down, tugging on the hem of her polo shirt, then let out a noisy breath.

"Spit it out."

"This is dumb, especially after I was mad you let Lou think the same thing." She fidgeted and began tapping her fingers on her thigh. "Okay, here it is. Jaxon wants to get back together. I don't know why because, like I said, we weren't together that long, and it wasn't great. But he's unhappy I broke up with him and says he misses me and he wants to get back together."

"Asshole doesn't deserve you, but I'm not seeing where I come in." He had an inkling, but wanted to hear her say it.

She put her hands over her face and spoke through her fingers. "I'm sorry, but I told him we're together."

Satisfaction rolled over the flash of panic. Fake was fine. It was the real deal that he didn't do. "Good. He'll leave you alone then."

She peeked through her fingers. "You're not angry?"

"Hell no. If it makes you feel safer, tell whoever you want we're together."

She dropped her hands. "No, I won't do that. I actually want a real boyfriend. Obviously, not him. But thanks. Jaxon has trouble understanding 'no' and it seemed simplest to say I was with someone else."

Owen wasn't boyfriend material, he was out of the running for that, but her comment made him want to punch his fist through the wall. She should be able to tell the guy no without having to bring in backup.

"Why do you need to find a real boyfriend?"

He must've telegraphed his irritation because she suddenly righted the chair. "Break's over," she said in an overly bright voice.

She rose to her feet, but she'd miscalculated because the space was so tight the only place for her to stand was between his legs. He stood too. They were so close her scent filled his head. Sunshine and blossoms.

They glared at each other. It felt like all the oxygen had been sucked from the room. Pink tinged her cheeks and her breathing quickened.

All he could think about was how he wanted to take her mouth. How he'd hitch her up onto the desk, step between her parted thighs, and slide his fingers into that silky fall of honey-brown hair. Then he'd dive in for a taste of that mouth, a taste he wanted more than his next breath.

But he couldn't do that. Couldn't let her know he wanted her with a yearning that made him insane. Because if he had her, theirs would never be a casual hookup.

He'd want more, she'd want more, then they'd be in a relationship. And that's precisely when he'd screw it up and end up hurting her.

Been there, done that, had the scars and ruined lives to prove it.

Whatever it was that had him thinking he couldn't live another day without the taste of her had to be caged in a corner of his brain with a chain and a padlock, never to be set free.

She stepped back. "This isn't a good idea."

She'd gotten that right, because even with the self-imposed restraints, he was afraid he wasn't strong enough to continue his resistance.

Basic truth?

He wanted Keeley Montaigne.

He wasn't good for her.

She wasn't good for him.

But he fucking wanted her.

***

Keeley stepped out of the office with the feeling she'd barely escaped the lion's den with her life. She pushed through the swinging door to the bar area. Of course, Josie was right there, looking suspicious. "Where've you been?"

"On break."

"You take a long-ass break, that means more work for me. You're in the wrong line of work if you want to be a diva."

Owen stepped through the door right after her. The expression on Josie's face would've been comical, except she'd obviously jumped to all the wrong conclusions. Keeley figured nothing she said would make the situation better so she ignored the comment and went to check on her tables.

The rest of her shift passed slowly. A headache had started with a dull throbbing behind her left eye, and by the time the last customer had paid their tab, all she wanted to do was get through the shutdown routine and go home to bed.

Plus, the headache made her short-tempered, and didn't help her deal with Josie, who'd been borderline abusive all night. Keeley gritted her teeth and ignored the snide comments. That plan worked until she headed for the restroom with the caddy of cleaning supplies. Josie passed her with a fake stumble and jabbed Keeley with her elbow. The second time that night.

Keeley felt the last fraying thread on her temper finally snap and she let loose. "Cut the mean-girl crap, Josie. No more throwing elbows. You don't have to like me, but you don't have to be so darned aggressive. Ignore me and I'll ignore you. But you jab me like that again, and I'll jab you right back." The words came out in a rapid stream of irritation.

"What are you talking about?" Josie had the aggrieved look down pat. "You bumped into me, and now you act like I assaulted you? Get real."

Owen had the chairs up and was mopping the floor. He paused, glowering at them as he leaned against the mop handle.

Keeley didn't care if Owen or Jen, who was at a booth writing on a clipboard, heard their argument. One of the cooks popped his head out the swinging door, looked alarmed, then retreated.

"Here's real for you." Keeley seethed, pulling up her shirt to show her lower rib cage. She pointed to the red mark that was already turning purple. "This is from the first time you elbowed me tonight."

"I *tripped* and accidentally brushed against you."

Owen was at Keeley's side in an instant, his expression furious as he scrutinized the bruise. He turned to Josie. "What the fuck, Josie? You did this to her?"

Josie morphed from self-righteously indignant to a teary victim in a heartbeat. "It was an accident, Owen. Keeley's slow and keeps getting in my way. I only want to do my job." Her eyes welled with tears.

"Either you're incredibly clumsy to be tripping and *accidentally* elbowing me while doing your job, or you're lying." The pain spiked in Keeley's head. "Given that this is the same mean-girl crap you tried fifteen years ago in high school, I'm going with lying."

Josie turned drenched eyes to Owen. "It's so unfair. I've worked here longer, but you treat her special, and then she acts like a diva to the rest of us. She's always been like that. Lots of girls hated her in high school because she thought she was better than everybody."

"This isn't fucking high school. Get over it."

"But it's not fair, Owen."

"I don't give a shit about fair. This is how it's going to be. You're to work with Keeley like you work with any other employee here, and that means you don't make comments, you don't bully, and you don't fucking jab them with your elbow. If you can't handle that, then you let me know and we can terminate your employment right now."

Keeley gave in and rubbed her thumb over her temple, where it felt like an icepick was skewering her brain.

Tears had Josie's mascara running down her cheeks. "You're so mean. It used to be fun working here. Now it's not."

"Don't give a shit about that either. We need to get this place closed down. Keeley, you're going home. Josie, if you want to keep your job, you're on refills."

"It's my job to do the bathrooms tonight," Keeley said.

"I'll do them. Get your stuff. I'll walk you out. Go home and deal with that headache."

Keeley groaned because the look in Josie's eyes told her Owen had confirmed everything she'd said about being treated differently.

Too tired to deal with it, she got her things from her locker, giving Owen a quiet thank you when he walked her out to her car.

CHAPTER EIGHT

"Got it, Dad?"

"I got it, I got it. Stirring's not rocket science."

Despite his response, Keeley kept an eye on him. She'd already caught him with the salt shaker, sprinkling away. They were following an oatmeal cookie recipe his mother had used when he was a boy. She'd seen a social media post suggesting baking with family recipes as a good activity to connect mid-stage Alzheimer's patients with their memories. Added benefit? Yummy cookies.

"Do you remember baking with Nana when you were little?"

He nodded. "Mama let me lick the spoon. The smell when they baked was the best."

"You'll have to let me know if these taste just as good."

She added the chopped walnuts to the mixture. Once they were folded in, Bruce carefully scooped dough to drop onto the tray. She slid the tray into the oven and set the timer.

Their marmalade cat Iggy sat on the wide window ledge, orange tail swishing as he watched birds at the bird feeder. Squirrels were his obsession, and more than once he'd thought he could pounce through the window. Good thing he was an indoor cat, or the wild animal population would be hunted into decline.

The wide window ledges were only one part of the kitchen remodel Abby and Bruce had done last fall. Quartz countertops, new cabinetry, and fresh paint worked together to make the space more welcoming and comfortable.

Bruce gave a jaw-cracking yawn. "I'm going to lie down."

"Okay, Dad. Our cookies will be done by the time you wake up."

Iggy trailed behind him. The cat was his constant companion. Keeley studied her father's gait. He seemed to be shuffling his feet more.

She sighed. Nothing would stop the progression of the disease, and it seemed like every week there was something new, something else to add to the list of what the disease had stolen from her dad, from their family.

Keeley sat at the kitchen table where she and her parents had shared so many meals and important family discussions. Their little family of three was all she had. Keeley'd had a little brother, briefly. Her mother had given birth to a little boy who'd died hours later. She'd been four when he'd been born, and what she remembered most was a deep sadness permeating their home. She'd always tried to be a good girl, not to cause trouble, and had tried to bring joy to replace the sadness.

For years her parents had kept a photo of the tiny infant on the mantel. She'd study his newborn face, searching for any clue of what he'd have looked like if he'd survived. Would he have kept the dark hair? Would he have had her dad's brown eyes, or Abby's gray eyes, or the mix Keeley had gotten with her hazel?

Her own pregnancy had ended after only a few brief months. She'd cherished that tiny life, but then it had been gone, disappearing in a rush of blood and pain. She'd learned at a young age that loving someone meant risking everything, since that person could be stripped away from you in an instant. Or, she thought, who they were could erode slowly over time by a memory-wasting disease.

Shaking off the melancholy, she rose to check the cookies. She hoped her friends' pregnancies were healthy and uneventful, and that all they had to worry about was picking out names and decorating nurseries.

While using a metal spatula to slide the cookies onto a cooling rack, her phone pinged with a text.

She prepped the next tray and had it in the oven before returning to the table to check her phone. Jaxon's name showed on the screen.

Ugh. He'd texted her after their breakup, trying to convince her to give them another chance. The texts had all been in the same vein: They were soulmates and belonged together. Their kind of love was destined by the stars. You couldn't argue with fate when fate had brought them together. Blah, blah, blah.

He'd finally stopped so she hadn't bothered blocking his number. So here he was again oozing about how it was fate that he'd run into her at the bar, and that he was still in town and they should get together for old times' sake.

Did he even remember their conversation the previous evening? She typed out a firm "no," and hit send. That was it, no explanation, no excuses. Then she blocked his number as she should've done months ago.

But a thought nagged at her: How had he known to find her at Easy Money? She wasn't buying that he'd happened to show up where she was working.

She sat with her chin in her hand as she thought of who she'd told where she was working: her parents, her friends in Sisters, Yousef.

Yousef was a gossip so he definitely could've told others, but while they'd met at a holiday party, Yousef and Jaxon didn't know each other. It wasn't like where she worked was a secret or anything, but it did make her wonder how Jaxon had known where to find her.

Abby came through the kitchen door carrying a grocery bag and wearing a trim quilted vest in deep purple over a long-sleeved t-shirt paired with olive green jeans. "It's warmed up a bit today. I think spring is truly on the way." She set the bag on the counter. "Those cookies smell heavenly. Your dad help you with them?"

Keeley nodded as she rose to put the kettle on for tea while Abby unpacked groceries. "He's napping. Baking wore him out." She sighed. "He's getting crankier, even a little mean."

Abby's sigh held a world of sorrow. "It's this monstrous disease. Your father is the kindest man I've ever known, and it's taking that part of him away from us."

"I know, Mom. It's hard for him, but it's harder on you."

Abby gathered Keeley in a hug. "It's hard on all of us." She released her daughter and together they put away the groceries.

Keeley plated the cookies, and in short order they were seated at the table, mugs steaming between them.

"I feel we haven't had time to catch up. Most days we pass each other while trading shifts caring for your dad. I'm thankful you're able to be with him more while Mrs. Troung is on vacation. It's a real help." Abby was a librarian and had cut back her hours to mornings only so she could be home for Bruce the rest of the day.

Abby bit into a warm cookie. "Oh, this is perfect." Wiping crumbs on a napkin, she said, "Tell me about the sisters. Are they feeling any pregnancy symptoms?"

"Not that I've heard. Delaney says Walker's been reading a book on pregnancy. He was looking a little green when he got to the part on childbirth."

"Oh, that's perfect. The bad boy is humbled." Abby laughed. "Now, tell me how it is working for Owen."

"For the most part it's fine. He can be grumpy." Keeley chose her words carefully. Abby hadn't been exactly subtle in her opinion that Keeley and Owen would make a good match. No sense in giving her mom false hope. "But he's also, I don't want to say kind, but he can be considerate in a grumpy Owen way."

Seeing a spark of interest told her she hadn't been as careful as she'd hoped. Keeley steered the conversation away from Owen. "Josie Whitlock works there and she's still as awful as she was in high school. She has the hots for Owen and decided I'm her rival. I've told her that's ridiculous, but she's hardwired to see me as her competition no matter what." Keeley's smile flashed. "She was complaining about something stupid from high school and Owen told her to get over it."

"Good for him. He's protective of you."

Keeley shook her head. "That's overstating things. Owen cares about you and Dad, so by extension, he keeps an eye on me. Add that my tires were stabbed after he told me my car would be fine leaving it on the side of the road overnight, and I think he feels some responsibility." She didn't know if she was trying to convince her mom or herself. There'd been that moment in the office that made her think maybe the heat wasn't one-sided. But that's all it'd been. A fleeting moment of feelings, soon to be forgotten.

"I think he's been hurt in the past so he's careful." At Keeley's raised eyebrows, Abby shook her head. "Whatever it is, Owen hasn't shared, but there's something painful there." She laid her hand over her daughter's. "No one gets through this life without some grief, but having strong love, sharing a life with someone who loves you deeply, makes it easier to bear."

***

Keeley steered her CRV up the driveway, the security light over the garage door coming on as she parked next to her cottage. Girls' night had been a blast. She'd spent the evening with Delaney and her sisters at her cabin. It'd started with Delaney and Keeley, then expanded to include Emery and Cam. They'd had so much fun. Delaney couldn't remember the last time she'd laughed so much. Walker had given them space and headed out to hang with his dudes at Easy Money.

Keeley and the sisters had spent the evening in digital detox, setting aside their phones and hanging out. They'd decided on crostini with everyone bringing their favorite toppings to go with Cam's fresh-baked baguettes, followed by a variety of delicious chocolates purchased at a new *chocolaterie* in town. They'd given each other DIY spa treatments so Keeley's face glowed from her facial, and her finger- and toenails were buffed and glossy with new polish called Cherry Bomb.

Emery had suggested they *not* spend the evening talking about their men and focus instead on other aspects of their lives. Fine with Keeley since she didn't have a man. Conversation had revolved around pregnancy and babies, as well as work and homes, and plans for the future.

It'd been great. Time with her friends always gave her an emotional boost. But Keeley couldn't help feeling her life had stalled.

Sure, she had a solid career, one she enjoyed and that gave her professional satisfaction. That was fine, but she was also back home living with her parents. She was there as they navigated Alzheimer's and its impact on their family: to emotionally support both her parents and to be part of her dad's care team.

But she couldn't help feeling her friends with their handsome husbands and beautiful homes were farther up the life curve than she was. She needed to renew her efforts to meet someone.

Lately though, dating seemed a chore. She couldn't lay that entirely at Jaxon's feet. Most of the men she met were perfectly fine, but none lit any kind of spark in her.

Blame for that lay entirely at Owen's feet. Working for him had been a strategic mistake because spending more time together had only deepened her stupid crush. The hope that more exposure would reveal his flaws and her crush would wither and die had been way too optimistic.

Once in bed with the doors locked and double-checked, she spent an hour scrolling through profiles on the dating app she'd joined. She swiped past dozens, and when none appealed, she told herself she was being too picky and went back for a second look.

One guy, Ric, was kinda cute in a nerdy sort of way. His profile said he was an entomologist with a state agency. He checked the gainfully employed box. His Instagram page showed he posted pictures of bugs. Lots of bugs. She chewed her lip, considering. Nerdy was okay, not everyone could be an Owen Hardesty. There was nothing wrong with insects being your passion. She tapped the "I'm interested" button and continued scrolling.

A chime sounded. Ric wanted to message her. Okay. With a couple of taps, they started chatting. Thirty minutes later she'd finally extricated herself from a text conversation about the life cycle of a particular species of parasitoid wasp that laid its eggs in the bodies of other insects and when the eggs hatched, the larvae ate the host.

Or was it the pupae that ate the host? Whichever, the end result was the insect host, after being eaten from the inside out, was dead.

She and Ric were *not* advancing to the next stage.

Keeley still had the creeps when she finally set her phone on her nightstand before she tried to fall sleep.

***

The next evening, Owen's Bronco was missing from the parking lot when she arrived at Easy Money for her shift. Jen was bartending, and for some reason, Owen's absence threw Keeley off.

"He's at his house," Jen said when Keeley asked.

"His house?"

"Yeah, you know, the house he inherited from his grandparents? A delivery for the remodel came in and he took the day off to deal with that and put in some hours."

One brief conversation with Jen and Keeley'd learned more about Owen than she'd ever known.

She worked her tables, chatted with customers, delivered orders, all the while mulling over the knowledge Owen had a house he'd never mentioned, and that he was remodeling.

Actually, there was no reason he should've told her, but it seemed important somehow. Also, his grandparents had lived in Sisters. She thought he'd been new in town when he'd bought Easy Money a couple years back, but grandparents meant family connections. She wondered if he'd visited as a boy.

Keeley didn't want to attribute the evening dragging to Owen's absence. Add in her dad's disease, and she was feeling a little down. A rarity for her.

When the last customer left a half hour before closing, Jen texted Owen, who replied they could close early.

Jen sent Dion and Josie home, then she and Keeley finished the closing routine. They walked out together, Jen locking the door behind them. Owen's Bronco was parked at the base of the stairs, indicating he'd returned sometime during the evening.

Jen's car was near the door while Keeley had parked at the back of the lot where a row of pine trees grew along a fence. It'd been the only area available when she'd arrived.

Lights were strung from tree to tree to illuminate the parking spaces. Jen started up her little Mazda and backed up, lowering the passenger window. Keeley fished around in her purse, searching for her keys and phone, chiding herself for not having them in her hand before leaving the bar.

"You good?" Jen peered through the window. Keeley knew Jen was meeting up with her boyfriend so Keeley waved her away.

"Yeah, I'm fine. See you tomorrow."

Jen drove off and Keeley continued across the parking lot, her hand still feeling around in her purse.

An indistinct sound brought her to a stop. She cocked her head and listened. A breeze whispered through the pines and it felt like the darkness from the moonless sky was closing in around her.

She shook off a feeling of unease. Until the sound repeated.

A footstep from near the back fence, then what sounded like something brushing against a tree trunk. It could be a raccoon or a skunk. Wild animals made their way into town all the time. But she didn't think it was a raccoon or a skunk. It sounded like someone moving against the rough bark of a tree.

She felt her phone and she let out a relieved breath. Now her keys. She opened her purse wider and used the flashlight on her phone to search. They weren't there. Her stomach sank. She'd probably left them in her locker.

When she'd come into the bar, she'd been chatting with Jen and not really paying attention, and rather than putting them in her bag she might've let them drop to the bottom of the locker.

Ugh. She'd have to bother Owen and ask him to unlock the door to Easy Money so she could check her locker.

The sound of a car passing on Main Street made a quiet whooshing sound. Footsteps sounded again, coming from behind her. She spun around thinking it might be Owen.

No one was there. Her gaze darted to the shadows around the trees, trying to locate the source of the sound, a difficulty with her heart pounding in her ears.

She'd reached her car, but without her keys she wasn't going anywhere. She turned back to the bar and again heard furtive steps that stopped when she did.

Sisters was a safe place. People didn't get accosted in parking lots. Though that was exactly what had had happened to Delaney in this very same parking lot shortly after Walker had returned to town.

She tapped the screen on her phone, putting it to her ear, slowly scanning her surroundings as she stepped back toward the building. The call was picked up on the first ring.

"Keeley, where are you?" Simply hearing Owen's voice helped settle her.

"In the parking lot. It's probably nothing, but I heard a noise and it scared me and I can't find my keys." She realized she was talking to a blank screen. He'd hung up on her.

She stared at her phone. What the heck?

A startled yelp escaped from her mouth when a form materialized from behind the tree she'd parked under. She barely registered the door of the upstairs apartment crashing like it had been flung against the wall, her attention zeroed in on the young man edging toward her.

"Gimme your purse."

Keeley jerked back. "What?"

"Your purse. Gimme your purse." Wearing dark jeans and a black hoodie with a beanie pulled low over his eyes, he was shorter than her and rail thin.

He was young, no more than a teenager. He made a jabbing motion and she gasped when light gleamed dully off a short-bladed knife gripped in his right hand.

She stepped backward, trying to put as much distance between herself and the knife as possible while keeping him in her line of sight.

He glanced over her shoulder, eyes widening. "Fuck. Dammit, bitch, gimme me the purse." He spoke fast, his voice cracking as he bounced on the balls of his feet. Then he lunged for her, grappling for the strap of her purse. She jerked away from him, phone flying from her hand to spin across the pavement. She flung her purse as far as she could hoping he'd go after it and not hurt her. Nothing in the purse was worth her life.

He darted after it, but had taken only a couple steps when a shirtless and barefoot Owen streaked past her, over two hundred pounds of pissed-off former Marine slamming into the younger man with the impact of a semi.

They both hit the asphalt, the knife skittering under the car. In seconds Owen had him face down on the pavement and was holding the mugger's hands with one of his own, his knee planted in his back.

Holy smokin' moly. Owen Hardesty was one beautiful man. The sheer physicality of all those gorgeous muscles in motion was a sight to behold. Then the reality of the situation crashed into her.

A kid had tried to *mug* her. Sisters wasn't New York or LA. She'd visited both cities and been perfectly safe. And now in her little mountain town, a kid had tried to take her purse by threatening her with a knife.

Owen's head swiveled as he scanned the area, then began to pat down his detainee. He found nothing in his pockets.

"Did you see anyone else?" he growled at Keeley.

She hadn't even considered her mugger might have an accomplice. She looked around. "I don't see anyone."

Owen snapped out orders rapid-fire. "Stay out of reach of this little shit and get your phone. Call 9-1-1."

"No, no. Don't call the police," the little shit wailed. "I'll get in so much trouble. I can't breathe, man, I can't breathe."

Keeping the kid's hands behind his back, Owen removed his knee.

Keeley gathered up her phone and purse, and took a moment to slow the breath wheezing in and out of her lungs.

She could've been hurt, but she was safe.

She needed to get herself together. Thankfully her phone screen hadn't been damaged. She fisted her hand with her index finger outstretched to keep it from shaking and called the emergency number. She was pleased her voice remained steady as she described the situation and gave their location.

When she disconnected, Owen ordered, "Now reach in my pocket and get my keys."

She shoved her phone in her purse and stepped over the kid's legs to slip her fingers into the slit pocket of Owen's sweats and tug out his keys. Her agitation must've been broadcasting out loud because he said, "Look at me." Her gaze found his and his calmness steadied her, settling over her like a warm blanket. "You're safe, Keeley."

Her breath came out in a whoosh. "I know. I'm sorry I'm such a wimp."

"Not a wimp. Just not used to this kind of situation. But you're safe now." When she nodded, he said, "Open the back of the Bronco. There's a black duffel in there. Open it, find the zip ties, and bring them to me. Got it?"

She nodded again.

She did as he'd directed, and in short order, Owen had the restraints in place. A siren wailed in the distance. He rose to his feet, leaving her mugger curled on the asphalt.

Owen swung around, and before she could draw a breath, his hands cupped her face, his thumbs brushing over her cheekbones. His gaze drilled into her, skimming over her face as if absorbing the details. His touch set off a power surge she felt from her head all the way to her toes. She wanted to burrow into him and hold on.

"You okay?"

She gave the briefest of nods. "Yes. You're here." She should totally shut up before she revealed too much.

He drew her closer, his expression fierce.

"Are you hurt?" she asked. "You hit the ground hard when you tackled him."

Intense was Owen's default mode, but she was witnessing his normal intensity on steroids. She imagined the adrenaline surging through his body amplified whatever was going on in his head.

The wailing of sirens drew closer.

"I'm fine," he murmured. His gaze followed his thumb grazing over her face and then lower to her lips, returning to burn into her eyes like blue flame.

He had to've felt the puff of her exhaled breath as his thumb pulled on her bottom lip. Her hands gripped his wrists. If he kissed her, and he sure looked like he wanted to, she'd need to hold on to him to keep from spinning off into the night.

He ducked his head, lips a whisper from hers, and…a patrol car sped into the parking lot, blue and red lights flashing, siren cutting off mid-wail.

The second patrol vehicle arrived right behind it.

CHAPTER NINE

Owen straightened and released her. She let go of him feeling like she'd come perilously close to the edge of something amazing or devastating. Maybe both. She pulled his keys from her back pocket to hand to him.

Leaving the headlights of their vehicles on, Sawyer and another deputy, a guy named Jake she remembered from high school, crossed to where she stood with Owen.

Sawyer put his hands on her shoulders and gave her a narrow-eyed scrutiny much like Owen had, but with a completely platonic vibe. "You okay, Keels?"

"I'm fine." She looked at her mugger where he lay motionless on the pavement. With his eyes closed he appeared very young. "He scared me, but didn't hurt me."

Sawyer squeezed her shoulders and released her. "You told dispatch you were mugged."

"He threatened me with a knife and demanded my purse. I threw it thinking he'd go after it and leave me alone. That kind of worked. I have two credit cards, but carry only a little cash. My phone's worth more than anything in my purse, but that's not what he wanted."

"Knife's on the pavement near the CRV's front driver's side tire." Owen used his toe to nudge the unmoving form curled on the ground. It was then she noticed blood oozing from a scrape on Owen's elbow. And he was standing there without a shirt or shoes. He had to be feeling the cold.

"I patted him down. Nothing in his pockets," Owen stated.

Sawyer and Jake each took an arm and hauled the kid to a sitting position. A scrape on his cheek looked painful. Jake replaced the zip ties with handcuffs.

"You recognize him?" Sawyer asked.

Jake shook his head.

"I know our local juvenile offenders, and he isn't one of them." Sawyer pulled off the beanie revealing tousled brown hair in need of a haircut. "What's your name, son?"

When that produced only a sullen scowl, Sawyer asked another question. "How old are you?"

"Fuck off."

Sawyer squatted to the kid's level. "Hell, you don't look much more than thirteen or fourteen."

"I'm sixteen, asshole."

"That's Lieutenant Asshole, and you being a juvenile made my evening a hell of a lot more complicated."

"I know him."

All the guys' heads swiveled in her direction. "I swear I know this kid. Did you go to Vista Middle School in Sacramento?"

"Fuck you."

Sawyer rose to his feet, frowning as he crossed his arms over his chest. "You gotta expand your vocabulary kid. 'Fuck' will only get you so far in this world."

"Fuck you again." His voice shook behind the bravado.

"Fernando." Keeley said the name and the boy's gaze flew up to meet hers, then he ducked his head when he realized he'd given himself away.

"You're Fernando. You were in Ms. Demaris's math class when you were in eighth grade."

He hunched his shoulders. "I'm not Fernando. I don't know you."

"His name is Fernando. I don't remember his last name. He was an eighth-grade student at Vista Middle School when I was subbing there. That would've been three years ago. I remember because I'd gotten my teaching credential like a month before. Pam Demaris took a temporary leave of absence and I subbed for her for several months."

Sawyer shook his head. "You're shitting me. A kid from your school shows up in Sisters and tries to mug you?" He crouched down again. "Listen up, Fernando. I'm going to read you your Miranda rights. Pay attention because there's going to be a quiz at the end."

Jake retrieved the knife and slipped it in an evidence bag, then used a flashlight to look behind the trees and under bushes. Keeley guessed he was looking for a backpack or anything else a kid might've had with him.

All through the conversation Owen stood at her back, not touching her, but his body radiating enough warmth it felt like he was. Which made her hyperaware of him.

She entertained the fantasy of leaning back and having him wrap his arms around her, holding her tight to his chest. Oh god, if only.

Her Owen crush was spinning out of control.

Done Mirandizing, Sawyer eyed Fernando. "How does a sixteen-year-old get to my town? Seems you'd need keys to drive yourself all the way from Sacramento, if you still live there. Curious, since you don't have anything on you. I'm guessing someone dropped you off. You tell me who that was, kid, and the DA might look favorably on your cooperation."

"You said I don't have to talk, so I'm not talking."

"A plus on the quiz, kid." Sawyer motioned to Jake. "Put him in back of the cruiser."

"I'll get the camera footage." Owen pointed to cameras mounted at the corners of his building. "I'm taking Keeley to my apartment. You want to get our reports you can come up."

Sawyer nodded. "All good. I'll join you once Fernando's on his way to the station."

***

Owen grasped Keeley's hand and pulled her with him across the parking lot.

His control was shaky. Her hand in his steadied him, but he couldn't stop the loop playing in his head.

She'd been working for *him*, had crossed *his* parking lot, and hadn't even made it to her car before a punk kid had pulled a knife on her. He didn't think the kid had any intention of using the weapon, but intentions didn't keep misjudgments from happening. She could've been badly hurt, or worse, before Owen could protect her.

That control had frayed perilously close to snapping when he'd had his hands on her. Kissing her would've been a colossal mistake. But god, he'd wanted that more than his next breath.

Kissing her would be an affirmation of life, proof she was okay, and it would put a dent in his craving, which he was having more and more difficulty controlling. And he knew if he kissed her, that control would slip.

He'd thought he'd been so fucking smart hiring her to work at Easy Money. Keep her close and be better able to keep tabs on her. That'd been the plan, and sure, that part had worked out. But Jesus H. Christ, seeing her nearly every freaking day, being in the glow of all that sunshine, only made the grinding need more acute.

He'd spent today working on his house and had been glad for the physical exertion. Using a sledgehammer, he'd broken through the plaster on a wall he was taking out. Then he'd run the Sawzall and used a pry bar to tear out the framing.

His idea was to remove the wall and open the kitchen to the dining area, where he planned to build an island with a work area on the kitchen side and stools on the other.

He'd thought of plumbing it for a sink but had decided against the idea. He'd caught himself wondering if Keeley'd like a kitchen island with a sink, and had confirmed he was truly screwed.

The lumber delivery had come at the right time to give him a break from her. He'd needed a day without anticipating working at the bar like a happy idiot because he'd get to keep eyes on her all night.

A day without seeing her walk into the bar and smile at him like a fucking ray of sunshine.

A day without hearing her voice, without smelling her scent of sunshine and blossoms when she passed by him.

A day to get control of his goddamn dick so he didn't have to fight a hard-on whenever she was around.

Normally he'd have checked on the bar operation before heading upstairs, but hadn't because he'd wanted to avoid Keeley. He should've gone downstairs at closing to make sure his employees made it safely to their cars. He'd screwed up.

"Wait, Owen."

"Why?" he snapped.

She looked startled and her hand tightened around his. He needed to dial back his shit. She didn't need him snarling at her because he couldn't deal with his own frustration.

"I think I left my keys in my locker. I'm really sorry, but would you mind unlocking the door so I can get them?"

"Later." He kept her hand in his as he climbed the stairs. His door hung open, evidence of how fast he'd exited his place after she'd called him.

All he'd heard was she was in the parking lot and scared, and he'd flown out of the apartment. He ushered her inside and pulled the door shut behind them.

Once inside, he forced himself to let go of her hand and step away from her. He crossed to the kitchen and opened a cupboard to retrieve the kettle from the top shelf. He filled it with water and set it on the cooktop.

Where the hell were the tea bags? If he kept busy, maybe he wouldn't haul her into his arms and pick up where that interrupted kiss left off.

She disappeared into his bathroom, returning minutes later with his blue and white first aid kit. She set it on the dining table and began taking out supplies.

"What are you doing?"

"Preparing to clean the scrape on your elbow. Your sweatpants are torn at the knee, so we'll see if you have a scrape there too."

"I'll take care of it myself."

He set a mug on the counter and finally found a box of tea pushed to the back of a drawer.

Did tea go bad? He hoped not because the box was years old.

The kettle started whistling and he turned off the burner and poured steaming water over the tea bag.

"Here." He set the steaming mug next to her.

"You made me tea."

"You like tea."

"I do. I'm not sure how you know that, but I do like tea." She gave him an assessing once-over. "Are you taking care of me, Owen?"

He crossed his arms over his chest, then winced when the movement pulled the road rash on his elbow.

"Look, princess, your mom gave me this tea when I was sick a couple years back. I can't stand the stuff, but she said it makes people feel better. You had a shock. I'm sticking with Abby's advice that the tea will help you feel better. Don't read any more into it than that."

"Got it. I'll let it cool while I take care of that scrape." She moved to the sink. "Now come over here so we can run warm water over it."

He was already shaking his head. "I'm good."

"You have dried blood all the way down your arm. I can see there's dirt in the wound." She narrowed her eyes. "If you don't let me clean it, I'm calling Mom so she can tell you to let me clean it."

He gave her his patented Owen scowl. She ignored him and reached for her purse to get her phone.

"Goddammit. Fine." He hated being outmaneuvered.

She smiled sweetly like she hadn't threatened him to get her way. She ran the water, testing it with her finger. When the temperature was to her liking, she pulled his hand under the stream. With liquid soap, she gently washed and rinsed, washed and rinsed, until the dried blood was gone.

She was standing too goddamn close. Her touch was soothing, her hair smelled like sunshine, and her shoulder brushed against the bare skin of his chest.

Earlier, relief that she was safe had nearly made him lose his shit, and if Sawyer hadn't shown up when he had, Owen would have kissed her. He'd have taken that mouth with his and put to rest the constant question of how they'd be together.

And here she was getting in his head again.

She held her breath when she directed warm water over the torn-up skin, washing away most of the dirt.

"Breathe, princess."

She let out a noisy exhale. "That has to hurt. I'm sorry."

"I've had worse."

She used paper towels to gently pat dry his skin. Head bent to her task, she used tweezers to carefully remove bits of grit from the wound. "I'm sorry. I'm sorry. I don't want to hurt you." The words were a murmured chant under her breath. It was fucking adorable.

Once she'd gotten the dirt out, she used a cotton swab to apply a thin layer of antibiotic ointment over the abrasion before taping a piece of gauze to cover it. She lifted her face to his. "I think that should do it."

"What, no lollipop?"

"I'm all out of lollipops." She raised up on her tiptoes and pressed a kiss to his cheek. "That will have to do. Now let's take a look at your knee."

"Knee's fine." His voice sounded like he was grinding rocks together. Why the hell had he made the stupid lollipop comment? It almost sounded like flirting, and he didn't fucking flirt.

Then she'd kissed him. A simple peck on the cheek and his brain had gone into system meltdown.

"Owen—"

"I said it's fine." He sounded like an ungrateful bastard, but there was no way in hell he could risk letting her put her hands on him again. He didn't trust himself not to lose all sense of decency and toss her over his shoulder and carry her off to his bed if she so much as breathed on him again.

The sharp rapping at his door was a welcome distraction. "Let Sawyer in. I need to grab a shirt and shoes."

When he returned wearing a hoodie and fleece-lined boots, Keeley was sitting at the table opposite Sawyer and sipping tea while she gave her statement.

Owen gave his, then got his laptop and pulled up video from the security cameras. Which made him furious all over again when he saw Keeley's frightened reaction to the little shit threatening her with a knife.

But she'd kept her wits about her and tossed her purse. Then the footage showed Owen as a blur of movement launching himself at the kid.

While he made a copy of the video, Keeley poked around in his kitchen and soon the aroma of brewing coffee filled the air.

Sawyer gave a grateful thank you when she brought him a cup. She looked at Owen, lifting an eyebrow in question. Yeah, because he was too scary to talk to. At his nod, she filled a mug for him too.

Owen leveled his gaze at Sawyer. "Any thoughts why a kid who knew Keeley would try to mug her for her purse?"

"Fernando's not talking so we've got nothing yet. He's a minor. We'll have to notify Child Protective Services and get him a public defender. He'll be held in juvenile detention while things get sorted out." Sawyer turned to Keeley. "Anything you remember about him?"

Keeley covered a yawn, shaking her head. "He was squirrelly like most eighth-grade boys. I think he got in trouble for something at the end of the year, but I don't remember the details."

It was nearly one a.m. and Owen didn't like her looking exhausted with dark circles under her eyes. "I think we're done for the night. Keeley needs to get home."

Sawyer gave him a knowing grin. Owen didn't even bother telling him to fuck off.

They trooped outside and down the stairs. Sawyer gave a brief nod before heading across the parking lot to his cruiser.

CHAPTER TEN

"Let's get your keys." Owen unlocked the back door of the bar, flipping on lights. The lockers were along the wall of a short hallway to the kitchen. Keeley went to hers and opened it. She held up her keys like a prize. "This makes me feel like such a loser. The keys were on the shelf when I grabbed my purse and I didn't even see them."

"You found them now. Let's go."

As they exited the building again, he asked her, "Is Josie still bothering you?"

Keeley shrugged. "Tonight was my first shift since 'the incident.'" She used her fingers to make air quotes. "She's giving me the silent treatment. That's a whole lot better than how she was Sunday."

"She's giving me the silent treatment too, because I didn't let her give me a blow job when I gave her a ride the other night." He stopped under the wash of light from the lamppost. "She pulls anything with you again, tell me right away. First time it happens, not after you're bruised and ready to take her down."

Owen jammed his hands in his pockets to keep himself from reaching for her. The urge to pull her into him and hold tight had him biting back an expletive. He was losing his fucking mind if he was fantasizing about hugging her.

As if sensing his tension, she suddenly looked dispirited. Her usual sunny optimism being replaced by sad eyes was a kick in the balls.

"Thanks for letting me back in for my keys. Um, listen, Owen, I'm sorry I'm a pain in the butt. I know you feel obligated to keep an eye on me. You've been really kind to my parents, and it seems that's put an extra burden on you concerning me. I'm grateful as well as sorry."

"That's bullshit."

"No, it's not. Friday night Mom asked you to leave your business to get me and you did that. Saturday you took care of my car. Then you gave me a job when I needed one. At least working for you means I'm giving something back. But tonight you risked your life and injured your arm protecting me when a kid tried to steal my purse."

Her lips moved into a ghost of a smile. "That's a lot when you've never had particularly friendly feelings toward me to begin with. You don't want my gratitude, I know that. But like I said once before, you have it anyway. But you've gone farther than needed to satisfy any kind of obligation to my parents. Going forward, I can take care of myself. You don't have to look after me, and I won't be a pain in your butt."

"That's still bullshit."

"You have a charming way with words."

Goddammit. He tipped his head back briefly to stare at the night sky, his jaw clamped shut to keep the string of profanity from spewing from his mouth.

She thought he didn't like her. The irony wasn't lost on him.

He was looking out for her in more ways than protecting her from physical danger. By keeping his hands off her he was saving her from heartache and misery.

If he was a lucky enough bastard to find she could love him, it wouldn't last because he'd destroy that love.

What Sawyer and Walker had that made them good husbands? He didn't have it.

He'd been a husband, been a father, and fucked up so badly he'd destroyed two lives. The gut-wrenching failures he'd left in his wake were huge red-letter evidence he posed an innate threat to any woman willing to risk a relationship with him.

He couldn't explain any of that to her, and it didn't matter. Nothing would stop him from continuing to watch after her as he'd been doing. She'd just have to deal.

They crossed the parking lot to her car. "How was the pie?"

"Gone."

"Right."

He sighed. "It was good, princess. Really good." Best pie he'd ever tasted.

She raised a brow. "You called me Keeley earlier."

"I've called you Keeley lots of times."

She shook her head. "Not before tonight. For some reason you think I'm snooty and snobby."

"What the hell? I don't think that."

"A princess is snooty and snobby. You might have said my name when talking to someone else, but I don't remember you ever actually calling me by my name. Until tonight."

"Don't read anything into it."

He thought he heard her mumble "heaven forbid" before he took the keys dangling from her fingers to unlock her car before handing them back. "Get in. Don't leave until I'm behind you in the Bronco. I'm following you home."

He didn't miss the eyeroll as she slid into her seat and shut the door. The window rolled down. "Didn't you hear a word I said? You don't have to look out for me anymore."

"I heard. Now you hear me. I'm not only following you home, I'm waiting until you get in your house, and then I'm testing the fucking door to make sure it's locked."

She opened her mouth to reply. Owen braced his arms on the door frame and leaned into her space. His was coming off too intense, but he couldn't help it.

"You've had your tires slashed. Your dad saw someone outside your house in the middle of the night, and tonight a punk kid, whom you knew, pulled a knife on you. Something is going on, *Keeley*, and until we figure out what that is, and all threats associated with you have been neutralized, I'm not standing down. Deal with it."

***

Keeley parked her CRV on Main Street and spotted Delaney across the street. She waited for a break in traffic to cross. A few shop owners had planted clay pots with pansies of deep purple, blue, and yellow, an optimistic decision since spring still hadn't fully sprung. But today was a beautiful day with the sun shining brightly, so maybe the warmer weather would stick around this time. One of her favorite views, the still-snowy peak of Payback Mountain, gleamed against the deep blue sky.

She joined Delaney and they meandered along the wooden boardwalk past an eclectic mix of shops. The boardwalk was a relic from the town's early gold mining days. The city maintained them as well as the historic buildings to preserve the old-timey atmosphere.

Keeley needed a distraction. Images from the night before kept buzzing around her head: the knife gleaming in Fernando's hand, Owen looking like the wrath of God as he'd taken down her attacker in a flying tackle, and the feeling of his warm skin against her lips when she'd kissed his cheek.

Then there was the realization nothing had really changed between her and Owen. While she worried she had hearts in her eyes whenever she looked at him, he still saw her as an obligation.

How was she going to kill her crush with Owen throwing himself into danger to protect her?

No matter that he was predisposed to being a protector and would have done the same for anyone, she had the sinking feeling that her crush was on a fast dive into something deeper. She wasn't too eager to examine the full extent of her feelings when Owen insisted on keeping his distance.

Except… There'd been that brief moment when he'd cradled her face in his hands, when his eyes had burned with a hunger that had made her heart yearn.

She didn't know what to make of that moment.

Maybe it'd been her imagination creating what she wanted and ignoring reality. He hadn't denied her assertion that he was looking out for her as a favor to her parents, but there'd been something about his touch that made it hard to extinguish all remnants of hope.

The grapevine worked fast and news of the night's events had reached Delaney. Thankfully her friend had restrained herself and let Keeley sleep until nine before calling.

Finally satisfied after Keeley'd gone over every detail of the evening, they'd agreed to meet in town.

Their destination was Retro Days, the shop run by their friend Mateo's mom, Antonia, which carried an eclectic mix of late mid-century furniture, housewares, toys, and miscellaneous other items.

Delaney stood with her hands on her hips. "What is it we're looking for?"

"Vinyl records. Dad grew up in the late sixties and seventies when rock music was big. There's an old turntable in the attic, and I thought if I found vintage albums he'd enjoy listening to the music."

"You know any of the streaming services would have all the music from that era he could want."

"I know, but according to Mom, when they were dating he'd pull out his records and play them for her. She gave me a list of some of his favorites. His doctor said tapping into solid old memories is sometimes helpful with Alzheimer's patients."

"I can see that. Okay, we'll look for record albums. What happened to his collection?"

"I guess when CDs debuted, he embraced the new technology and got rid of his records. Too bad."

Delaney pulled open the door, the bell above it making a tinkling sound. Speakers played The Doors intoning that this was the end.

Entering Retro Days was like stepping onto the set of an old TV show.

At the counter with a customer, Antonia waved with her usual smiling friendliness. "Hello, girls," she sang. "We've got a lot of new old things in. Have a look around."

"Oh, my gosh, look at this, Delaney." Keeley pulled her friend to a display of vintage toys and books. "Nancy Drew books with the yellow spine. My mom has the complete set."

"We spent that one summer reading nothing but Nancy Drew, remember?" Delaney picked up a doll with bright orange hair. "Do you remember Trolls? I wonder if they still make these."

They were browsing through bins of action figures when Antonia approached.

"Good thing you two came in, because I thought I'd have to hunt Delaney down." Antonia looked amazing in a top with a vibrantly colored flower-power design paired with bell-bottom jeans and chunky boots. Her long black hair was shot with streaks of silver.

She stood with her arms crossed but couldn't hold the stern look. She broke out in a beaming grin when she took Delaney into a hug. "I heard the news. How are you feeling?"

"I'm fine," Delaney shrugged, "except for my now tender boobs. I swear they grew a size overnight, which, by my husband's behavior, is a fascinating development. Other than that, I wouldn't know I'm pregnant."

"You and Walker will be the best parents," Antonia assured her. "This whole town is abuzz with the news you and your sisters are all pregnant at the same time. Do we have due dates?"

Delaney shook her head. "Nothing official. None of us has gone to the doctor yet, but by our calculations we're all due in the weeks before Christmas."

Antonia put her hands to her cheeks. "Holiday babies. Oh, that will be wonderful. Clara must be over the moon."

"She is. We FaceTimed her with the news. She's got another two weeks on her trip. I think she's a little anxious to be home and assure herself that we're all well."

"Of course she is. That's only natural." Antonia turned to Keeley. "And what's this I hear about you, young lady?"

"Me? I'm not having a baby."

"Not a baby but, ooh la la, you've got one handsome boyfriend. That Owen Hardesty is both a good man and a good-looking man. Three months ago, someone broke into my store. Do you know what they took? Legos. I had two vintage Lego sets and they stole them, as well as three G.I. Joe dolls still in their original boxes. Hunky Owen helped me put in a security system with an alarm and cameras. He suggested I put tracking devices on my more valuable inventory, which I've done. He looks after our community."

"They're a cute couple," Delaney added, her eyes dancing with delight.

Keeley held up her hand. She could feel her cheeks growing warm. "Sorry to quell the rumor, but Owen and I are not together."

"Oh." Antonia looked deflated.

"I wouldn't write them off," Delaney remarked. "Get those two together and you can practically see the sexy vibes bouncing between them. It's only a matter of time."

That perked Antonia up. "Sexy vibes are an excellent start." The bell over the door chimed and two older men entered the store. "Let me see if I can help these gentlemen. You girls have fun poking around."

A half hour later they walked out having found three classic rock albums from the list of artists Abby had provided.

"Let's go to Three Sisters. I'm jonesing for a cinnamon roll," Delaney suggested. "Hey, do you think I'm having a pregnancy craving? Walker will have to run into town every other day if my pregnancy craving is Rico's cinnamon rolls."

"Cam makes really good cinnamon rolls too," Keeley reminded her.

"True. Her apple pie cinnamon rolls are to die for. Once we open for the season, that'll work. I have to plan ahead for these things."

"Okay, friend, let's go. Even if it's not pregnancy related, we can still get cinnamon rolls."

"True story."

They walked the short distance down Main Street and stepped into the heavenly smells of Three Sisters Bakery with its wondrous blend of coffee, cinnamon, and baking bread.

As they stepped in, a dark-haired woman with a little girl was heading toward the door.

Delaney stopped short. "Melanie?"

The woman's eyes widened in recognition. "Oh my god. Delaney? And Keeley?"

Melanie continued to clutch the little girl's hand as she gave the women one-armed hugs. "I can't believe I ran into you two. I was trying to get up the nerve to call you." She looked flustered. "This is my daughter Adelyn."

She put a hand on Adelyn's shoulder. "Addy, these are friends from when Grandma and I lived here before you were born. This is Miss Delaney, and this is Miss Keeley."

"Hi there, Addy." Keeley smiled at the little girl. She guessed Addy to be around five years old. She had a sturdy little body, and shared her mom's dark hair and brown eyes.

"I love the sparkly unicorn on your shirt," Delaney said.

"It's an alicorn because it has wings." When she spoke, Addy showed a gap where she'd lost her two bottom baby teeth.

"Really?" Delaney cocked her head. "I've never heard of an alicorn."

"They're mythical creatures. I like reading about mythical creatures."

"Me too." Delaney grinned.

"Are you living in Sisters now?" Keeley asked Melanie.

Melanie ran a hand down her daughter's braid. She cleared her throat before responding.

"We're visiting but are thinking about moving back to Sisters. Mom moved to live close by when Addy was a baby, but I know she'd like to come back here." She shook her head. "I guess it's the perspective of age, but when I was a kid, I didn't appreciate that Sisters is truly a beautiful little town." She glanced at Delaney and squared her shoulders. "I got your email, Delaney. I'm sorry I couldn't be more helpful. I heard you and Walker got married. I'm so glad." The words came out in a rush. "I hate that I had anything to do with separating you two or his wrongful imprisonment."

"I know we'd like to better understand what happened."

Melanie seemed to give herself a shake. "I've got to get. We're in town with my mom. Addy and I came in here while she's meeting up with a friend. We're heading back home to Stockton this afternoon." She turned to address Delaney. "I know we need to talk. Maybe we can set something up, with Walker too, if he'd like. I think we all want to understand what happened back then. I can't this trip, but soon." She looked down at her daughter. "Mom and I both want to move back to Sisters, and if we can make that happen, it'll be this summer so Addy can start kindergarten here in the fall."

Delaney nodded. "Let's exchange numbers so we can stay in touch."

***

Keeley spent the afternoon hanging out with her dad. She brought down the turntable from the attic and they played the records she'd bought. They sang along with Mick and the boys while Iggy gave up watching squirrels in exchange for the spinning turntable.

Keeley enjoyed her dad's laughter as Iggy's head spun around following the record. She stroked the orange cat, making him purr, while listening to her dad's story of him and three college friends driving through the night to attend a music festival featuring The Band. Which was great until he'd insisted he wanted to call one of those friends. Reminding him the friend had passed away was awful. It was like he was losing him for the first time.

Her mom came home from the library, which gave Keeley half an hour to change and get to Easy Money.

CHAPTER ELEVEN

She was glad she'd kept expectations low about anything changing between her and Owen because when she showed up for her shift, his face morphed into his usual made-for-Keeley frown. By the way he acted, the events of the night before last never happened. Fighting the melancholy left over from interactions with her dad, she stowed her purse—keys carefully *in* her purse this time—tied on her waist apron, and hit the floor.

Three hours later Keeley took the last stool at the end of the bar, arching her back as she settled onto the seat. It felt like she'd been moving at a dead run for every one of those hours.

Owen's Mid-Week Minis were a popular draw for Happy Hour, and it had brought in a sizable after-work crowd who'd devoured the mini pizzas with their drinks. They'd hit the lull between Happy Hour and dinner, and she could finally take her half-hour break. At least being busy had boosted her mood.

Owen slid a plate of the mini pizzas and a glass of cranberry juice in front of her. "Eat."

That was exactly why Owen confused her. He'd been all gruff and grumbly since she started her shift, but then felt compelled to put food in front of her.

"Why are you feeding me?"

"I don't want you passing out from hunger."

"Right."

He busied himself checking supplies in the well. She didn't think he was paying attention to her until he raised his head and skewered her with his typical grumpy glare. "Is the douche with a man-bun bothering you? That why you were upset when you came in?"

"Who's the douche with a man-bun?" Then it clicked. "Oh, you mean Jaxon. He spends a lot of time on that man-bun, I'll have you know."

He waited. "Well?" he finally asked.

"Well, what?"

"Keep up, princess. Is he bothering you?"

"No. I mean he was, but I blocked him on my phone."

"He being aggressive?"

"Not particularly, more manipulative than anything. I don't understand why he wants to get back together so badly. I thought he'd already moved on."

"You're selling yourself short." He filled an order, then returned. With arms braced, he leaned on the bar. She struggled not to sigh. "That's not why you were upset."

She shifted her focus to her glass, using the tip of her finger to wipe at the condensation on the side. "No, it's Dad. We were having a good time this afternoon. I'd gotten some vintage records and was playing them on an old record player of his that I found in the attic. We were singing along to the Rolling Stones, then his mood flipped on a dime, and he's yelling at me because I won't let him call a friend who's been dead four years."

"Fuck."

"That sums it up pretty well."

Owen used a towel to wipe the bar. "You and Abby are doing your best, and the records were a good idea. Even though it didn't end well, it was still a good idea and he was enjoying himself until he wasn't. Take the wins where you can."

Her phone vibrated with a text from Sawyer. He'd created a group text with her and Owen. She read the message.

Sawyer: Fernando admitted to being dropped off at EM parking lot. Won't ID driver. Instructions were to steal K's purse. Driver

was to pick kid up half hour after bar closed. Payment of three hundred dollars if he had the purse.

Keeley: Did he admit to knowing me?

Sawyer: Yeah, he knew you.

Owen slipped his phone back in his pocket. "That attack wasn't random, you were targeted."

"It seems like, but I still don't understand why. I don't see how this has anything to do with my tires."

He shook his head. "There's a connection. Not understanding what the connection is doesn't mean there isn't one. Starting now, Easy Money house rule is no one is to go out of this building alone. You don't take the trash out, and you don't walk to your car alone. The rule applies to everyone, but I'm most concerned about you. If I'm not here, you get one of the others to walk out with you."

Orders came in and Owen got busy.

She studied him contemplatively. Maybe she was slow, but evidence was starting to mount that maybe Owen's contradictory behavior was because he was conflicted.

Throughout her shift she'd watched him moving behind the bar, his gaze constantly sweeping as he clocked incoming customers, kept tabs on the dudes at the back table who'd grown progressively louder, and kept tabs on her.

Because he did. Others noticed too. She'd been catching up with her parents' neighbor Janey, who'd come in with a coworker from the bank. She introduced her friend as Sherry. As a teenager, Keeley babysat Janey's three sons. Since the boys were doing well in high school, the oldest graduating as salutatorian, it was nice to hear the little heathens had adapted to civilization. "You and Doug did a good job with those boys."

"Thanks, sweetie. How are you doing? Are you dating anyone?"

"Nope. I've been busy, but I should get back into the game. It's hard to work up any enthusiasm though."

"I don't think you'd have to look too far. I think someone is smitten."

"Oh? Who?" Keeley glanced around. She wasn't sure what she was looking for, maybe someone with emoji hearts floating over their head.

Janey and Sherry had both burst into laughter.

"Owen's had his eyes on you ever since we came in. He pays attention to everything that's going on, but he pays special attention to you, my girl."

Sherry fanned herself with her hand. "That man's one tall drink of water."

Watching him as he ran the blender, Keeley agreed.

At some point since Sunday, he'd gotten a haircut and it looked *good*. Shorter on the sides, tousled hair longer on top.

She'd seen him shirtless twice now, and could attest that his lean build had been bulked up with muscle that rippled and flexed as he moved.

The evening of the attack, when all he'd worn were sweatpants riding low on his hips, she'd greedily watched him whenever she thought he wasn't looking.

Strong, broad shoulders tapering to a lean waist, he was a study in the perfection of the male form. She was surprised he hadn't followed the trend of getting inked. He'd been in the Marine Corps, and he'd been a cop, but his skin remained unmarked except by the bullet scar near his shoulder.

"I think that special attention goes both ways, don't you, Janey?" Sherry asked, her voice teasing.

Cheeks burning, Keeley had smiled brightly. "Okay, ladies, what can I get for you tonight?"

After Janey and Sherry had finished their meal and left an overly generous tip, Keeley'd done some watching of her own, trying to see Owen's behavior through their eyes.

And time and time again she found his gaze locked on her. Usually, he was scowling, but what if that scowl reflected more than basic grumpiness? What if he didn't actually dislike her? It was an intriguing thought, but did she really want someone who wasn't happy about wanting her?

She chewed her bottom lip in contemplation.

Looking at the past week objectively, Owen had decidedly put himself in her orbit. Maybe it was because of his friendship with her parents. He certainly appeared invested in her safety.

There'd been that moment after tackling Fernando when he'd cradled her face in his hands. Her heart gave a heavy thump remembering the feel of his calloused palms, the gentle stroke of his thumb over her cheek, the look in his eyes that was anything but disinterested.

Munching on a tasty mini pizza with caramelized onions and mushrooms, she eyed him speculatively. If he did have feelings for her, what if she cleared the air between them? Maybe there could be something there and her tiny crush could actually bloom into something real.

There was only one way to find out. All she had to risk was humiliation and never being able to face him again.

Before she could put her intention into words, her phone buzzed and she pulled it from her apron pocket to read the text. Her eyebrows went up when she saw the name. "What the heck?" she muttered.

She tapped to open the text, frowning as she read the message.

"Everything good?" Owen sipped from his glass of soda water.

"More like everything's weird," she replied. At Owen's questioning look, she said, "Pam Demaris texted to say she'll be in Sisters this weekend and thinks it'd be fun to get together for lunch."

Owen braced his arms on the bar, gaze riveted on her face. He possessed an extra *something* that made her feel like he paid attention to her with his entire body. Maybe this was his cop look.

She'd bet he was good at interrogating suspects. "She's the teacher you were subbing for when Fernando was in her class."

"Yeah. Suggesting we get lunch together is weird because we aren't friends. When I subbed for her she was difficult, calling to make sure I was doing what she wanted, kind of hovering in the background even though I had it handled.

"Then when she returned to work, I was subbing for another teacher and she tracked me down to accuse me of stealing a bin of colored whiteboard markers from her classroom. It was totally stupid, but she wouldn't let it go and reported me to the principal. Thankfully, the principal thought it was stupid too and hired me for the temporary position I've had for the past two years."

"How has Demaris acted toward you during that time?" Owen asked, indicating to Jen to take care of customers while he gave Keeley his attention.

She shrugged. "Still weird. Her room was across the hall and I felt like she was always watching me, waiting for me to mess up so she could report me. Yousef says she's jealous of me, but I don't see it."

"You said Yousef and some others had a going-away party for you the night your tires were slashed. Was she in that group?"

"No. She doesn't really hang out with the other teachers, even the ones on her team."

"But you did. Did you have a lunch group, other teachers you ate with every day?"

"Yeah. There were about six of us on our hall who ate together in Yousef's room. Pam was invited, but chose not to join us. Mostly, she kept to herself or let students eat in her room."

"Did you tell Sawyer about her?"

"No, why would I?"

Owen crossed his arms over his chest, brows lowered. "We're looking for a motive for your tires being slashed. You're pretty and popular with your coworkers, and I bet the kids loved you. Dude's probably right that she's jealous. She hasn't been friendly with you and she has a connection to the little shit. She could've been the one to drop him off. And now out of the blue she wants to meet for lunch? I don't believe in coincidences."

He thought she was pretty? It was vain and small of her, but his compliment was like a surprise cupcake topped with frosting and sprinkles that's created to make you happy.

Telling herself to focus, she brightened when an idea occurred. "I could agree to meet her and figure out what she wants. It'd be like I was undercover."

"The hell you will. If she's the one who dropped off the little shit to pull his stunt, I don't want you anywhere near her."

"I don't know why Fernando would be doing her bidding. Beyond that, why would she want my purse?"

"Could've been a tactic to scare you. But the kid using a knife takes it up a notch."

"I still think I should meet with her. It's not like she'll try something in broad daylight. I could even meet her here."

"No."

She sipped her cranberry juice, considering him over the rim of the glass. "You're not being reasonable."

"Fuck reasonable."

She snorted out a laugh. Setting down her glass, she decided to go for the gold. Heart hammering like a deranged woodpecker on speed, she took a deep breath and asked, "Do you like me, Owen?"

"What? Why the hell would you ask me that?"

"Because other people seem to think you do, but you always act like I'm a huge pain in the butt, and I guess I want to know."

His scowl turned so ferocious she felt like she'd poked a sleeping bear. He grabbed the towel he'd hung over his shoulder and began wiping down the bar. "I don't have time for this heart-to-heart shit."

"Right, okay, never mind. I thought I'd ask, but I can see this was a bad idea. Forget I said anything." She rose and knew from the heat, her face was flushed with embarrassment. "I'll get back to work, you know, because it's my job." He stopped wiping the bar and stared at her like she'd sprouted horns. Now she was furious. "You don't have to be such a jerk about it."

"How am I a jerk?"

God, she was losing it. "You just are."

She wished she could flee the scene, run home, and bury her head under her pillow. But her dad had always told her to start as she intended to carry on, so she did exactly that.

For the rest of her shift, she treated Owen with determined pleasantness, hiding her hurt behind a sunny smile.

***

Awkward. Keeley hated she'd made things awkward with Owen. They remained that way through closing. After walking out with Dion, she was glad when she could drive away from all those emotions. She turned into the driveway of her parents' home, mind still on her conversation, or rather lack of conversation, with Owen, when she brought the vehicle to an abrupt stop. A flash of light had caught her attention. She peered through the windshield at the neighbor's yard. Having no streetlights wasn't unusual in residential areas in the mountains. Sisters had mandated all streetlights along Main Street be Darksky Approved. Away from the business corridor, drivers had to rely on their headlights and knowledge of the area to navigate safely.

She searched for the flash of light, what she'd thought was the glow of a phone visible from under a grouping of trees. She waited, but it didn't reappear. She continued down the drive to park next to her little cottage, the security light at the corner of the building coming on. Recent events were making her paranoid.

She sat for a minute and let the quiet soothe her. Asking Owen whether he had feelings for her had *not* gone well. Not that he'd actually responded to her question. He'd been grumpier than usual for the rest of the evening.

Maybe she should have fessed up and admitted *she* had a crush on *him*. That probably would have freaked him out. The truth of the matter was, as much as she might wish otherwise, Owen Hardesty wasn't going to be her future. She'd have to double down on her efforts to carve from her heart all the messy feelings he pulled from her.

Keys and phone in hand, she walked past her attached garage to the corner of the cottage where a stone pathway led to her door. The sound of running feet had her head whipping up.

Again? Memories of Sunday flashed through her mind. She spun around and spied a dark form hurtling toward her. A surge of panic and a moment to brace herself and then impact. Her body slammed into the wall, her head colliding with the corner of the building hard enough she saw stars. She was trying to figure out what'd happened when her attacker grabbed her purse and ripped it from where she'd hung it on her arm.

Keeley stared in dazed disbelief at the figure fleeing down the drive toward the street. She was too stunned to give chase. Figuring it better to sit before she fell, she slid down the wall with a groan, landing on her butt. Blinking to clear her vision, she brought her hand to her head and felt the stickiness of blood.

Eyes closed, she tried to gather her thoughts. She'd been assaulted, but the attacker had fled. She was okay, or at least mostly okay.

Blue fleece jacket. Blue and green New Balance shoes. Phone in the side pocket of stretchy pants. She worked to commit the details she'd only had seconds to note to memory.

Opening her eyes, she leaned forward to gather her phone from where it'd fallen on the walkway and tapped the screen to make the call.

An engine turned over, the sound coming from up the street. Tires screeched as a vehicle raced into the night until the sound faded to nothing.

Moments later Abby rushed across the courtyard from the house to crouch beside her daughter.

"Oh my god, Keeley, you said you weren't hurt but you're bleeding." Abby turned Keeley's head to the light. "I called 9-1-1, but I need to call back and have them send an ambulance."

"I don't need an ambulance. I'm hurt, Mom, but not badly enough to go to the hospital. They stole my purse."

"Let's get you out of the cold. I want to see if you need stitches." She pressed a folded tissue to the cut. "If you do, you're going to the emergency clinic, young lady, and without an argument."

Abby rose to her feet and looked around. She looked fierce, like she was ready to take down the assailant.

"Whoever it was is gone, Mom. They ran toward the street, and I heard a car start and take off."

Abby stooped to help Keeley to her feet. "Come on, baby. Let's get you inside. I asked dispatch to tell the responding officers to come in without sirens and to go to your cottage. I don't want your dad to wake up. He has such a hard time sleeping."

"Good thinking."

Headlights flashed as a vehicle turned into the driveway coming to a stop with a crunch of gravel. Keeley recognized Owen's Bronco.

"You called Owen, Mom? Why?" Her voice shook.

"Because he cares about you, that's why. Didn't he protect you from that young man with a knife? He's involved, and so I called him. Plus, dispatch said the sheriff's deputies were tied up with a car over the side of the road at the other end of town. Possible DUI. They're sending someone, but it'll be a minute."

The driver's door of the Bronco slammed shut, cutting off Keeley's retort. The security light showed Owen moving toward her like a predator stalking its prey. Or like a man whose woman was in danger.

Wishful thinking on her part, but no matter what she'd said to Abby, she was glad to see him. He was strong, capable, and without a doubt, he'd protect her at a time when she was feeling particularly vulnerable.

Owen joined them, his gaze boring into Keeley with single-minded intensity. He wore his heavy wool Pendleton over the long-sleeved shirt with the Easy Money logo he'd worn that evening. From either the adrenaline or the cold night air, she wasn't sure which, she began shivering so hard her teeth chattered.

"Darn it, a light's come on in the house, which means Bruce is up." Abby turned to Keeley. "I need to get him settled or we'll be up all night." Abby grasped Keeley's hand. "I'll check on you when I can."

"I'm okay, Mom. I'll text you how I'm doing." Keeley still held the tissue to her forehead.

Abby hugged her daughter, then for a brief moment leaned her head on Owen's shoulder. "I'm glad you're here, Owen. Take care of my baby."

"I will. Don't worry, Abby."

"I know you will." Abby pulled her robe tight and scurried back to the house.

Owen used a firm hand under Keeley's chin to turn her to the light. His gaze traveled over her face. "You can't seem to stay out of trouble, can you?" he murmured.

And then he replaced her hand with his on the tissue and tugged her to his chest, pulling his jacket around them both and wrapping his other arm around her. With his cheek resting on top of her head, he spoke quietly, "Tell me what happened."

She breathed deep, the smell of him, his warmth, invading her senses. The shivering eased. If she could stay like this for the rest of her life, she'd be happy.

Tears stung her eyes. Her words were muffled because her cheek was against the wall of his chest, but he seemed to hear her as she walked him through the attack. "And then she stole my purse," she said on a hiccup. "God, I sound like a baby."

"She?"

"Yeah, I'm certain it was a woman. Why is it that all of a sudden people are so interested in my purse?"

"That's the question." Owen's hand slipped to the back of her neck where it felt warm and heavy. "We'll deal with your head, then we'll deal with the rest."

"I'm tired and sore, and I just want to go to bed, but before I can do that, I need to call my credit card companies to tell them my cards were stolen. I'm sorry I got you damp." She lifted her head and swiped at the moisture on his shirt. "I'll put a Band-Aid on the cut and it'll be fine. I'll go to the doctor in the morning if I need to."

"Let me see." He lifted the makeshift pressure bandage, peering at the wound in the glow of the security light. He swore under his breath. Expression grim, he said, "You need stitches, princess. I'm driving you to the clinic."

"I need to call the credit companies first, before she can use my cards. I don't want to go to the clinic."

He took her hand and pressed it to hold the tissue. "Keep the pressure on." Then he swung her up in his arms and moved toward the Bronco. She gave a yelp and curled an arm around his neck. "I can walk."

"Yeah? I can also carry you."

"Dammit, Owen. Would you listen to me?"

"Talk all you want, but you're going to the clinic and getting that cut stitched, and having a concussion check."

"You're bossy."

"When I need to be."

She groaned when he settled her in the passenger seat.

The interior lights shown on his face that was back to glowering. "Do you have pain anywhere besides that hard head of yours?"

"Maybe my shoulder's sore." She leaned back in the seat, exhaustion dragging at her. "I don't need stitches. The bleeding's already stopped."

He leaned in, face inches from hers. "Do you trust me, Keeley?"

"Of course I do." She said it with a certainty that surprised her.

"Then trust me on this. You need stitches. I had medic training in Afghanistan. I could stitch it for you, but it wouldn't be pretty and would hurt like hell. So I'm taking you to the fucking clinic." He pressed his lips to hers in a brief, hard kiss. "The answer to your question is yes."

The door slammed shut and her brain went static.

The answer to her question was yes?

CHAPTER TWELVE

Keeley had a moment thinking she actually did have a concussion or had hit her head hard enough to become delusional. No way had Owen Hardesty kissed her. It was brief, it was a bit rough, but her tingling lips told her it wasn't her imagination.

She had big questions that should take precedence over everything else. Like who'd mugged her and why. But in that moment, whether her crush liked her was all she could focus on. She could hardly wait for him to buckle his seatbelt and start the Bronco before asking, "Yes, as in you friend like me, or yes, as in you like me like me?"

"That one. Text Abby, tell her I'm taking you to the clinic. Then call dispatch and tell them to send the responding officer there to get your statement."

He drove toward the clinic. She would've believed he was calm, sitting back in his seat, driving with easy competence, except for the tension around his eyes.

Underneath the cool exterior she suspected was a mountain of rage. She wasn't sure where that rage was directed, but she knew it wasn't toward her.

Thank god, because she had all sorts of warm tingles dancing along her skin, and him being mad at her would ruin them.

She contemplated his response. "Wait, if you like me, why have you always treated me like I'm a disagreeable pain in your butt?"

"Because you are a pain in my butt. You stir me up when I don't want to be stirred up. But, princess? We're not talking about this now. Do what I told you to do."

Rolling her eyes was a mistake because it made her head hurt. "You are one frustrating man," she muttered.

She put the bloody tissue on her lap and got out her phone. She texted her mom that she was on her way to the clinic, and then made the call to dispatch.

A wet trickle on her forehead told her the wound had started bleeding again.

"There's a bandanna in the glovebox. It's clean. Use that."

She found the bandanna and flipped down the visor to use the mirror. Even though it made her look like a retro hippie chick from the 80s, she folded the bandanna into a headband and tied it around her head.

Owen parked in the brightly lit parking lot behind the clinic. She opened the door and he rounded the hood. When he looked ready to scoop her up in his arms again, she put up a hand. "Nope, I'm walking in."

If she was cradled in his arms again, she might refuse to let him go.

The automatic sliding doors of the clinic opened and they walked in and joined the short line to check in. Keeley glanced around. A couple leaning against each other dozed on a bench. An elderly man held the hand of an equally elderly woman as he walked with her to the waiting nurse. And a twenty-something young man wearing sunglasses sat with a shoeless, swollen foot propped on another chair.

There was nothing more depressing than an emergency room in the middle of the night.

Sitting next to Owen under the ugly fluorescent lighting, she filled out paperwork attached to a clipboard. With her insurance card in the possession of the thief, she gave silent thanks her primary doctor was with the clinic, which meant her information was already in their system.

The triage nurse who introduced himself as Juan called her in fairly quickly. She tried not to look surprised when Owen rose to come with her.

He caught her look. "I'm making sure you don't sweet-talk them out of stitches."

"Why would I do that?"

"I know you. You can be stubborn."

She was still shaking her head over that when Juan took her vitals. Her blood pressure and heart rate were higher than normal, but she attributed that to Owen's broody presence. The man wound her up.

Juan confirmed that yes, indeed, she needed stitches and she'd be called back shortly. Owen snagged a packet of wipes, and when they got back to their seats in the waiting room, he tipped up her chin and used the wipes to clean the blood from her face. Given the dark stain on the wipes, she must've looked like an extra in a horror movie.

Owen's touch was gentle despite his jaw clenching hard enough she thought he was in danger of cracking a molar.

"Are you okay? You seem tense."

His gaze dropped to hers and she caught her breath. That rage she'd thought he was bottling up? It looked ready to break loose and wreak havoc.

She gripped his wrist. "Owen."

He leaned toward her, his expression fierce. "Someone hurt you, so no, I'm not fucking okay. I'm going to find who's responsible and make sure they never touch you again."

Hoo boy.

A deputy she didn't recognize came in, and Owen pulled back the anger. He rose to speak to her, then they came to where Keeley was seated. The officer introduced herself as Deputy Beth Guerrero. Keeley went over what had happened and gave all the details of her assailant she could remember, then answered a boatload of questions. Owen brought the deputy up to speed with what had happened Sunday night.

By the time Beth left, Keeley felt like all the energy had been sapped from her body. Her shoulder throbbed, her head throbbed even more, and all she wanted to do was go home to sleep. Waiting to be called back, she leaned back in her seat and closed her eyes, letting her mind drift.

She must've fallen asleep because the next thing she knew Owen was speaking in her ear. "C'mon, princess, they're calling you."

She blinked her eyes open and found his face inches from hers. An arm around her shoulders held her close to his side and her head rested on his shoulder. How had that happened?

Her name was called again and Owen pulled her to her feet.

Thirty minutes later, a PA named Anayah was pressing a bandage over what she assured Keeley was a neat row of stitches that shouldn't leave much of a scar. Keeley hadn't wanted to look in the mirror. Owen's low voice carried from the hall where he'd gone to use his phone.

"I gave your cute boyfriend a bag of supplies," Anayah said. "Keep the wound dry and covered with a bandage for at least two days. See your primary, or come back to the clinic if there's any sign of infection.

"We don't think you have a concussion, but if you develop any of the symptoms we talked about, same thing, see your primary or come back. Any questions?"

Keeley shook her head slowly, not sure if she should correct the boyfriend comment.

"Don't worry, hon. You're tired. I gave the boyfriend the same information so you're in good hands."

Oh geez. "Um, he's not really my boyfriend."

Anayah laughed. "I'd say it's only a matter of time then. Let that cutie take you home, get some Tylenol in your system, and get some sleep."

They stepped into the hall and Owen draped an arm over her shoulders, pulling her into his side.

Anayah gave her a laughing goodbye. "Right, not your boyfriend," she whispered so only Keeley could hear.

Owen shoved his phone into his pocket. "I gave Abby an update. She's going back to bed now."

Keeley yawned. "Good, because Dad will be up early no matter what. Thank goodness Mrs. Troung is coming in tomorrow so Mom will have help."

He didn't speak as they drove through the night. He parked the Bronco in front of her garage, got out, and rounded the hood to her door, steadying her when she slid out of the vehicle.

"Give me your keys."

She should've known he wouldn't drop her off and leave.

His head swiveled, gaze searching the area as they made their way to the cottage door. He unlocked the door and had her wait in the entry while he conducted a search.

She hated feeling vulnerable. Hated that the attack made her scared of sleeping alone. She could always go to her parents' house and spend the night in the guest room.

The whole thing had her completely pissed off. She should be able to sleep in her own home without feeling afraid.

"All clear." Owen reached behind her and turned the dead bolt on the door.

Maybe she was getting punchy because she stared at him in confusion. "How are you getting out if the door's locked?"

His grin flashed, breaking the tension that seemed to have settled around him. "You're exhausted, princess. Go get ready for bed."

"What are you going to do?"

He shoved his hands in his pockets. "Stay with you. I'm not leaving you alone after what happened."

"I'll be okay. She got my purse. I don't think she's still a threat. I wish I knew why she wanted my purse, but that's what she was after."

"We'll talk tomorrow."

As much as she wanted to go straight to bed, she crossed the living room to the alcove where she had a desk and a two-drawer filing cabinet. She only had two credit cards so it shouldn't take long to contact the companies.

She finished one call with the happy news nothing had been charged, then dialed the next. The agent was competent, sincerely sympathetic for her awful night, and confirmed that nothing had been charged with that card either.

Plugging in her phone next to her bed, Keeley yawned again, suddenly so tired she could hardly keep her eyes open.

In the bathroom for an abbreviated bedtime routine, she finally gave in and looked at her reflection in the mirror.

Oh lord, she looked like a hot mess.

All color had leached from her skin, making her eyes look overly large with dark smudges under them to give her a hollowed-out look.

The bruising around the bandage on her forehead had turned an ugly purple. She brushed her teeth thinking she needed to find blankets for Owen to use on the couch.

Rinsing her mouth, she exited the bathroom. Not seeing him, she went to her bedroom. And came to a screeching stop in the doorway.

He'd taken off his shoes and pulled back the bedding and now that long body was stretched out on one side of the bed, hands behind his head as he rested against a pillow. He still wore his jeans, but with his arms stretched up a thin strip of muscled abs was revealed.

His eyes were closed, but they popped open when she threw a pillow squarely at his chest, one of the small decorative pillows he'd shoved onto the floor. "What the hell are you doing?" he grumbled.

"What the hell am I doing? What the hell are *you* doing in my bed?"

"I told you I was staying."

"Yeah, on the couch."

"Your couch is a loveseat and at least three feet too short for me. No thanks. Your bed's a full size. Barely adequate, but it's miles better than the couch."

She closed her eyes against the headache the Tylenol had yet to reach. Opening them tiredly, she said, "Look, I know Mom asked you to look after me and I appreciate you taking that to heart and making me go to the clinic even when I didn't want to. Truly I do. But, Owen, you looking after me doesn't extend to sleeping in my bed. *I* need to sleep in my bed."

"There's room for both of us." He sat up, swinging his feet to the floor. "Look, princess, until I can get a security system installed, I'm sticking close. Right now, that means you and I are sharing this bed."

She opened her mouth to object, but he held up a finger. "We're both exhausted. I promise I can keep my hands to myself. You're safe from being attacked in your sleep."

"Don't make fun of me."

"How is that making fun of you?" Exasperation edged his tone.

"If you don't know, I'm not explaining it to you." She hated resorting to such a juvenile response, but she was too tired to find the words to explain.

"For fuck's sake. You got an extra toothbrush?"

She nodded. "I left one out on the bathroom counter."

He disappeared, and she considered her options. She was tired, they both were, and Owen made her feel safe. As much as she didn't want to admit it, the attack had rattled her and she didn't want to be alone. As he'd told her before, she needed to deal.

Owen returned. He turned his back and undid his belt, dropping his jeans to the floor. He slid between the sheets, jammed a pillow under his head and lay on his side facing the wall. He pulled up the covers and she was surprised he didn't start snoring immediately.

Whatever.

Retrieving her pajamas from under her pillow, she retreated to the bathroom to change. With flannel pants and a long-sleeved t-shirt decorated on the front with a sleepy sloth hanging from a tree and the words "Slow Moving in the Morning," she looked more like a survivor of the zombie apocalypse than anything remotely sexy.

She didn't have the energy reserves to argue any further about the sleeping arrangements. They'd sleep side by side and she probably wouldn't even notice that he was there.

Of course she noticed he was there. A half hour later she flipped onto her back for probably the hundredth time and let out a heavy sigh. Apparently, exhaustion didn't guarantee sleep.

She was too aware of the man lying next to her to relax. He smelled good. His deep, even breaths were mesmerizing, and he threw off heat like one of those radiant heaters for patio dining.

After she flipped her pillow one more time, Owen turned to his back with an arm stretched over his head. In the faint glow from a nightlight, she saw the shadow of his arm as he brought up his hand to jam his fingers through his hair.

"I'm sorry I'm keeping you awake," she whispered.

He sighed, then turned so he was facing her. "Come here." He wrapped his hand around her waist to tug her snugly into the curve of his body, his arms going around her. He whispered in her ear, "Now relax, darlin', and go to sleep."

With the feeling that life couldn't get much better, surprisingly, she did just that.

CHAPTER THIRTEEN

Owen woke with daylight streaming through a window, the woman of his dreams in his arms, and an erection that threatened to get him in a shitload of trouble nestled against her ass. He disengaged and rolled out of bed, adjusting himself with his back to her. He pulled on his jeans and when he felt in control enough to face her, he found he needn't have worried because she was still out cold.

He stared at her, for once looking his fill. Wavy brown hair that he knew in the summer would streak to a honey blonde. Faint freckles across the bridge of her nose, and lips he wanted to kiss, *really* kiss, and not like the stupid peck he'd given her the night before.

She wore a bandage on her forehead over stitches because of an injury that should've never happened. It fucking pissed him off that she'd been attacked. He'd let her go home by herself and she'd been hurt. That wasn't happening again.

He'd been an idiot, admitting he had a thing for her, putting his hands on her, kissing her, brief as it was, as if he had the right. He might as well pull his beating heart out of his chest and offer it to her because getting involved with her would end with the same result. He'd fuck it up, and he'd hurt her, and he'd still end up destroyed.

He was used to being left, but with Keeley, he wouldn't survive when she did.

He held fast against the desire to touch her, to brush her hair off her forehead, to stroke her cheek until she woke and then catch her lips in a kiss that could only lead down the path to perdition.

He left the bedroom, closing the door quietly behind him.

Waiting for the coffee to brew, he pulled his phone from his pocket and found a couple dozen messages. Most were from Delaney demanding to know what was going on.

Since it was Sawyer he wanted to talk to, he texted his friend the basics of Keeley's night with directions to pass the info to Delaney. He wanted to forestall her coming by to check on her friend for herself. He also asked Sawyer to come to the cottage so they could strategize.

He looked in the refrigerator and found mostly what he considered girly food: yogurt, avocados, kombucha.

What the hell was kombucha?

He grabbed a loaf of bread and read the bag that identified it as twelve-seed.

Who needed twelve seeds in a piece of toast?

He spied a small bowl with eggs marked with an X on the end and figured they were hard-boiled. He rummaged around and came up with provolone cheese and decided breakfast sandwiches were on the menu.

When Sawyer drove his truck up the driveway, Owen was sitting at a little table on Keeley's postage-stamp-size patio eating his sandwich and working on his second cup of coffee while scrolling through the news on his phone.

While still chilly, the sun shone strongly, and the day promised to be a truly warm spring day.

"Where's Keels?" Sawyer took the chair across the table from him, a travel mug in his hand.

"Still asleep."

"That so?" Sawyer grinned.

"Not what you're thinking, bro. I may want that, but that's not where we're going."

"Why the fuck not? You've been into her for a while."

"I'll screw it up, and I don't want her hurt."

Sawyer cocked his head as if trying to figure out a complex math problem. "Of course you'll screw it up. We all do. But if you love each other, you'll work it out. That's life."

Owen was already shaking his head. "I'm too fucked up for her, and she's too smart to love me."

"We're all fucked up, but our women love us anyway. Look at Walker. Dude was so fucked up he didn't come home for the good part of a decade. But when he finally did, he and Delaney worked it out, and now look what he's got. The woman he loves married him and they have a baby coming. Nothing better than that."

Owen kept his mouth shut.

Sawyer wasn't ready to give up. "You tell Keels what's holding you back?"

"No, and I'm not going to."

Sawyer shook his head as if gravely disappointed. "You're a good man, and I think you two would be great together. But if you can't pull your head out of your ass to figure that out, then don't fuck with her by sleeping with her. She's not a hookup."

"You her big brother all the sudden?"

"I've always been her big brother. Same for Delaney."

"You're such a Boy Scout."

Sawyer's grin flashed. "Yeah, and the ladies love me." He dropped the smile. "Our girl's been the target of an attack twice now. I want your take on what's going on."

"Someone wanted her purse. That's what the kid wanted Sunday. That's what the woman who attacked her got last night."

"I read the report." Sawyer scratched his chin. "Shit isn't adding up."

"Agreed. Keeley didn't call the credit card company until after we got back from the clinic. That means the assailant had her card for a good two hours." He nailed Sawyer with a look. "There wasn't a single charge."

"Which could mean there was something else in her purse they were after," Sawyer concluded.

"That's what I'm thinking."

The sliding door to the patio opened and Keeley stepped out, a mug of coffee in her hand. She'd pulled a hoodie over her pajama top and wore shearling boots on her feet. She sat at the table and curled her legs under her, her eyes closed as she gripped her mug with both hands and sipped slowly.

Sawyer peered at her forehead. "Jesus, Keels, that looks painful. You gonna be okay?"

Keeley nodded with her eyes still closed. She took another sip of coffee.

"Give her five minutes for the caffeine to hit her system before talking to her," Owen muttered.

Keeley raised her eyelids. Owen could think of about a dozen things he'd rather be doing with her while she still had that sleepy look in her eyes. And not one of them involved the cop sitting at the patio table with a knowing smirk on his face.

"You want an egg sandwich for breakfast?" The offer was out of his mouth before he could block it.

Then Keeley gave him a sweet smile that made him feel like he'd offered to slay dragons for her. "That would be lovely. Thank you."

Sawyer shook his head when offered breakfast and Owen headed inside. At least busying himself in the kitchen gave him a chance to lock down his control.

This was the second time he'd been around when she'd woken in the morning, and it made his desires—not only the sexual ones, but the desire to have a life with someone he wanted to share quiet mornings with—harder to resist.

Sawyer seemed to have stripped away the bullshit Owen'd been telling himself, and seeing Keeley looking so goddamn appealing was weakening the chains he'd put on his own wants and desires. If he was going to withstand her appeal, he needed time to get himself under control again.

He buttered the toasted bread, added cheese and egg, gave it a quick zap in the microwave, and when he turned around she was right there.

He shoved the plate at her. "Here."

"Thanks." She set the plate next to her mug on the counter, then turned back to him. Grabbing ahold of his shirt, she went up on tiptoes and kissed him.

Not the little pecks they'd shared before. No, this was a warm laying of her lips on his with an added little hum of pleasure that vibrated through him all the way to his dick.

A snap echoed in his head as the self-imposed restraints disintegrated, obliterated by the intoxicating feel of her lips moving on his.

Her lips parted as he took control of the kiss, swiping his tongue to taste the warm lushness of coffee and an additional element that was quintessentially Keeley: sunshine, which, he discovered, tasted a lot like honey.

He moved his hands under her clothing and stroked the warm skin of her back. No way could she miss his erection jutting insistently through his pants.

She moaned against his mouth, a sexy sound that made his head spin. Hands cupped under her ass, lifted her, then set her on the counter, shoving aside the tub of butter and pushing a knife into the sink with a clatter.

Then he was between her spread thighs, rubbing against the heat pulsing through the flannel she wore.

Damn. He was ready to go off in his pants like a randy teenager.

His hand grazed the skin of her rib cage, his thumb brushing the side of her breast. He groaned. She wasn't wearing a bra.

With his thumb he brushed the tip of her nipple and had her moaning again, a throaty sound that by itself could get him off. He broke the kiss as reality snuck up on him. "Fuck."

"Yes please," she responded. "But lock the door, m'kay?" Her eyes were soft and slumberous, and when she licked her lips, he was ready to scoop her up in his arms and dive back into bed.

Holy shit. He withdrew his hands from her skin and raised them up, taking a careful step back like she was a bomb primed to detonate with the slightest of vibrations.

Why that conjured images in his head of Keeley in the midst of an orgasm he'd orchestrated, god only knew.

The single ounce of self-preservation he'd managed to retain was yelling in his head to fucking knock it off.

Not only was Sawyer sitting outside probably thinking of the best way to castrate him, but Keeley deserved better than to be jerked around by a guy who could never be what she deserved.

"Fuck, Keeley. No, not fuck. Wrong word."

Her response of "yes, please" ping-ponged around in his head to accompany another round of erotic images of a naked Keeley. He shook his head to clear it. "Never mind. I'm sorry. I shouldn't have let things get this far."

Perfectly arched brows lowered over hazel eyes. "*I* kissed *you*, Owen. I'm the one who initiated whatever this is. And I'm perfectly fine with how far things have gone. In fact, I'm pretty sure I indicated I'd be happy if they went farther."

"Right. Sure. But they can't. We can't." He scrubbed his hand over his face.

"You weren't acting like kissing me was a chore. Or like having your hands on my breasts was distasteful. In fact," she glanced at his crotch where things had yet to subside, "evidence suggests you enjoyed what happened as much as I did."

He turned away so he wouldn't have to lie to her face. "That's a physical reaction."

"I see. You'd have responded like that with any woman."

"Right. Yeah."

"You're such an asshole. And a liar." Keeley pushed herself off the counter. "At least I can admit I have feelings for you and feel good about it. You say you like me then have a freakout when we actually do what people with a mutual attraction do."

"I've been clear I don't have relationships. Sure, I like you, but that doesn't change anything."

Asshole that he was, he shoved away from the sink and strode out of the house.

***

Jerk. Keeley stood in her kitchen. *Sure, I like you.* Who says that? She rubbed her forehead with a balled-up fist, then winced when it pulled at the stitches.

What the heck had just happened?

She'd gone with the impulse and kissed him, and, oh boy, had Owen responded.

She'd put that kiss right up there as the number one kiss of all kisses she'd ever experienced.

He'd been into it until it seemed his brain had caught up with his body and he'd slammed on the brakes. Of course he could say no, his feelings didn't have to match hers. But that's not what she got from him. Something was holding him back, and he wasn't willing to explain.

Deciding she couldn't do anything about the situation in that moment, she refilled her coffee mug and picked up the plate with her egg sandwich and carried both out to the patio.

Sawyer was on his phone sounding like he was wrapping up a call while Owen sat in his chair, a scowl on his face and arms crossed over his chest. She gave him her sunniest smile for the express purpose of messing with him.

Sawyer tossed his phone on the table and leaned back in his chair. He pinched the bridge of his nose and released a sigh that sounded like it came from the depths of his soul. He dropped his hand and said, "That was a detective from Sacramento PD. A woman's body's been found buried under trash in a dumpster behind an office building."

His gaze zeroed in on Keeley. "Her clothing matches the description you gave of your assailant last night. Medium height, medium frame, blue fleece jacket, and blue and green New Balance shoes."

Keeley set down her sandwich, nausea suddenly making her stomach roll.

Owen swore under his breath.

She licked her lips and asked, "How was she killed?"

"Preliminarily, it looks like head trauma. Rigor had set in already when the body was found by an individual searching for recyclables around seven a.m. That puts the time of death a minimum of two hours before that."

"Have the police ID'd her?" Owen asked.

Sawyer nodded slowly. "She had her phone in her pocket, ID in the phone case. Photo on the driver's license matches the body. Forty-two years old, lived in the Sacramento suburb of Carmichael. Her name is Pamela Lynn Demaris."

Keeley set her mug on the table with a thunk. "That's not possible."

"Identification is preliminary, but unofficially SPD believes it's her. I'm sorry, Keeley." Sawyer's gaze remained steady. "There's more. Your purse was found in the possession of a homeless woman trying to use one of your credit cards at a convenience store about a mile from where the body was found. The Sacramento police want to talk to you."

Keeley felt the blood drain from her face. "Do they think I killed her?"

"You were with me all night," Owen snapped. "No one's going to believe you had anything to do with it."

"Being with Owen gives you a solid alibi," Sawyer affirmed. "Plus, you were in the emergency clinic. You had nothing to do with her death, but the detectives will still have questions. I gave them your contact info. They want to talk with you this afternoon so be expecting a call to set up a video conference."

"A kid Demaris knew tried to take your purse." Owen pinned her with a steady look. "Someone brought him to Sisters, and that could've been Demaris. Fernando could've been following orders from her, and when that didn't work she decided to snatch the purse herself. But she didn't use the credit cards. What else do you carry in your purse, princess?"

"Nothing significant."

The men shared equally dubious expressions.

"I've never even looked in a woman's purse," Sawyer claimed.

"Me either," Owen grumbled. "Who the hell knows what women carry in those things."

"It's not like we have the nuclear codes." Keeley remembered at the last moment not to roll her eyes. "Really, I have nothing special in my purse. The only things of value are credit cards and my phone, which I don't always carry in my purse. I have my driver's license and insurance card in my wallet. Other than that, probably a hairclip, pens, tampons. Maybe some receipts. That kind of thing." She shrugged. "Nothing interesting or of value."

Sawyer leaned forward. "Let's try this. Think back over the past several months and the interactions you had with Demaris. Is there anything that stands out as odd or out of character? Also, consider anyone else you've been in contact with where things felt off. And I mean anything. This could be here in town, at work, in your social life."

She nibbled at her breakfast sandwich. "My tires being slashed was unusual. Owen coming to rescue me was unusual."

"Anything between you and Demaris in the weeks leading up to you getting the flat tire?" Owen asked.

She shook her head slowly.

"You said before Yousef thought Demaris was jealous of you," Owen reasoned. "We established she was a loner while you were accepted as part of the in crowd. That could lead to jealousy."

She glanced at Sawyer. "Owen and I already talked about this. I don't like the term 'in crowd' because it makes us sound cliquish, which we weren't. We invited new teachers, substitute teachers, secretaries. We welcomed anyone who wanted to join us for lunch, or when we went to the cantina after school on Fridays. Even the custodian, Angie, joined us.

"The group was fluid because everyone was welcome. Pam was invited, but she preferred opening her room so kids could eat there during lunch and she chose not to join us for happy hour."

Sawyer picked up his phone. "Give me Yousef's last name and phone number. I want to talk with him."

"I don't want Yousef bothered."

"That's not how this works." Owen's words were clipped. "Cops will talk to anyone with insight into what was going on with this woman. There's a killer out there only a few degrees separated from you. There's not a chance I'm letting them get any closer than that."

She told herself not to read anything into his comment. She chewed her bottom lip as a memory surfaced.

"There was something at the holiday staff party in December. It was kind of pathetic more than anything else." She had the attention of both men. "The party was at our principal's house and I brought Jaxon. At the time, we'd only been dating a few weeks.

"Anyway, Pam was flirting with him. She'd worn this tight, lowcut dress and she was drinking. The evening progressed and she was drinking more. The drunker she got, the more aggressive a play she made for Jaxon."

"Could be she was trying to make you jealous," Sawyer suggested. "How did Jaxon respond?"

"I wasn't jealous. Maybe that should've told me something about my lack of feelings for him. I could tell Jaxon was flattered by the attention. He was eating it up. But then when she wouldn't leave him alone, I think he was embarrassed."

"Do you know if they saw each other after that night?" Owen asked.

Keeley leaned back in her chair. She wanted to be helpful, but she also wanted to crawl back in bed and pretend this morning had never happened. And the cut on her forehead hurt. "I don't think they did, but I can't say for sure. Jaxon and I were dating, but didn't see each other more than once a week or so. We were both busy."

"You broke it off with him?" At Keeley's nod, Owen continued, "Why?"

She shrugged. "We weren't really clicking, and he was secretive about his work. The more I got to know him, the less I liked him. That was in February."

"What kind of work does he do?" Sawyer asked.

"He's a CPA. He'd worked for a firm, but wanted to make more money so now he does freelance work. I'm not sure what that means if you're a CPA. I do know he didn't have his own office. He worked from home, or sometimes he'd go to the location of the business he was working for."

"You said he was bothering you for a couple weeks after the breakup?"

"Yeah. He kept calling, then he wanted to meet up one last time. He said he wanted to reclaim our courtship. His words.

"He sounded so pathetic, plus I wanted to make it clear we were done, so I agreed." She grimaced. "We met at a coffee shop and it was plain weird. He was agitated. His head went up every time someone came in, and he kept looking out the window and checking his phone. He led off with the idea we should get away so we could focus on us. He proposed a vacation to Mexico."

"You're shitting me," Owen muttered.

"I'm not, and it gets better. He said he had a short-term rental in Acapulco picked out but wanted to put it in my name and for me to pay for it. He'd pay me back as soon as he could, and by the way, we'd need to *drive* to Mexico and would have to take my car."

She laughed. "He seemed stunned when I turned him down. I think he understood I wasn't budging on that, so he pivoted and asked if he could borrow five thousand dollars."

She caught the men giving each other a knowing look. "I know what you're thinking. Jaxon is nuts. He said he needed the money to help him get through a rough patch, but that things would be looking up for him soon, and he'd pay me back with two percent interest."

"Fucking incredible." Owen's frown grew deeper.

"It's so crazy it's funny. I told him no, and left. After that, he stopped bothering me. I took for granted that he understood we were done."

"The next time you saw him was when you're working for me and he came in?" Owen asked. "How'd he know where you were working?"

"I don't know," she replied. "That was my second day at Easy Money, and I hadn't told more than a few people where I was working."

"What'd he want, Keels?" Sawyer asked.

"To get back together." She sighed. "I was so irritated with him. I turned him down, but he kept pushing so I ended up telling him Owen and I are together to get him to back off."

"Oh yeah?"

"We're not." Keeley glanced at Owen. His expression gave nothing away. "Together, I mean. Owen said he was okay with Jaxon thinking we are."

"You said he'd started texting again and you had to block him," Owen pointed out. "And Demaris texted wanting to meet up for lunch."

"I didn't respond to Pam's invitation."

Sawyer leaned forward in his seat. "Two people contacting you out of the blue at about the same time, and then one of them turns up dead? Add in that they knew each other. And a third person used to be Demaris's student. The whole thing strikes me as suspicious."

"I don't like it," Owen muttered. "You need to bring this asshole in for questioning."

"Agreed. What's Jaxon's last name?"

"Romero."

He tapped on his phone. "Okay, send me Jaxon Romero's contact information." Once he had it, he said, "I've got to take off so I can get the ball rolling." Sawyer rose, directing his next comment at Owen. "You'll keep doing what you're doing."

It wasn't a question. "Damn straight," Owen replied.

Keeley narrowed her eyes, but before she could ask what he meant, Abby stepped out of her house to make her way across the courtyard. Sawyer greeted her with a wave as he headed to his sheriff's vehicle.

Abby looked like she hadn't gotten much sleep. She bent over her daughter, brushing Keeley's hair off her forehead.

"Oh, my baby. That looks painful. How are you feeling?"

"Like I'm ready for some painkillers." She glanced at Owen. "There's more, Mom."

"I don't like the sound of that. Tell me."

Keeley was relieved Owen took the lead in relating what they knew about Pam Demaris's death.

She still couldn't believe it.

Why would Pam have stolen her purse? It didn't make sense.

God knew teachers weren't the best paid of the professions, but they weren't in a dire enough situation they'd need to steal.

Maybe Pam had been involved in something that had led to desperation. That might explain the need for money, but not why she'd specifically target Keeley.

"I'm so sorry that woman is dead." Abby pulled her jacket closed with shaking hands. Keeley worried the news had rattled her mother. "I can't imagine why she'd target Keeley."

"I was wondering the same thing," Keeley said. "Here's a thought: What if she had an addiction to illegal drugs or gambling? Or was in debt to someone who was a threat to her and she needed money fast? Add in jealousy, if Yousef is right, or that she's never liked me. She decides to resort to crime to pay her illicit debts so she targets me because, you know, two birds, one stone."

"That's as good a theory as any, other than that she didn't use your credit cards," Owen said. "Could be she hadn't had time before she was killed."

They tossed around some other theories, but in the end, that's all they were, theories.

CHAPTER FOURTEEN

Keeley sat on her couch, her feet curled under her with her laptop propped on her knees as she searched for lesson ideas for the beginning of the school year. In a couple months she'd be starting a new job teaching a special day class at Sierra High School, and she needed to start preparing.

Owen had headed home for a shower and a change of clothes. Maybe he'd take a nap as he hadn't gotten any more sleep than she had.

He'd insisted she take the night off from work, but then given further orders she was to report to him if she planned to leave home.

Being bossed around was getting old, but late that afternoon she dutifully texted she was going out. He'd immediately responded.

McHunk: Where to?

Keeley: I'm not a teenager.

McHunk: Definitely not. Where to?
Keeley: ☐ Lone Pine Ranch. Shane + Emery = BBQ

McHunk: Ok.

Keeley: Thanks, Daddy.

McHunk: Don't even.

Hours later and feeling better after her own nap, she turned onto the long dirt road that wound through the foothills of Payback Mountain to Lone Pine Ranch.

She was driving "legally" since the detectives from Sacramento had sent her wallet via messenger service. They'd kept the rest of the contents of her purse as evidence, but at least she had her driver's license.

Wearing jeans, a flannel shirt partially unbuttoned over a white tank top, and cowboy boots, Keeley parked her CRV near the barn. She'd always loved the rustic charm of Lone Pine Ranch with Shane and Emery's log cabin house and the wide-open spaces framed by the gorgeous peaks of the Sierra Nevada mountains.

Shane's dog Bruno trotted up to her, with Walker's homely mutt Bud following close behind.

Keeley dropped to her knees. "Hey there, Bruno. Hey there, Bud." She gave both dogs the lavish welcome they deserved, Bruno rolling onto his back for a belly rub. "Oh, aren't you a handsome boy?" she crooned as his tail swished in the dirt. A pair of jean-clad legs came to a stop next to her. Rising to her feet, she brushed her knees.

Owen stood with his hands in his pockets and an unreadable expression on his face. With his long legs encased in faded Levi's with white paint splattered on one leg, the sleeves of his navy blue Henley pushed up to his elbows, and worn work boots, he looked ruggedly masculine in a way that lit a fuse low in her belly.

On top of that, his scruff was growing sexily scruffier. The fuse burned even hotter.

"I didn't know you'd be here."

"Emery called to invite me. Jen is tending bar tonight with the new guy as backup."

"That's nice. I'm glad you're here." She tilted her head, trying to get a read on his mood. Something was going on with him. "What?"

With a shake of his head, he gathered the front of her shirt in one big hand and pulled her to him. "You. Just you."

Then his lips were on hers and she could hardly breathe.

Mouth, tongue, teeth, he used them all to kiss her thoroughly and completely.

She clutched his shirt and could barely hold on. The kiss lit the fuse to the dynamite and the explosion of need threatened to obliterate her.

She could no longer convince herself what she felt for him was a tiny crush. It was much bigger, and she had the uneasy feeling it could destroy her.

After thoroughly devouring her, Owen let her go. He still wore that impenetrable expression, but his eyes had gone electric blue.

Without saying a word, he turned on his heel.

"Oh no you don't." Keeley grabbed his arm and held on. "You don't get to kiss me like I mean something, then walk away like I don't."

He stopped, eyes glittering when he whipped around, his hands going to her elbows. "You do mean something, Keeley. You mean too damn much. You started it this morning and now that I know how it is when we kiss, I only want more."

"I haven't made it a secret that I want more too."

"I can't give you more." He released her and his eyes went flat. "I'm committed to protecting you. That hasn't changed. It's better if we stay away from each other for both our sakes." He stalked off to where the rest of their group was gathered, the dogs running along with him.

Jerk. She didn't need Owen Hardesty, and certainly didn't need the emotional roller coaster he put her on.

He kissed her like he meant it, and then said they needed to stay away from each other. And, oh yeah, he was her *boss.* How was that supposed to work? Fuming, she crossed the wide yard to join her friends.

Delaney pulled her into a hug, whispering in her ear, "Wowza. That was some kiss. What's going on with you and Owen?"

"He's a jerk and I'm not talking about it. I won't let him ruin my night."

Delaney squeezed her hand. "Fair enough." She lifted the hair Keeley had combed over her forehead so it hid her stitches, and winced. "It still hurt?"

"Some, but it's healing."

Cam and Emery joined them, and there were more questions.

After the initial fuss and discussion over the attack and her stitches, and then Pam's murder, Keeley held up a hand. "That's the end of that. I don't want violence and death to be what we talk about all evening. It's all I've thought about all day and I need a break. The mystery will still be there tomorrow, so let's enjoy each other's company tonight."

Her appeal for a modicum of normalcy worked.

Shane knelt to feed wood into a fire burning in a steel ring circled by folding chairs. Delaney leaned against Walker in a loveseat sipping ginger ale. Sawyer had Cam backed up against a fence in a lip-lock that was getting heated, and Emery brought a bowl covered in plastic wrap from the house to place on a folding table already groaning under the weight of trays of sliced vegies, and bowls of watermelon, baked beans, and potato salad.

Shane's friend and ranch hand Harding, with his warm brown skin and long beard gathered with a hair tie, stood at the grill with Gage and Mateo as he used tongs to flip a rack of ribs and chicken quarters.

Still trying to find her equilibrium after that power-packed kiss, and the subsequent heated words, Keeley did what she loved to do. She moved among the friends to chat and catch up with everyone.

Delaney's not-just-morning sickness had apparently started after lunch and had finally eased enough she thought she could eat. Working together, Keeley helped Cam and Sawyer set up two long folding tables under a giant tree that grew in the middle of the yard.

"We're having a boy," Cam insisted.

Keeley felt like she'd walked into the middle of a conversation.

"Could be, but I think we're having a girl," Sawyer replied. "I want a girl with her mama's blonde hair and gorgeous eyes."

"Or she could have her daddy's dark hair and gorgeous eyes. But we're having a boy. We can name him James Theodore after his great-grandpa and great-uncle. We could call him JT for short."

Sawyer stood and stared at his wife. "That's perfect." He shook his head, his eyes reflecting emotion. "But I still think we're having a girl. She could be Clara after your grandmother."

Keeley arranged the chairs as Sawyer drew Cam into his arms in an embrace so full of love it seemed to glow from them like a moonbeam.

Owen sat with a beer bottle balanced on his knee. He appeared to be engaged with whatever Walker was saying, but she could see the broodiness under the social façade.

More than once she caught his gaze on her. She figured turning her back to him conveyed her *leave me alone* message pretty well.

Bringing a tray from the house with little bowls of pickled onions, dill pickles, and a variety of olives, Keeley spied Owen and Mateo with Shane, their heads under the hood of a pickup.

Shane went to the driver's seat to turn over the engine while Owen cocked his head as if listening. Using a wrench, he adjusted something in the engine compartment. Listening again, he seemed satisfied with whatever he'd done and signaled for Shane to turn off the engine. He glanced over, and Keeley gave a start when their gazes clashed and she realized she'd been standing doing nothing other than staring at the man.

The sun went down in the western sky, lighting up thin wispy clouds in shades of purple and orange, and a breeze whispered quietly through the pines. It was the perfect backdrop for the evening. The people Keeley considered her chosen family filled their plates buffet style and sat at the long tables, flickering lanterns holding back the dusk. She deliberately chose not to sit in the empty seat beside Owen, instead taking the spot between Mateo and Gage.

She bumped shoulders with Mateo. "Hey, friend, how's firefighting?"

"Doing some controlled burns to try to get ahead of wildfire season."

They chatted, trying to draw Gage into the conversation.

Dark haired and broody, Gage had the look of a wounded warrior. She didn't know his story, all Emery'd shared was he'd had a rough upbringing and some trauma that had brought him to his friend's ranch to heal. He seemed laid-back, but she had the feeling he kept a lot hidden behind a dry wit and slow smile.

Here she was with two sexy and handsome men, but neither of them rang the same bells for her that Owen did. Regardless, she enjoyed the meal and conversation even while being acutely conscious of Owen seated across the table. She noticed the corded muscle of his arms as he passed a platter, his long fingers as he cut his meat with a knife, his hooded gaze on her as he sipped from a bottle of beer. He was like a life-size magnet with a constant pull she found nearly impossible to resist.

She tuned into the conversation around her. Predictably, talk swirled around pregnancy and babies. Sitting at the head of the table, Harding beamed from ear to ear. "I'm gonna have me a baby to watch after," he told Shane, rubbing his gnarled hands together. Keeley pegged Harding's age at somewhere between seventy and ninety. "Y'all don't need to worry about childcare because Harding's got it under control."

"Shane and Emery can't hog Harding. You guys have to spread the love," Delaney complained.

"I got plenty of love to spread around. But I can only take care of one baby at a time," Harding said.

Happy pregnancy pheromones seemed to radiate from the couples. Keeley turned to Emery. "Twins run in families, right? You have twin brothers, so maybe you and Shane will continue the tradition."

"Bite your tongue, girl," she said, her voice emphatic. "I don't have a preference for girl or boy, but I've put my order in for a single." She held up an index finger. "One baby at a time."

Emery pinned Shane with a *watch out mister* look when she caught him grinning. "What are you smiling about? You know how my brothers are. It'll be a miracle if they survive to adulthood."

"Twins would certainly give us a jumpstart on our family."

"Says the man who won't have *two* babies growing inside him."

"Darlin', I'm game for whatever we get. It'll be fun."

"Here, here." Walker held up his beer in salute.

Keeley decided time with her besties had been exactly what she needed.

Between being attacked twice, and whatever was going on between her and Owen, her batteries needed a positive charge. After a couple hours with her friends, she felt calmer and in a more settled frame of mind.

They finished dinner and she helped with the cleanup. She said her good-byes with lots of hugs and walked across to her car under a sky strewn with stars, fishing her keys from her purse. Pam had stolen the brand new purse she'd gotten for an excellent price at a sale several weeks ago. Keeley had no idea if she'd get it back or if the police would hold on to it as evidence. She'd been forced to dig out her old purse from the back of her closet.

Footsteps approaching from behind didn't alarm her like they would have had she been anywhere else.

"Wait up." Owen trotted up behind her.

Cam stuck her hand out the window to wave as she and Sawyer drove away, headlights bright in the darkness. Keeley turned to face Owen. Given the look on his face, she could already guess what he wanted. Suddenly she was tired of it.

They stood in the glow from the light over the barn door. Owen jammed his hands into his pockets.

"Look, Keeley, about that kiss. I'm sending mixed messages, and that's not what I want to do. I wanted to be clear."

"Got it." She opened her car door.

He shifted his weight from foot to foot. "I don't want to hurt your feelings."

"My feelings are my own concern. Is there anything else?"

The slow shake of his head made her think she'd surprised him. Good.

"Right, okay. I'll follow you home. I brought a sleeping bag so I can bunk on the floor."

"No," she said succinctly, glaring at him. "You will not bunk on the floor. I'm fine. I don't need or want your protection."

"Fuck that. I don't trust that asshole Jaxon, and we don't know who killed Demaris. You're vulnerable living alone."

"My cottage is mere feet from my parents' home. I'm fine. I don't want you there, Owen."

"Right." He sighed. "Before I forget to tell you, I've contacted a security company to work out a plan for a system that includes your cottage and your parents' house. A rep will be at your house in the next couple days."

She shook her head at his change of subject.

Fed up, she got in her car, started the engine, and backed up to turn around. All the while Owen stood, hands still in his pockets, and watched her leave.

***

Owen stretched, then cursed when he rapped his elbow against the Bronco window. Jesus, it was cold. He'd unzipped his sleeping bag and spread it over himself, but it had slipped off sometime after he'd finally gotten to sleep. That would've been about oh-dark-thirty. He sat up, bringing the seatback to the sitting position, and scrubbed a hand over his face. He'd sell his soul for a cup of coffee. The sun shone brightly through the trees ringing the Montaigne property.

Shit. He'd slept later than he'd intended. He'd meant to make sure Keeley stayed safe through the night, then get out of the firing zone before she spotted him.

He leaned his head against the headrest, fingers jammed through his hair, and closed his eyes because the stabbing rays of sunlight hurt his brain.

He'd pissed her off last evening. Maybe that was better because maybe if she was pissed off, it'd be easier to keep his hands off her.

A sharp rapping had him jerking open his eyes and knocking is elbow on the window again.

Keeley stood outside his truck, as pretty as a sunbeam and wearing a poppy orange Vista Middle School hoodie with flannel pants. She brought a mug to her lips that read "Don't make me use my teacher voice" and sipped slowly.

The bandage on her forehead infuriated him all over again. He opened the door and stepped out, his cramped muscles complaining, and inhaled the scent of coffee.

"That's fucking mean."

Blinking slowly, she took another sip.

He eyed the coffee level as he brushed past her. She still had about an inch to go before being conversational. He went into her cottage, used the john, and splashed cold water on his face. In the kitchen he noted she'd made a full pot. He got a mug and poured his daily dose of sanity and went to join her where she sat at the table on her little patio.

He blew to cool his coffee then drank deeply, warmth sliding through his body. He'd much prefer waking up next to Keeley to sleeping in his SUV, but at least he had coffee.

"You slept in your Bronco."

She must've gotten to the halfway point. He sipped from his mug, taking his time answering. "Yeah."

"I told you I don't want your protection."

"Tough shit."

The bright sun brought out the gold flecks in her eyes and the golden freckles across the bridge of her nose.

"You're staring."

"Wouldn't stare if you didn't have freckles."

She rubbed a finger self-consciously across the bridge of her nose. "I need to remember to put on sunblock or they'll get worse."

He clamped his mouth shut to keep the words he wanted to say from tumbling out. That he loved her freckles. That she was perfect as she was.

She dropped her hand. "Anyway, about you sleeping in your Bronco. Pam was murdered. I get that, but I don't see how that puts me in danger. If it did, the sheriff's department would do something about it. I don't know why you're doing this overprotective big brother thing. Is it because Mom asked? Or Sawyer? Is it because you're a big strong alpha and think it's your job to protect the little lady?"

He scowled at the alpha comment. "I sure as hell don't feel like your brother."

She snorted and added an eye roll.

"What?"

"Let me get this straight. You kissed me last night, but then regretted it. When I'm leaving, you make a point of telling me you're unavailable. Then you spend the night outside my house because you think I'm in danger." She huffed out a breath. "I can't figure you out."

He scrubbed a hand over his face. "I shouldn't've kissed you."

"Whatever. You're not the first man I've made the mistake of having feelings for." He opened his mouth to speak, but she held up a finger. "I dated a guy during my last year of college. We were good together, we had fun. I thought he was someone I could build a future with. Then I got pregnant."

Owen's gaze whipped up to hers. "What happened?"

"I was twelve weeks along when I miscarried." She gave him a fleeting smile. "That baby daddy had already dumped me with a *Sorry, I can't do this* excuse. You stepping back is nothing new."

"Fuck." Owen stared hard at her. "You deserve better than that."

"That's right, I do. And I'm going to make better happen for me."

CHAPTER FIFTEEN

Keeley walked through the back door of Easy Money for her evening shift. She stowed her bag and tied on her waist apron. Owen was in the kitchen changing the CO_2 tanks. He gave her one of his all-encompassing looks then went back to his task without a word.

Which was pretty much the way the evening went. Keeley was determined to keep their relationship firmly in the employer/employee camp and he seemed to feel the same. The Friday night crowd was enjoying the country rock band performing popular covers, and were having a good time dancing.

"Hey, there. When's your break?"

Keeley took a step back from the big man who'd stepped into her path. Jay Berringer was the assistant manager of Sisters Hardware and was generally a good guy. Unless he'd been drinking. She'd had her eye on his table as he and his two friends had become increasingly loud. Time to cut them off. But first she'd have to deal with the big guy.

"Not for a while yet, Jay. Can I get you anything?"

"Oh yeah, sweet thing. You can get me something." He gave her a leering, gap-toothed smile while he puffed out his chest and adjusted his belt. "Always thought you were a looker. How about you take your break now and we have ourselves a get-to-know-you-better dance."

"Nope, no get-to-know-you-better dance for me, Jay. But thanks."

"You don't need to play hard to get. I'm a friendly guy. I can show you a good time." He slurred the word "show" so it sounded more like he'd slow her a good time.

"I don't need a guy for that. How about I get a round of Cokes for your table, on the house?"

A hand on her shoulder drew Keeley back and Owen stepped forward. "Hey there, Jay." He kept moving, his hand going to Jay's shoulder as he turned the man and had him headed back to his table. "Heard a shipment of that new siding came in. I'll be in to take a look at it."

Keeley had never fully appreciated Owen's skill in diffusing a situation. He could certainly get in someone's face if circumstances warranted, and he did. But he adeptly maneuvered Jay back to his table with his buddies while keeping it nonconfrontational.

Behind the bar, she filled three glasses with Coke, added a fresh bowl of bar mix, and when she would have lifted the tray, Owen was there.

"I got it." He hefted the tray to take to Jay's table.

A vibration had her digging her phone from her apron pocket. The notification showed a voicemail from an unknown number. Phone to her ear, she listened as she transferred clean glasses from the wash rack to the shelf, arranging them by type. Message over, she stared at the screen, trying to make sense of what she'd heard.

"What's up?"

"Listen to this. Jaxon left a message using a different number." She tapped speaker so Owen could hear and pressed play. Sounding agitated, Jaxon spoke, voice shaking.

"Keeley, I need help. I'm in trouble. I wouldn't call if it weren't an emergency. Something bad's gonna happen, and only you can help me. There's these bad dudes and they want to hurt me. Or they could hurt you. Police questioned me about that woman's death. I had nothing to do with it. Come to that gas station past the Welcome to Sisters sign tonight when you get off work so we can talk. Come alone." His voice dropped. "I think they'll kill me. You're my only hope."

"There's no way in hell you're meeting that fucker."

"Gee, Owen. I'm so glad you stopped me from meeting a man of questionable character, by myself, at a gas station that's closed for the night. Also note I played the voicemail for you."

"Right, sorry. That was knee-jerk."

"Forgiven."

"Send the voicemail to me." While she was doing that, he said, "You have any idea what trouble he could be in or how you could be involved?"

She shook her head. "Nope, no idea. It's weird. I know I've said Jaxon and I didn't have much of a relationship, but we really didn't. I never met his family, he never met mine. That holiday party was the only time he met any of my friends. I never brought him to Sisters. We weren't that involved."

"He thinks you were involved." His gaze went sharp. "Did you sleep with him?"

"That's none of your business."

"Maybe not, but it tells me something about your relationship."

She rolled her eyes. "Whatever. The answer is no, we didn't sleep together. I was waiting for more of a spark between us, and it never happened."

"Good." He motioned to Jen. "You've got the bar. I'll be in the office." He turned to Keeley. "I need your phone."

"You could ask nicely," she said, even as she handed it to him.

"Thank you very much for handing me your phone."

She couldn't help grinning at his overly polite tone. "He can't believe I'd meet him."

"I have no idea what he believes. I don't trust him. Back in a minute." Owen disappeared through the swinging door.

The band had finished their set and began dismantling their equipment. Keeley helped bus and wipe down tables and seats, and Jen closed out tabs as customers wound down their evening.

Owen returned, handing Keeley her phone. "I called the number he used. No answer. I'm taking you home. Sawyer's not on duty, but he'll meet me. We'll take your car to the gas station to meet Romero. We'll see if he shows."

"Why take my car?"

"Catch him off guard. He won't be fooled for long, but maybe we can catch him by surprise if he thinks it's you."

***

Keeley rinsed and put her toothbrush back in the cup. She wondered if Owen and Sawyer had met up with Jaxon. He said he was in trouble, but she couldn't figure out why he thought she could help him other than thinking she'd give him money. Once Jaxon saw Owen and Sawyer, he wouldn't stick around. He was confrontation-averse, especially with larger and stronger men.

She'd pulled a long-sleeved sleep shirt over her head when a loud knocking sounded from her front door. She rushed to the door anxious to hear what Owen had to say. With her hand on the dead bolt she paused, the hairs on the back of her neck standing on end. She backed slowly away from the door.

"Who is it?"

"Keeley, it's me. Let me in. I need to talk to you."

Jaxon.

He knocked again, louder this time.

She scurried back to the bedroom to grab her phone and dialed 9-1-1 on her way to the kitchen. The heavy weight of a chef's knife in her hand gave her a marginal feeling of security. She let out a startled yelp, the knife clattering to the floor when a sharp rapping came from the sliding door to the patio. Jaxon was a shadowy shape through the glass.

"9-1-1, what's your emergency?"

Keeley scooped up the knife, and hastily flipped off the indoor lights and turned on the patio lights to make it harder for him to see in. She backed up to the wall and slid to the floor. With the knife in one hand and her phone in the other, she recited her address to the operator. "My name is Keeley Montaigne. Jaxon Romero is outside my house, pounding on the doors. He's scaring me."

The dispatcher assured her the call had gone out and officers were responding. Keeley answered several questions: No, Jaxon had not threatened her. Yes, she could see him, he was peering through the glass door. No, she didn't see a weapon.

Jaxon's voice sounded muffled through the glass. "Keeley, let me in. I knew you wouldn't meet me at the gas station. I bet that's where you sent that asshole you're with. I had to get him away so we can talk. I need your help. You've got something of mine I need back, and I need to borrow some money."

Jaxon paced back and forth across the tiny patio, pausing to peer through the glass, cupping his hands around his eyes. It was her first good look at him. His face looked like it'd been used as a punching bag. One eye was swollen shut, his lip was puffy and split, and his jaw appeared to be the color of a ripe plum.

"Stay on the line with me, Keeley. Officers are seven minutes out."

A lot could happen in seven minutes. She texted Abby to tell her that she was safe, asking her also to call Owen, and to stay in her house, adding that the sheriff's department was responding.

She hated that her parents were once again being affected by whatever this mess was she somehow found herself in.

Jaxon's voice carried through the window. His movements were becoming agitated. He was running his hands through his hair, bouncing on the balls of his feet, and kept looking over his shoulder into the darkness edging the patio.

"Talk to me, Keeley. I could end up *dead* and you don't care. I could *die*." He paced back and forth, at times using both hands to grab his hair and pull. "Open up, dammit." Spittle flew from his mouth. He kicked a clay pot she'd bought to plant with geraniums, shattering it and sending shards flying.

He shoved a chair, sending it into the window, but luckily the glass didn't break. Keeley scrambled to her feet when he grabbed the chair and hoisted it up, holding it cocked over his head. He turned toward the sliding door. She caught her breath, sure he would throw it through the glass.

Then he froze with the chair over his head, his attention riveted on something to the left of the patio.

Owen entered her range of vision, gun steady in his hand.

Jaxon stood motionless. It was like watching a balloon deflate as he seemed to shrink before her eyes. Owen's voice was a low rumble through the glass. Whatever he said convinced Jaxon to slowly lower the chair to the ground. He turned his back to Owen and went to his knees, raising his hands behind his head and lacing his fingers together. Keeley drew in a deep breath as what felt like a fist around her lungs eased enough for her to breathe.

In uniform, Sawyer appeared in the circle of light as he moved behind Jaxon and cuffed him. Owen set the safety on his gun and tucked it into a shoulder holster under his jacket. He searched Jaxon, pulling a wallet from his back pocket as well as keys, and a phone from the front, placing all items on the patio table.

"Keeley, are you there?" The dispatcher spoke in her ear.

"Yes, yes, I'm sorry. We're good. Deputy Sawyer McGrath is here along with former police officer Owen Hardesty. They have Jaxon in custody." Feeling lightheaded, she breathed deep to get oxygen to her brain. "Everything's fine."

Keeley heard the faint wail of a siren and spoke hurriedly. "Would you ask the deputies to come in without sirens? My dad is an Alzheimer's patient and he'll get agitated if they wake him."

"Sure thing."

Keeley ended the call with the dispatcher and the sirens cut off a moment later. She tossed the knife into the sink and then opened the sliding glass door. Owen spoke over his shoulder to Sawyer as he approached the doorway, his gaze locked on hers.

He didn't stop until his arms circled around her and he'd pulled her into him.

She released a ragged sigh and breathed him in. "Jaxon thought you'd go to the gas station and he'd be able to get to me here," she murmured with her face pressed to his neck.

He dipped his head, his mouth next to her ear. "I figured. He'd have to've known you'd never meet him at a gas station at night, and he knows we're together. I'd gone up the road only a quarter mile before I realized his plan. Felt like an idiot I didn't figure it out sooner.

"I called Sawyer to let him know and circled back. Jaxon parked his car to block the driveway and I had to park on the street. It took me too damn long to get to you." His hand went to the back of her head. "I'm sorry he scared you. I should've never left you alone."

"You came back and you stopped him."

He dropped his forehead to rest against hers, eyes closed. He seemed to need her touch as much as she needed his.

"I'm so damn tired of fighting this thing between us," he whispered.

Then his mouth was on hers and she felt like he'd thrown off whatever restraints had been holding him back.

He kissed her with an all-consuming urgency that found an answering need in her. With her body fused to his, it was impossible to ignore his response.

His lips moved along her jaw to the slope of her neck. "Tell me to stop. I can't fight you any longer and I don't want to hurt you."

"I don't want you to stop." Her voice sounded breathy.

Voices from the patio had Keeley peering around Owen's shoulder. More officers had joined Sawyer.

Owen loosened his hold, his hands sliding down her arms to tangle his fingers with hers. "Did you tell Abby you're okay?"

She shook her head. "Not yet. The cops will want a statement from me. I'll text Mom an update and get shoes, then come out."

She didn't want to leave the security of Owen's arms, but forced herself to let him go when Sawyer approached. Jaxon sat in one of the patio chairs, hands cuffed behind him, his head hanging dejectedly to his chest.

After reassuring her mom everything was under control and there was no danger, she retrieved her Uggs from her bedroom. Two deputies were escorting Jaxon away in cuffs when she stepped onto the patio and pulled the glass slider shut behind her.

Sawyer had his arms crossed and a serious look on his handsome face. "Tell us what happened."

Owen moved behind her, a hand on her shoulder as he stayed close. She recounted what Jaxon had said. "He really thinks his life is in danger."

"Not liking you being targeted again, Keels. You have any idea who it is your pal Jaxon thinks wants to kill him?"

She shook her head. "He's not my pal, and I don't know. Maybe this has something to do with his work. He was always secretive about what he did and who he worked for, so maybe it was something shady? I don't know how he thinks I could save him." She frowned. "Though he did say I have something of his he wants back."

Owen's hand on her shoulder tightened. "What does he think you have?"

"Maybe the cops can ask him because I have no idea. It's not like he ever stayed over and left things at my apartment. I would've noticed anything of his when I moved." She paused, considering. "I wonder if he's delusional."

"Sacramento PD didn't get anything when they questioned him?" Owen asked Sawyer.

"They're trying to figure out the connection between some interesting facts: A woman's dead. She knew Keeley, and she'd met Romero. As far as they know only that one time, but it's still a connection."

"Keeley is the link between the two of them."

"She is, and neither of us likes that. Romero's under arrest so he's not a threat for the time being."

"Did you notice his face?" Keeley asked. "Someone beat the crap out of him."

"Yeah, I noticed. I'm heading to the station so I can talk to him." Sawyer gave a nod as he prepared to leave. "We'll touch base tomorrow."

Owen and Keeley gave their statements, photographs were taken of the patio, and when Keeley brought out a broom and dustpan, a deputy took it from her to sweep up the broken bits of pottery. All the while she was aware of Owen frowning, arms crossed over his chest, his gaze locked on her, his blue eyes burning.

She felt like the other cops couldn't clear out fast enough. She wanted Owen, and that he wanted her as badly made her nervous and ravenous.

A cool breeze picked up and Owen disappeared into the house, returning with a coat to drape over her shoulders. It took some time before all law enforcement was gone and the patio was clear. Moths flew erratically in the glow of the patio light. Keeley absorbed the quiet as a light gust stirred the pines. She let it soothe the anxiety left over from the incident with Jaxon.

Owen took her hand and pulled her into her cottage, locking the sliding door behind them. They stood with their fingers linked together, staring at each other, the air between them charging with energy.

While waiting for the cops to be done, Keeley'd been feeling the weight of exhaustion, but now with Owen's gaze burning on hers with a heat that threatened to sear her skin, her heart thrummed and anticipation replaced drowsiness.

"I don't do relationships." It sounded like the words were forced past his teeth.

She nodded slowly.

"I'm a risk. We do what I want to do tonight and I'll likely end up hurting you. I'm a bad bet."

"Are you warning me off, Owen?"

"No. I want you too much for that. But I can't promise anything. You need to know that."

"Maybe you *are* worth the risk." She stepped closer, bringing up his hand and pressing it between her breasts where her heart beat heavily. She went onto her tiptoes and pressed a kiss to his lips. "I'm not asking for promises."

"You want a husband and family. I can't give you that." The pain in his eyes arrowed straight to her heart.

"You've been hurt. Badly."

He tipped his head back, eyes closed, his thumb stroking between her breasts. "I've been something." When he brought his gaze back to hers, she recognized regret. "I care about you, and it would kill me to hurt you. That's why I want it clear that whatever we do tonight, it's not the beginning of something more."

She thought her heart would break for him. "I have these feelings for you, Owen, feelings of need and desire that have no place to go. When I'm with you, when we kiss, those feelings consume me, and they get tangled up in yearnings for more.

"I hear you when you say you can't give me a future. But you can give me the present. Give me something of you, even if it's only for tonight."

CHAPTER SIXTEEN

Owen brought his hand to the curve of her neck, his thumb under her jaw, and dipped his head to capture her lips. This kiss felt different. His tongue sliding along hers offering her the promise of something more. She knew that was a false promise even as the heat of his mouth fueled a fever that built, degree by degree.

Burning up, she shrugged out of her coat.

He moved into her, his hands lowering to stroke, long and slow, over her rib cage, over her hips, and under her buttocks. He hitched her up and walked her back to settle her on the kitchen counter. She spread her legs and he moved between her thighs. She sighed when they were lined up exactly right, heat to heat.

Pushing his jacket off his shoulders and onto the floor, she slid her hands under his shirt. He shuddered when she stroked her palms over all that glorious skin. His chest, his ribs, his belly, then lower to his belt. The only illumination in the room shone through the windows from the patio, casting bands of shadow and light.

He sucked in a breath when she worked his belt loose, then the button of his jeans, and when she slipped her hand into the opening and found him, he pushed into her palm with a low groan.

"Bedroom," he growled.

Forced to release her prize when he scooped her off the counter, she shifted her focus. With her tongue she stroked the hot skin at the juncture of his neck and shoulders. When she couldn't resist, she sank in her teeth. Only a little. He jerked with an uttered oath. "You marking me, woman?"

164

"Hell yeah," she murmured and soothed the bite with her tongue.

She could feel his erection nudging through her clothing. She pushed against it and he staggered, bumping against the wall.

A giggle escaped her mouth. "You'd fail a drunk test, officer." She rubbed again.

"You try walking a straight line when you're about to erupt in your pants." His voice held a thread of desperation. "You're going to be the end of me, but damn, it'd be a good way to go."

She laughed against the skin of his throat.

He carried her into her bedroom and laid her on the bed, then turned to switch on the lamp on her nightstand. With a sweep of his arm, he cleared her decorative pillows to the floor.

She loved watching him move with the incredibly fluid grace he possessed. He tugged on the back collar of his shirt to pull it over his head, revealing his rangy build with defined muscles. She figured he had to work out.

His jeans were open at the fly and she gulped at the heavy length of his erection encased in navy briefs. The fever raging inside her had ratcheted up until it felt like she could be burned to ashes.

He took his wallet from his back pocket and retrieved a couple condoms he tossed onto the nightstand.

His skin looked golden in the lamplight.

"You don't have tattoos."

"No, neither do you."

"Yeah, but I wasn't a Marine or a cop. Both occupations where getting tattoos is the norm."

His frown deepened. "My biological father was heavily tatted. I wanted nothing to do with the guy. I look like him, can't help that, but I won't get inked like him."

"I have so many questions about that."

"Later," he growled. Hand on her ankle, he brought up her leg, pressing his lips to her shin, then moving to the back of her knee.

"Later," she agreed, her breath catching in her throat.

Leaning over her, he took both of her hands in his and raised them over her head. Muscles bunched and flexed deliciously across his chest as he propped himself over her, lowering his head until his lips were a hair's breadth from hers.

Heat rising from her belly, over her breasts, and up her neck threatened to ignite her in a fiery ball of need.

"You good with this, princess?"

"Yes, yes, yes," she chanted as she strained against his hold. "Consent clearly given." Since he had her hands, she wrapped her legs around his thighs to pull him into her. "Sweet baby Jesus, I've got to get out of these flannel pants so I can feel you."

He chuckled. "Let me help you with that." He released her hands and moved his to her hips so he could peel off the cotton pants. She had a moment where she wished she wore sexy underwear, but surprise sexy times meant you had to take what you got.

Then her brain went blank because he also yanked off his briefs.

She wasn't inexperienced. She was familiar with the male anatomy.

But, holy moly. She hadn't experienced quite that much male anatomy.

She tugged off her top and when she moved to unclasp her bra, he caught her hands. "I get to do that, princess."

The puckered scar caught her attention and she raised a hand to touch it, gently rubbing where a bullet had violently ripped through his body. He sucked in a breath when she levered herself up to press her lips to the emblem of her warrior.

"Jesus Christ," he muttered. "You turn me inside out."

He braced himself over her again and she trailed her fingers through his chest hair and down his narrow waist, and over the rippled washboard of his abdomen.

Her hum of appreciation when she reached the velvet hardness of him and began fondling his erection turned to a whimper of frustration when he pulled out of reach.

"We'll get to that, baby. There's no hurry."

He played his fingers over, then under the elastic of her cotton panties while at the same time nudging a bra strap off her shoulder. He used his nose to push aside the cup and expose her breast. "You...are...perfect." The words were spoken between open-mouthed kisses to her breast.

She reached for him again, but he moved away. "Still no. Not yet."

"How come you get all the fun?"

"Don't worry, princess, you'll have fun. So much fun." The huskiness of his voice was like adding gasoline to an already raging fire.

He nudged her up and she arched her back so he could unclasp her bra. Then he began worshipping her breasts with his mouth while slipping his hand under her panties to stroke and fondle. Panting, her breath coming in gasps, she was climbing toward a climax when he raised his head, blue eyes burning, and withdrew his hand.

At her groan of disappointment, his smile turned wicked and he moved down her body, his movements excruciatingly slow.

His warm lips and tongue trailed over her ribs, dipped in the hollows of her belly, and when he tugged down her panties, slipped silkily lower still. His gaze locked with hers as he continued tasting and licking, his hands stroking, until he was *there,* causing sensation to blaze through her system like a solar flare.

She closed her eyes at the pleasure, letting herself absorb everything she felt.

He urged her on, mouth, tongue, clever fingers pushing her to climb higher and higher, then higher still, until she spun out in a universe of dizzying galaxies, grounded only by his strong hands grasping her hips and his tongue gently soothing her.

When she could breathe again, she murmured, "I think I experienced the Big Bang." He gave a startled laugh and she stretched languorously. "I now know what it is, the biggest and best orgasm in the cosmos. I feel weightless."

"Yeah? Think you could do another?"

When his grin flashed, she realized she'd never before seen him look unguarded, joyful. That he could feel like that when fully engaged in her pleasure was humbling.

He got to business again, this time reversing the direction of his lovemaking, using mouth and fingers to work his way up her body.

He kissed, licked, and nipped over her belly and breasts, her neck and earlobe, until his mouth was on hers and his erection nudged exactly where she wanted it to be.

Then he muttered a curse and pulled back. "Wait. Condom."

The wrapper crinkled as he took care of business and then he was back.

Gazes locked together, he thrust forward, shallow at first, then stronger, deeper. They moved together, tension coiling, pressure building.

He took her hands, their fingers linking together. All humor evaporated and she had the feeling neither of them expected the shift of emotion to something that felt weightier. His jaw tensed and she could sense him exerting iron control to hold back on his release.

"I want you with me, princess." Hands still holding hers, he changed the angle of his lovemaking.

"Oh god, that's so good."

Trapped by his intensity, she rode the building tide of sensation. He was right there with her as power swept over and through her, her second orgasm cascading in a wave of pleasure that brought him with her as they hurled over the crest together.

He collapsed on top of her, breathing heavily. When he eventually rolled over, she put an arm over her eyes to hide the rawness of her emotions.

She realized he'd been right when he'd said he'd hurt her. Because while for him their being together was temporary, she felt like she'd absorbed him into her soul. He was a part of her now in a way she wasn't entirely comfortable with.

She heard the swish of a tissue being pulled from the box beside her bed and guessed he was taking care of the condom. Then he scooped her up, holding her with casual strength as he pulled down the bedding and deposited her on the sheet.

He joined her, pulling her into his arms. "We'll figure this out, princess," he murmured in her ear as he held her close.

She had a fleeting thought she should practice some self-preservation and sleep on the couch, but instead drifted to sleep in the arms of the man she was worried she'd fallen in love with.

***

Owen woke the next morning and immediately realized he was in deep shit. Much like the first morning he'd woken up in her bed, Keeley was sound asleep, spooned into him, her sweet ass nestled against his groin. He wanted her. Bad.

They'd fallen asleep naked and at some point during the night had woken cuddled together much as they were now.

Her rubbing against him had been enough to set him off. It'd felt like an explosion of nuclear proportions because, good god, the heat, passion, whatever you called it, had consumed them.

Warm skin, lush lips, and a woman he couldn't get enough of had nearly resulted in him going in bare. It'd been a close call.

Keeley'd been astride and about to take him inside before his brain had engaged and he'd grabbed a condom.

There was no excuse for that lack of control. Even with that thought in his head, he took a moment to absorb the feeling of absolute contentment he experienced with Keeley sleeping securely in his arms after making love into the night.

He breathed deep, filling his lungs with the scent of her, then loosened his hold. He had to take a step back before it was too late.

Last night he'd reached a tipping point. All he could think about was having her. He'd wanted Keeley so badly he'd rationalized giving in to the temptation. It'd be only once. He'd made sure she understood he couldn't give her anything more. She agreed this was what they both wanted.

But nothing about what they'd experienced together felt like a one-time thing. It'd felt like he'd let her past every defense he possessed, and she'd taken hold of his heart and could rip it out of his chest if she chose to.

Carefully, he eased away. Luckily, she slept like the dead and he managed to disentangle himself and roll out of bed without waking her.

After using the bathroom, he dressed, then made his way to the kitchen. With the coffeemaker doing its thing, he ate a banana.

He found a notepad and a pen and scratched out a note, placing it by the coffeemaker. He filled a mug and let himself out through the sliding door to the patio.

The sky overhead was the deep blue he'd only ever seen in the mountains. With his eyes closed, he tipped his face back to feel the warmth of the sun on his face.

The squawk of a Steller's jay had him opening his eyes to spy the bird perched on the top of the patio umbrella. Owen moved around the table, straightening the chairs. There were a couple shards of pottery that'd been missed while cleaning in the dark, but otherwise there wasn't anything to indicate an asshole with a screw loose had been outside the window terrorizing Keeley only hours before.

Sawyer had texted to say Romero wasn't talking and there was no new information. Sipping his coffee, Owen made his way across the courtyard to the house where he climbed onto the deck and rapped lightly on the kitchen door. It was early, but Bruce would be up, and if Bruce was up, Abby was up.

Abby opened the door, stepping aside when she saw him. "Come in, Owen. I saw your SUV so I made enough breakfast for everybody. How's my girl?"

"Still sleeping."

Bundled in a thick brown sweater, Bruce sat at the table working a puzzle, its pieces contained on a tray. Owen knew it was part of his therapy.

Bacon sizzled in a pan on the range. Owen set down his mug and swiped a piece of bacon already draining on a plate as he leaned back against the counter.

He knew how things looked. Abby wasn't dumb, and she'd know his Bronco parked in front of Keeley's garage meant they'd likely slept together. He'd rather address the truth head on than tiptoeing around it.

"Keeley and I are involved."

Abby's smile brightened like a sunbeam, much like her daughter's often did. "Oh Owen. I'm so glad. You must know I've wanted to see you two together for a long time. You complement each other so well. You'll be good for each other."

Bruce spoke from the table, "Who? Who's good for each other?"

"Owen and Keeley, honey. Don't you think they make a good couple?"

"Hell yeah. Good move, Marine."

Owen scrubbed a hand over his scruff. "Hold on. We're involved, but I'm not good for her in the long term. I wish it was different, but I don't want you to get your expectations up."

Abby stepped in front of him and laid her hands on his cheeks. "You are a good man, Owen, and I love you. There's something in your past that makes you feel that way, and I'm sorry for it. But you deserve happiness, and I think you and Keeley will bring happiness to each other. Don't punish yourself by not going after something good, something you want. You both deserve more."

Her words held such sincerity and were spoken with such conviction he could almost believe she was right. Almost.

Abby patted his cheek then went to the pan to move the last of the bacon to a paper towel. Owen sat at the table. "How'd you rate bacon?" he asked Bruce.

"I like bacon. Today's the day for bacon."

"I like bacon too, but don't get it much."

Abby spoke over her shoulder. "Bruce gets bacon once a month, so you came on his lucky day." She poured the bacon grease into a can and wiped the cast iron pan. "I'm making scrambled eggs and there are biscuits in the oven. You'll eat with us? Then you can tell us what's on your mind."

"Biscuits, bacon, and eggs? As Bruce says, hell yeah."

"Good. There's a cantaloupe in the fridge and a bowl on the counter. Would you prep the melon?"

He scooped out the guts and was cutting the rind off the cantaloupe when Keeley walked through the door, a mug of coffee cradled in her hands. She kissed Abby on the cheek, then shocked Owen by going up on her tiptoes to kiss him on the lips.

Stupid thing was, if she were truly his, he could see exactly that moment playing out on different occasions stretching on for the rest of his life.

He blocked out that dream because yearning for something that could never be would only make him more miserable than he already was.

His gaze searched hers and she gave him a shy smile before setting her mug on the table to wrap her arms around Bruce from behind. "Good morning, Dad."

"Good morning, daughter."

She kissed Bruce on his cheek and took the seat next to his. Her folks' orange cat left his perch on the windowsill and leapt onto her lap. She stroked him and drank coffee, her gaze steady on Owen.

Abby scooped eggs into a bowl. A timer chimed and she opened the oven and pulled out a tray of golden biscuits. In minutes they were all seated at the table with a breakfast that beat the shit out of his usual oatmeal.

Keeley smiled at her dad when he slipped a bit of bacon to the cat on her lap. The cat knew he had a good deal and was purring his heart out.

"Tell us what happened last night that brought the police to our home again," Abby said.

CHAPTER SEVENTEEN

Owen raised a brow at Keeley, who tapped her mug and shook her head. "You tell them."

So he did, giving Abby and Bruce the rundown of the events from the previous evening. He finished by saying, "I don't want Keeley left alone, and I don't want her staying at the cottage. She's been attacked or threatened three times. I can take care of her at Easy Money, but she's more vulnerable here."

Keeley sat up, the cat jumping off her lap. "Wait a second," she began, but he held up a finger.

"This is nonnegotiable, princess. You're not staying here."

He bit into a biscuit smeared with Cider Mill Farm boysenberry jam. Swallowing, he said, "I can't remember the last time I had homemade biscuits, Abby. These are damn good."

"Damn good," Bruce repeated.

Keeley, more alert now, her hazel eyes glittering sharp green, said, "You can't order me around, and then be all charming to my mom."

"I'm never charming."

She rolled her eyes at him. "You can be, and you know what I mean."

He wanted Keeley to understand, but there was a more urgent consideration. "Is there someplace you two can go for a few days where you'll be away from whatever is going on?" he asked Abby.

"I don't want to go away," Bruce protested.

Abby put her hand over her husband's. "Only for a few days, Bruce, and I'll be with you." She addressed Owen. "Bruce's sister lives in the Bay Area, and we've been thinking for a while we'd like to visit her while he still can. I can call her."

"Do that. I'm taking Keeley to my house. She'll be safe there."

"Now wait a hot minute, mister. You've skipped a step or two. One of those steps being actually asking me if I'm willing to stay at your house."

"You'll end up there anyway."

"Oh, will I?"

"Yeah, you will. I'm saving time."

She was probably right, but he couldn't stop a grin. She looked fucking sexy in a sweatshirt that kept slipping off her shoulder, then add to that, this was the first time she was the one acting grumpy. He wished they were alone so he could scoop her up and take her back to bed.

With her brows pulled down in a scowl, she took her phone from her pocket and tapped the screen, then held it to her ear. Glaring at Owen, she spoke into the phone, "Delaney, give me a call when you get this. I might need to bunk at your place for a few days. PS, I hope the not-just-morning sickness isn't kicking your butt." She disconnected the call and arched her brow at him like a dare.

Abby rose from her seat. "I'll let you two figure yourselves out. After I clean up the kitchen, I'll call Carla. She'll be happy to have us."

Keeley rose to her feet. "Let us clean up, Mom. You go make your phone call."

Owen stacked plates and brought them to the sink.

"No, I've got it." Abby made shooing motions. "You both go on. I'll let you know our plans after I've talked to my sister-in-law." She paused. "You'll still be in town so you'll take care of Iggy?"

"Of course, Mom. I'll check on him every day." Keeley gave her parents hugs. "Talk to you later."

Owen got the mugs he and Keeley had brought over, hooking them on a finger. He opened the door and followed her out. She stopped midway across the courtyard and turned, primed to blast him, and he had to fight the instinct to duck.

"Let's get something straight, pal." If words were bullets, he'd be a dead man. "If there's a reason you think I should do something, you talk to me and explain yourself. Don't talk around me, and don't make decisions that concern me without my consent. I'm not in the Marine Corps, and I'm not a rookie police officer. You're not the boss of me. Well, except at work, then you are the boss of me, but I still don't take orders."

He rubbed the back of his neck and sighed. "Okay, fine. You're right."

"You're admitting I'm right?"

His eyes narrowed. "Don't get used to it, princess. I want you safe, but maybe I could have gone about it better."

The wheels were turning in her head and he figured she was deciding if she still needed to give him shit. Then she smiled and he felt like the sun had come out from behind a dark gray cloud.

She went up on her toes, whispering, "You're forgiven," before pressing her lips to his. He responded before he could stop himself. The mugs clanked together as he brought her flush against him, taking her into a deep kiss with the flavor of coffee swirling between them.

Still fused at the lips, she went back down to her heels, her hands gripping his arms. He was breathing heavily when they broke the kiss. Her grip tightened. "Wow. I'm a little bit dizzy."

He shook his head. "Last night I told myself that we'd have one night. We'd have great sex and get it out of our systems, and then each go our separate ways before anyone got hurt."

She pressed her fingers to her lips like she wanted to contain the taste of him at the same time the sunshine went out of her expression. "Right. You don't want a relationship with me."

"That's not exactly right."

"What exactly is it, then?"

The sound of a vehicle engine carried ahead of a black truck coming up the driveway.

"Not going there."

"I think big strong Owen Hardesty is running scared because he has inconvenient feelings."

He could feel his face settle in a scowl.

The truck parked behind Owen's Bronco in front of the garage, the sign on the door reading Ballard Security.

"Who's that?"

"Friend of mine. He's a little early." He took her hand like he hadn't just stated he didn't want anything serious with her. "I want you to meet someone."

Talk about mixed signals.

***

A tall man wearing a ball cap over dark blond hair stepped out of the truck. A broad grin split his face when he spotted Owen. When they were a foot apart, he grabbed Owen in a hug, holding him tight and slapping his back hard enough Keeley thought he could've knocked over a horse.

"God dammit, it's good to see you." He held Owen at arm's length, studying his face before releasing him. "You look better than you have in a long while, brother." His green gaze swept to Keeley and he shot a wicked grin back at Owen. "You gonna introduce me to your girl? If she's the one that's got you back with the living, I'm already a fan."

Owen said, "Jesus Christ, Luke," but Keeley had a fluttery feeling around her heart when he let the "your girl" comment stand. He made a motioning gesture. "Luke Ballard, Keeley Montaigne."

"Crappy intro, man." Shaking his head, Luke held out a hand. "Hello, Keeley. This guy tell you I'm here to set up a top-notch security system for you?"

"Hi, Luke." She narrowed her eyes. "I've seen you before at Easy Money several months ago."

"I drop in when I can to see my best bro."

"That's nice. Owen told me someone would be coming out to install a security system. I didn't realize it was today, but you're certainly welcome. When you have your estimate, I'll need to go over it with my parents and see what best fits our budget."

"There's no cost."

Owen put his hands on his hips. "That's bullshit, Luke. You give me an estimate like you would for anyone else."

Luke's expression turned dead serious. "You aren't anyone else." To Keeley he said, "This guy tell you he saved my life?"

Keeley looked from one man to the other. "You were his partner? You were with him when he got shot?"

"He told you about that? Yeah, that was me." He nodded at Owen. "That's progress, brother."

Owen's face was back to its standard scowl. "We don't need to go into all this."

"I know he was shot, but not the details."

Ignoring Owen, Luke turned to Keeley. "We were in the LAPD Detective Bureau together and partners for five years. That is, until the night things went sideways in a shithole of a house in South LA.

"I thought I was a dead man until our boy here charges in like he's special forces, guns blazing. Bullets are flying. He takes one in the vest. Thank the gods he was wearing it. Vest takes a round and you're going down, but not Owen.

"I'm not in good shape so he grabs me by the shirt and tosses me over his shoulder. I feel the impact when he takes another. But he stays on his feet and runs through a hail of bullets to get my dumb ass out of there."

"You were shot too, on top of already being messed up."

"I was messed up because the fuckers were working their way up to killing me, but wanted to have some fun first. I was hit on the way out, but survived thanks to you." Luke's gaze shifted to Keeley. "Ask him who was awarded the department Medal of Valor."

"Shut up, Luke."

Keeley wasn't surprised Owen had earned the recognition, or that he had never mentioned it. He wasn't someone who sought the spotlight. Without thinking, she slid her hand into his. His grip tightened around her hand.

"In light of that, your girl's family needs security? I put it in and there's no charge."

Owen shook his head stubbornly. "You already put security in at Easy Money at no cost. You don't let me pay for this? I'll get someone else to do it."

"How about you do it for cost? And my family pays that cost, not Owen." Keeley gave Owen the side-eye.

Luke pulled on his bottom lip. "Okay, sounds like a plan. Let me get what I need from my truck and we'll get started."

Luke walked to his truck and Keeley turned to Owen. "You have a hard time with gratitude. You do big things for people, but are uncomfortable when they want to show appreciation."

"Maybe. I don't like people making a big deal." He brought her hand to his mouth and absently pressed a kiss to her knuckles.

"You could just say thanks. It works."

"Okay."

"Okay?"

"Yeah. It'll take Luke an hour or so to work out a plan. Why don't you get your stuff together." He rolled his eyes before giving her a half smile. "Keeley, I'd like you to stay at my house so you'll be safe. Would you please accompany me?"

"See? That wasn't so hard. Really formal, but yes, thank you for asking." She went onto tiptoes to kiss his cheek. "I'd like to see your house."

She turned to the cottage, then looked back over her shoulder. "Oh, and Owen? You may be relationship averse. Don't let it scare you, but this feels like a relationship."

178

***

Keeley showered and dressed, then fielded a call from Delaney while packing a small suitcase. Putting her friend on speaker, she set the phone on her nightstand while she folded a pair of jeans.

After she'd told Delaney she'd be staying at Owen's and would no longer need to bunk with her, Delaney said, "You're staying at his house? I know he's doing a lot of work on it and Walker and Shane helped him with a job that took three strapping men to do, but I've never seen it myself. He's pretty private and I'm thinking that him being willing to take you there to keep you safe is a big deal. Am I right that you and Owen are together now and it's official?"

"It's complicated. A friend of his is here to put in a security system and Owen didn't correct his assumption we're together. But I don't know. Last night we, um, were together together, if you know what I mean."

Delaney's shriek nearly popped Keeley's eardrums, and she was three feet from her phone. "You and Owen did the deed? Oh my god. Was it good?"

"Oh yeah, it was good. *Very* good. That's all I'm going to say about it."

"With all those sparks between you two, I don't think there's any way it could be bad. I'm so glad you each got out of your own way." Delaney paused, and when Keeley didn't say anything, asked, "Are you okay? I know you have strong feelings for him. He feels something too, but Owen's harder to read. It'd be bad if you're more into him than he's into you."

"I do have strong feelings for him. And I know he feels something for me. I don't want to overanalyze it. This is new and we're in a weird situation with me being caught up in something sketchy, which makes him all protective.

"Where things currently stand? He made a point of saying he doesn't do relationships, but this morning felt really relationship-y.

Include in that him thinking he can be bossy and make decisions for me."

"Alpha male is going to act alpha male. Call him on his shit and you'll be okay. Ask me how I know." Keeley could hear the humor in her friend's voice, but then her tone changed. "Sawyer told Walker about Jaxon being outside your house last night, but you gotta fill me in. They were way too skimpy on details."

Keeley explained how Jaxon had texted asking her to meet him, but that it'd been a ruse. Continuing the story, she continued, "So then Jaxon shows up at my house and starts pounding on the door and yelling."

"That would've scared the crap out of me."

"He sure scared me. He was ranting, demanding that I help him. He said he was in danger and could be killed."

"Killed? Do you think he was serious?"

"I'm not sure. He tends towards the dramatic so it's hard to tell if he was being performative to manipulate me, or if he's really in danger. He also said I have something of his and he wants it back."

"What do you have of his?"

"That's the thing, I don't have anything of his. You can add delusional to his issues. Oh, and get this, he said he needed money."

"What a jerk. No offense, but I don't know what you ever saw in him."

Keeley had asked herself that a lot lately. "Honestly? I want what you have, Delaney. You and Emery and Cam. I want a husband and a family so I'm trying to put myself out there to meet guys. I thought Jaxon was kinda cute, but that soon wore off. I seem to attract the weirdos."

"Owen's not a weirdo."

"No, but he's also taken pains to tell me there's no future for us together."

"Maybe if you could get him to open up about whatever it is that makes him think that way, you could help him work through it. It's obvious he cares about you."

Keeley nodded even though her friend couldn't see her. "I'll think about it."

"Good. So what happened with Jaxon outside your cottage?"

"I called 9-1-1. The dispatcher was calm and reassuring, but officers were seven minutes out and Jaxon was on the back patio. He was pacing back and forth and becoming increasingly agitated. Then he picked up a chair and raised it over his head. I'm sitting on the floor with the dispatcher on the phone and a butcher knife in my hand getting ready to scramble out of the kitchen so I won't get cut by flying glass if he throws the chair through the window. Then Owen's there, gun drawn, so calm and in control."

"Oh wow. Sawyer wasn't with him?"

"He was on his way. Owen was a cop, and it showed. I couldn't make out what he was saying, but Jaxon simply deflated. All the bravado and energy evaporated out of him. Owen gave him orders, and Jaxon obeyed. Then Sawyer arrived and cuffed him."

"Hot damn. I bet Owen was all *me big protector man, my woman's in danger,* which led to get-it-out-of-your-system sex. That's the best kind."

She wasn't wrong.

Owen appeared in the doorway. "You ready, princess?"

"I still need to pack my toiletry bag. Five minutes." Owen disappeared and she said to Delaney, "I've got to go, friend."

"Okay, but remember you're welcome to hang out at our place or stay overnight if that's what you want to do. Don't hesitate to call."

"Thanks, Delaney. You're the best."

"That's what bffs since fifth grade are for." She paused. "One last observation? Every time Owen calls you princess, he's announcing you're his."

CHAPTER EIGHTEEN

Owen drove along a narrow road past A-frame and log cabin homes set back from the road. A glance at the Bronco side mirror confirmed Keeley was still behind him in her CRV. He tapped his fingers on the steering wheel.

Last night had been incredible. Amazing. But making love with Keeley had done heavy damage to the walls he'd built between them because now they were kissing and holding hands, and acting like goddammed lovebirds.

Bringing her to his house was going to mess with his head. There was no other place he was confident she'd be safe. But having her in his home was like giving him a glimpse of heaven with the realization it could never be reality.

He'd damn well keep her safe from Romero and whatever that fucker was involved in, but would she be safe from him?

That she seemed to want his sorry ass nearly as much as he wanted her was a problem because all she had to do was blast her sunshine his way and he couldn't help himself.

She offered herself openly and with affection, and he'd rather cut open an artery than reject her. He needed a strategy to keep her from being hurt, and he had a bad feeling to do that he'd have to explain his past, something he'd never shared with anyone except his mom and stepdad.

As much as it went against every instinct he had to pull back and protect himself, he'd have to tell her straight up why they couldn't be together. The deaths of the two most important people to him were on his head.

Once she knew that, she'd realize why he was a bad bet. He'd hate doing it. Hate her seeing him for what he really was, but it might be the only way he could ensure she kept her distance.

In the meantime, he'd start working on rebuilding those walls around his heart without being an asshole.

He went around a bend in the road before it straightened out. His neighborhood sat on what was basically a long bench of land at the border of Sisters that edged up to the National Forest boundary. His grandparents had chosen well when they'd bought the house some sixty years before. The spot provided the best of both worlds by being near town, but not too close, and they'd handed it down to their grandson.

With his property abutting the National Forest boundary he was protected from development behind him, and with the edge of the bench dropping off across the street, there'd be no development there either.

He liked having neighbors, and liked having them far enough away that they didn't bother him.

Owen lifted his hand to a couple kids whizzing by on mountain bikes and turned onto his paved driveway. He passed the front of his property with its widely spaced pines and cedars on either side before reaching the clearing where the house sat.

He wondered how Keeley would see his place, what she'd think of it, and didn't like that it mattered to him. Because that confirmed how much *she* mattered to him.

To his eyes the house looked homey with its stone chimney and wide wraparound porch, but some people liked fancy, and his home wasn't fancy.

He pulled up in front of the detached garage. Half of the garage was a shop and there was space in the other half to park his Bronco if he chose.

Keeley parked next to him and stepped out of her CRV, her purse slung over her shoulder. She shut the door, turning in a circle to take in his place.

It was like when she'd come to his apartment for the first time. Seeing her at his home would make it even more difficult to keep her separate from his life.

Owen stood with his hands in his pockets.

She turned to face him. He hadn't remembered to brace himself and had to absorb the impact of her beaming smile. He coughed when it felt like his breath had backed up in his lungs. Who could resist a woman whose default setting was sunshine and light?

"Owen, your home is lovely. You've got the forest behind you, and I bet from your front porch you have a stunning view of the valley."

"You're not wrong."

"Front porches are my favorite architectural feature."

"You have a favorite architectural feature?"

"Yes, I do. I have strong opinions about houses. One being that every home should have a front porch. They add so much character. Do you have a swing? I didn't see one, so if you don't, you must get one. Then you could sit in your porch swing and watch a thunderstorm sweep across the valley as you sit wrapped in a blanket, sipping hot tea, and knowing you're where you are meant to be."

"That's mighty specific. I'll have to see what I can do about a porch swing. The house is over sixty years old, and it needed a total rehab, so fair warning, much of the interior is a work zone."

"Oh, that's exciting. I want to see what you've done."

Point proven. In his experience most women balked at staying some place rough, but Keeley saw it as an adventure.

She tilted her head. "Is it hard to be here with your grandparents gone?"

"At first, yeah. Not anymore. I'm changing the interior enough that it won't look like their home." He shrugged. "This was a good place for me when I was a kid. I spent my summers here. The memories are good."

"Did you know Walker and Sawyer when you stayed with your grandparents?"

"Yeah. We played Little League together. Hung out. My grandparents contributed some cash to the lawyer fund to help clear Walker's name when he was in prison."

"They sound like good people. I wish I'd met them." His grandparents would have loved Keeley. They'd accepted Gloria when he'd married her, but that relationship had never warmed.

Keeley turned her head to take in the sweep of his land. "You've got a good defensible space."

He was glad for the change of subject. Her parents being on top of fire mitigation on their property, he wasn't surprised she was aware of the added responsibility the wildfire threat brought to their community.

Every person who lived in the mountains had to be vigilant about fire safety, but some people lived in a fantasy world, thinking wildfire would never be a problem for them.

"I had to clear out a dozen trees. Hated doing it, but it was the only way I'd have a chance if there's a fire. I've also spent a lot of time and money hardening the house."

She opened the back of her SUV and reached for her suitcase, but Owen was there ahead of her. He lifted a brow when he hefted it out of the rear cargo area. "You pack some bricks, princess?"

She grabbed a smaller bag. "No, but I didn't know what I'd need so I packed several books, and my laptop, and I brought my hair dryer."

"Okay."

"No snarky comments about women packing too much?"

"Why the hell would I do that? You need what you need."

"That's quite civilized of you." They walked toward the back of the L-shaped house. "If you hardened the house, I'm guessing even though they look like it, the shingle siding isn't really made of wood."

"You'd guess right. They're fiber cement. I sealed all the gaps and installed specialized soffit vents to keep embers out. Pain in the ass, but it's done."

"That's smart, and the shingles look nice. And you've got a metal roof."

"Yeah. Living up against the forest, I've got to be smart. I've been thinking about putting in a pool. I like to swim, and I'd get a pump so I could use the water in case of a fire."

He led her across the yard where he planned to build a deck, but where currently he housed a rollaway for the debris created by the remodel.

He unlocked the back door, stepping back to let her walk into the mudroom ahead of him. He followed her in and left her suitcase next to the pocket door inside the kitchen. She put her bag and purse on the suitcase.

When she started toeing off her trainers, he shook his head. "Leave them on. Work zone, remember?"

"Right."

They stepped into the kitchen, and she paused to look around. "Wow. You said sixty years old?"

"About that. They bought the house as a new build in the early sixties and the kitchen was remodeled in the eighties."

"Your appliances are Harvest Gold. I've never actually seen that color other than in magazines. They're classic."

"Never bothered me when I was a kid, but I hate the color now. Those'll be gone when I get to the kitchen part of the remodel and replace them with stainless steel."

"I wonder if in another sixty years people will look back on stainless steel appliances with the same horror we reserve for Harvest Gold and Avocado Green from the seventies."

"Not my problem. I like a clean look."

"Will you give me the grand tour? I want to know your vision."

"My vision is to get rid of everything that made the place look dark. That includes the paneling, small windows, and small rooms."

"That's a good start."

He gestured across the kitchen. "I took out a wall there to open the kitchen to the dining room and built the island. It's done except for the countertop and cabinet doors, which I want to match to the rest of the kitchen. I'm waiting for inspiration on that.

"The island will have stools on one side, and cabinets on the other." He glanced around the space. "The Formica's butt-ugly and the sink's chipped. I've been waiting to pull those out until I figure out what to replace them with. I was thinking stained concrete and a stainless sink."

"Concrete countertops?" She gave a shudder. "That'd be like having a sidewalk in the kitchen."

"Ha. More like making good use of a functional material. Concrete is durable, heat resistant, and stain resistant if it's sealed properly. You can even incorporate surface designs like making it look like marble. Plus, it'll complement the stainless appliances."

"It sounds…industrial. I was going to say soulless, but I don't want to hurt your feelings."

He frowned, considering. Maybe she had a point. "What would you do?"

"Don't get me started or I'll be showing you my dream kitchen Pinterest board. I started it when Mom and Dad had their kitchen redone."

"How about you tell me."

"Okay, you asked for it." She grinned.

"My philosophy is the kitchen is the heart of the home. By removing the wall, you've made the dining area part of that heart. A family has meals there, but it's also where kids would do their homework while mom and dad are making dinner.

"It's where mom pays the bills while dad makes school lunches after the kids are in bed. Big talks happen at the dining table, like where to go on vacation or whether you can afford to put in that pool."

He turned away like he was picturing her ideas in his kitchen. But the reality was the home she described hit him with the force of an earthquake and made him yearn for something he could never have.

"Go on, I'm listening." His voice sounded gruff even to his own ears.

"With that philosophy behind it, I'd want the kitchen to feel warm and inviting."

He turned back to her. "And concrete countertops are cold and uninviting."

She hunched her shoulders. "No offense, but that's my feeling. My dream kitchen applied to your space would have a white apron sink, since I *love* apron sinks, and would be complemented by a light gray quartz countertop. Not a solid gray but something with a bit of pizzazz."

"Pizzazz."

"You're laughing at me on the inside. I'm on to you."

She tapped her finger on her lip as she stared at the cabinets currently painted what he thought of as shit brown.

"To finish the idea, the top cabinets would be glass fronted and painted a light sage green, and then I'd have vintage-style light fixtures to bring it all together. Add your stainless appliances, and you get a modern farmhouse look that's warm and welcoming as well as functional."

"You've given your dream kitchen some thought."

"I have. What type of flooring will you put in?"

"I'm thinking a porcelain tile that looks like wood."

"Ooh, that's a good choice. That's what's in the kitchen at the big house at Cider Mill Farm and it looks great." She tilted her head. "About the kitchen, you're the one who has to live with the design choices, so make sure you get what you like."

"Even if it's concrete countertops?"

"Even then. Now show me the rest."

Piles of lumber and coils of wiring and extension cords snaked here and there. He'd almost reached for her hand to walk her through his project before he caught himself. Distance, he reminded himself. She could keep from tripping without his help.

"I like the windows you put in."

He made an effort to focus. "That was one of the first things I did. They're double-paned for energy efficiency. I put that to the test this past winter and my energy bill was considerably lower than the same time last year. They'll pay for themselves."

The living room was done except for flooring and paint. The walls had been primered, but that was it.

Keeley tapped on the paint sample card he'd taped to a wall. "I love this cream color. It would complement the sage green in the kitchen, and you could bring in more color with an area rug in a jewel color like burgundy or red, and maybe an earth brown couch."

He pictured her ideas and decided they'd work. Like really work.

"What did you do with your grandparents' furniture?"

"Kept a few pieces I liked but got rid of the rest. The style looked dated, and not in a good way. Lots of overly ornate pieces. I want simple, well-made furniture."

He led her down the hall. She peeked into a half-done bathroom, and the first bedroom where he'd knocked out a wall to the adjoining bedroom to make a bigger room with a walk-in closet.

As with the other rooms, it was complete except for paint and flooring.

He'd thrown his sleeping bag in a corner. She poked her head into the other bedroom he intended to use as a home office, then led her to the open doorway at the end of the hall.

"The master bed and bath are the only finished rooms in the house."

She stepped into the room. He could admit to being gratified by her audible gasp. "Oh, this room is beautiful. And you have a pewter bed frame. I love the lines. Is it vintage?"

"Guess so. It was one of the pieces of my grandparents' I kept."

"Wise man. It's a classic design and gorgeous." She ran her fingers over the metal. "Your ceiling fan complements the style."

Since that had been the idea, he appreciated the comment.

She stepped into the bathroom and let out another gasp. He came up behind her. "This is a beautiful bathroom, Owen. Other than your misguided ideas about concrete countertops, you have good instincts for what goes together. And see? You used quartz here." She smiled over her shoulder. "The tub itself is a work of art. I don't usually take baths, but that tub looks inviting enough I think I might need to."

"Tub's here if you want." The mental image of her naked in his bathtub, of her and him together and naked in his bathtub, had his blood heading straight south.

He wanted to reach for her, to pull her into his arms. To make use of the bed only feet away. He needed to get a grip.

He didn't want things to be awkward, so he said, "Look, there's only one bed. I've got my sleeping bag and will sleep in the other room. You can sleep here."

Keeley was usually an open book with every emotion revealed on her face, but in this instance, he couldn't read her. "Okay."

He opened his mouth, then snapped it shut. He hadn't expected her immediate agreement, maybe because she wasn't shy about expressing objections if she had any.

Though it was good she didn't object, he felt disappointed she hadn't expected to share his bed. And why would she expect anything different when he'd made a point that last night had been a one-time thing?

His phone pinged with an incoming text. Welcoming the distraction, he tugged his phone from his pocket.

"It's from Sawyer and he included you on the text. The prints they'd pulled from your car after your tires were punctured?"

"Yeah?"

"They're a match to Pamela Demaris."

"Pam slashed my tires? Why would she do that? This keeps getting more and more bizarre."

"Good question. Sawyer says he'll text an update on the case later." Owen gave her a thoughtful frown. "You and I need to talk. Demaris was connected to Romero, and we need to figure out how."

CHAPTER NINETEEN

The next morning, Keeley wandered into the kitchen and found a sticky note from Owen on the refrigerator saying he'd be back soon. She wore boy shorts and a tank top with a fuzzy robe belted over them. Definitely sexier than her sleepy sloth pjs, not that Owen had seen her in them.

Last night he'd said good night and disappeared. Later she'd heard a saw running, and a peek out the window had revealed lights on in the garage. She had the feeling he was taking desperate measures to avoid her. Fine. Whatever. She rubbed her eyes and yawned.

While construction was going on around it, the kitchen was still functional. Owen had brewed a pot of coffee and set two sturdy mugs next to it before he'd left for wherever he'd gone. Thank goodness because the machine looked way too complicated to have to figure it out in the wee hours of the morning. She checked her phone. Okay, maybe not wee hours, but eight a.m. was still early.

She opened the door of the Harvest Gold refrigerator. Contents were sparse and she immediately determined there was no creamer or milk to be found. And there wasn't much by way of breakfast food.

There were bottles of condiments in the door and lunchmeat in a bin, but no bread. A single apple looked lonely on a shelf next to a half dozen bottles of water. A peek in the cupboards revealed peanut butter and a bag of chili-flavored Fritos. Owen had lunch food for when he worked at the house, but that was it.

She had her phone out and was contemplating texting him when the outside door opened with a gust of fresh air. Owen carried a couple grocery bags in one hand and a white paper bag with the Three Sisters Bakery logo in the other.

Good grief, what was it about this man that made her want to grab that face and kiss him long and hot until they were both breathless?

Sure, he wore faded blue jeans ripped at one knee that fit his butt just right. Scarred work boots and a heavy canvas jacket enhanced the manly-man image. Add in the tousled hair, deep blue eyes that sharpened when he looked at her, and lips she really wanted to kiss, and it was no wonder she was a goner.

He must've caught something of where her mind had gone because in a swift motion he set the bags on the floor and moved toward her, grabbing her by the elbows and lifting her until they were eye to eye.

"You look at me like that, princess, and I have a hard time reminding myself why we're not going there." Even as he said it, he was backing her up against the wall. Her robe fell open and his gaze raking over her body felt like a line of fire burning her from the inside out.

"I have no idea why we're not going there. That's on you," she murmured. Her hands gripped his unbuttoned jacket and pulled him to her. "Kiss me or I'm going to go crazy."

He closed his eyes and breathed deep. Even in her caffeine-deprived state she recognized his internal struggle. But then a groan rumbled from deep in his throat and his lips slanted over hers. And consumed her.

His mouth took her deep, his tongue deeper still, her fingers diving into the lush thickness of his hair. His hand cupped her rear through the tiny shorts and pulled her into him until they met, heat to heat. The kiss spun out, gentling as he moved his mouth to nibble on the sensitive skin below her ear.

When he released her, he stepped back and sucked in a lungful of air. "Goddammit, Keeley." He brought up his hands to bracket her face. "I need to tell you, to explain why I can't do this. Why we can't get into a relationship."

She was going to point out that they certainly were in a relationship of some sort, but the torment in his eyes had her swallowing the words. "Okay," she managed.

He stepped back and using both hands, jammed his fingers through his hair. His expression held a mountain of pain.

"I was married, and I had a little boy."

Surprise held her silent even as a dozen questions bounced around her brain.

"They're dead. I'm responsible for that. I should've told you earlier before this whole thing started."

He snagged the bags from the floor and set them on the counter. Without looking at her, he pulled out a container of creamer and set it next to the coffeemaker.

"You bought creamer. My favorite brand."

"I pay attention."

"Thank you."

When he continued unpacking the groceries, she leaned against the counter, head tilted as she watched him. "Have you ever talked about this?"

He shook his head.

"Tell me what happened."

"Let's get breakfast first. We can talk after."

She nodded. Peering into the bakery bag, she asked, "What'd you get?"

"Bagels."

He set bananas and strawberries on the counter along with a loaf of bread and a tub of cream cheese. Then, after using a serrated knife to slice the bagels, he stuck them in an ancient toaster oven.

She rinsed the berries, sliced them and a banana into small bowls she'd found in the cupboard, all the while telling herself not to get used to the cozy domestic scene she and Owen made. He believed whatever had happened with his family made him unworthy or undeserving of having a family in the future.

Owen laid a piece of plywood over a couple sawhorses and placed folding chairs on either side. In minutes, they were sitting at the makeshift table with an excellent breakfast.

Keeley slathered cream cheese over her toasted cinnamon raisin bagel and took a bite. Chewing slowly, she wondered what'd happened to Owen's family.

He sat across from her looking a little lost. She wished she could help ease his pain but wasn't sure he'd let her past his defenses. So she asked him questions about the remodel and how he planned to furnish the house, thinking maybe a simple conversation would help him feel more comfortable.

***

Eating toasted bagels and drinking coffee while Keeley chatted openly, Owen felt some of his tension ease. He figured that was her goal, and was grateful for the reprieve it gave him.

His entire adult life he'd followed a hard-and-fast rule that no one needed to know his shit. But it was different with Keeley. It didn't matter they had no future together, he wanted her to *know* him. To understand him in a way no one else did. It wouldn't change anything, it couldn't, but maybe by knowing, she'd get *why* he couldn't be with her, and she wouldn't hate him.

"I don't like talking about what happened. Other than my mom and stepdad, I never shared it. But if anyone has a right to know, it's you." They'd finished their meal and he rose to his feet, face set in serious lines.

"Let's go out to the porch. No swing, but I have a couple chairs out there."

"Okay." Mug in hand, she followed him out the door. They sat side by side in camp chairs, a chilly wind gusting.

She pulled her robe tighter around her. He rose and ducked back in the house, coming back with a fleece blanket he dropped over her legs.

Sitting again, he stared into the distance where Sisters lay nestled in a forested bowl.

He fucking hated it but prepared to bare his soul.

"After high school, I didn't know what the hell I wanted to do with my life. I'd taken auto shop classes and got a job as a mechanic changing oil, brake fluid, replacing filters, because that's all they'd let an eighteen-year-old kid do. I figured I'd do that until I could work out a better plan. I was seeing this girl. Her name was Gloria. I was young and dumb. We both were, and she got pregnant."

"Oh Owen."

"Yeah. We weren't in love. At best you could say we were in lust. But my mom had gotten pregnant, and that dude hadn't stuck around. Mom kept contact with his family, but there was nothing they could do to get him to take responsibility." He shrugged. "I wasn't going to be that guy. I wanted to do the right thing. I bought her a ring, we got married, and I joined the Marines.

"Joining the military was the only way I could see to provide for my family. I'd get regular pay, medical benefits, and housing."

"That's honorable."

He shrugged. "Maybe. Mom was okay with it. We'd been living in Fullerton in Southern California. She'd married Eddie, my stepdad, and he wanted to move to Phoenix with my stepsister, but I didn't want to go with them. If I joined the military, I'd have base housing for me and my family.

"Add to that, I was a wild kid and Mom thought I needed the discipline I'd get in the military. She wasn't wrong. My grandparents lived here in Sisters. They wanted me to go to college, but I wasn't ready for that."

Keeley's expression turned somber. "What did Gloria think?"

"Mixed bag there. She liked being engaged, liked going to parties with a fiancé who was a Marine. She wanted to keep doing what we'd been doing.

"We got married at a courthouse, and a week later I'm in boot camp at MCRD, San Diego." His gaze followed the flight of a crow skimming the treetops.

"Gloria was working as a receptionist for an insurance company and living with her parents. I didn't see her until Family Day, which is the day before graduation from boot camp. She already had a baby bump and had ultrasound pictures of him. That made the baby more real."

He caught Keeley's gaze with his own. "The idea of being a dad scared the crap out of me, but I was excited too. I'd get to be the kind of dad I'd never had."

He studied her. "You were pregnant once."

She nodded. "Yeah. I was scared and excited too. But I'd had a better role model with my mom." She brought the blanket around her shoulders. "What happened after boot camp?"

"I reported to Camp Pendleton. Gloria hated base housing. Complained our place was too small. She said I wasn't spending enough time with her, and living on base was too far from Fullerton for her to visit her friends and family as often as she wanted."

He paused. "I was committed to the military and working my ass off. Any time I had free I tried to do what she wanted. I painted a room for the nursery and tried to make sure she'd have everything she needed for the baby before I deployed because I knew that was coming. She still wasn't happy."

"She sounds young."

"Actually, she was a few months older than me, but it doesn't matter. We were both young."

He shrugged. "The thing was, I felt like I was growing up. I'd accepted my responsibilities, I was being trained for military service, I was providing for my wife. But she still wanted to do what she'd always done.

"She'd go home for long weekends. Then I found out she was partying. She said she wasn't drinking, but I don't know what she was doing.

"One weekend I thought I'd surprise her and showed up at her parents' house. She was at a party. I tracked her down and found her making out with some asshole. She was seven months pregnant and letting a guy put his hands up her skirt at a party. I lost my shit and beat the guy bloody."

Talking about it brought the memories flooding back, but something about Keeley's quiet, unwavering presence allowed him to keep the emotions in check.

She paid attention, he'd give her that. She watched him with those gray-green eyes, hanging on his every word. But he hated showing her what a failure he'd been.

"Thing was, I wasn't giving Gloria what she needed most. She was lonely and felt like she was stuck in our apartment on base with nothing to do. She said I didn't understand her, that I didn't even try to understand her. Then I got my mobilization orders. The baby was due in a couple months, and I was being sent to Afghanistan."

"You felt like you were abandoning her."

"Yeah. I did. But I got on that plane and flew to the other side of the world. Seven weeks later I got a text and a bunch of pictures of Gloria holding this tiny baby boy. She'd had her mom with her."

"Oh my gosh." Keeley was so open her emotions were written all over her face. "You were a daddy. That must've been so hard to be away from your family. Hard on Gloria, but hard on you too. That's an awful sacrifice we ask of our soldiers and their families." She reached out and took his hand, her palm pressing to his. "What did you name him?"

"She'd wanted to name him after her dad, so he was John Robert Hardesty. She called him Robby since her dad went by John.

"We'd talk on the phone when we could, but it felt like she was always mad about something. She was exhausted and had to figure out the parenting thing by herself. She was upset because she was struggling to lose the weight she'd gained.

"There wasn't a fucking thing I could do for her except listen and send home a paycheck. When my deployment was over, I went back home and tried to be the husband she needed, and the father my kid needed."

"It must've been a shock to go from a war environment to home."

He gave a humorless laugh. "The first week back I was so fucking overwhelmed. When you're deployed, you don't have to think about what you should be doing, because you have a mission, you have orders, and your job is to execute them.

"Stateside, I was figuring it out as I went along and not doing a very good job of it." He ran his fingers through his hair. "Most important thing for me? I wanted to get to know my son. The kid was amazing. He was doing this army crawl thing using his elbows to scoot himself across the floor. He was the cutest damned thing with the bluest eyes."

He shouldn't have been surprised when he saw the sheen of tears in Keeley's eyes.

"Oh, that's sweet," she whispered.

He gave a grunt of agreement. "Gloria was trying, I could tell she was. She didn't like how much I had to work, but I tried to make it up to her.

"Then I'd get time off and it was like she was punishing me because she'd go visit her family and leave me with Robby. I didn't really mind, though. I had him all to myself, and if she was gone, we weren't fighting."

He rubbed a hand over his beard. "Turns out that wasn't a good solution because she was seeing someone else. I didn't find out until later. I was sent back to Afghanistan a day after Robby's first birthday.

"I got back to the barracks one night and my lieutenant was there with a major. They told me there'd been an accident." His voice went flat. "Gloria, Robby, and this guy she'd hooked up with were in a car accident. Some asshole kid street racing hit them. Fucker was going over a hundred miles an hour and he tore the car in half." He gazed into the distance. "There were no survivors."

Tears streamed down Keeley's cheeks. "Oh god, Owen. I'm so sorry. I can't imagine how much that must've hurt."

The wall he'd built around his heart wobbled like it'd taken another hit.

This was why he didn't talk about this.

He rose abruptly. She rose too, dropping the blanket and moving into him, wrapping her arms around his waist.

He stood rigid, arms at his side. She didn't seem to care and held him tighter like she could inject some of her sunshine right into him.

Maybe she could, because he felt warmer in a way the coffee couldn't hit.

He couldn't help but bring his arms around her shoulders, holding her to his chest, his cheek resting on the top of her head.

Never in his life had he felt something that was a balm to his soul, but Keeley hugging him was exactly that.

"I'm okay. It's been long enough it no longer feels like I've been ripped apart with no way to put the pieces back together," he murmured into her hair.

She tipped up her head so she could look in his eyes. "I know what you mean. When I lost my pregnancy, I felt so raw. I also felt betrayed by my boyfriend, who was such an asshole."

Owen's mouth tilted up at one corner. "That's a pretty strong swear word, Miz Montaigne."

"I reserve my swear words for those who truly deserve it. Gives them more impact that way."

"True statement. Fucker abandoned you when you needed him most."

"He did, which also made me question my judgment. Why hadn't I seen that in him?" She shrugged. "Mom made me get therapy, and that helped. The pain from that time never goes all the way away, but I can deal with it now."

"Moms are like that. My mom also pushed me into therapy. It helped."

She beamed at him and in that moment, wild horses couldn't have stopped him from kissing her. He bent his head and their lips met in a kiss that lit a fire in his veins at the same time it soothed the jagged edges of his heart.

Then realization set in.

He'd convinced himself he could have a platonic relationship with Keeley, and kissing her was *not* something people in platonic relationships did.

"I'm sorry." He gripped her shoulders and took a step back. "Listen, Keeley, you need to know I'll never get married again or have kids. No matter how hard I tried, I wasn't enough for my wife, and the result was she died, and my boy died. I let them down."

"That street racer was responsible for their deaths. I know that. But Gloria wouldn't have hooked up with the guy she was with if we'd had a better relationship." He released her and stepped back, shoving his hands in his pockets.

"Gloria made the choice to be with him. She could also have made the choice to honor her vows." Owen was shaking his head before she even finished speaking, and Keeley felt she had to make him understand. "From what you told me, Owen, you tried to make it work. She didn't."

"Doesn't matter. I'll never put myself in a position where the people I love most can be taken from me. I could never go through that again and survive."

It looked like a shadow dropped over her features. "I see. It's better not to love at all." She drew in a shaky breath. "You have a deep well of compassion inside you, Owen. It's hard to see you closing yourself off from living a full life."

"I haven't closed myself off from a full life. It's a different life than what I once had. That's all."

"A full life means being open to other people, to feelings, to strong emotions."

He narrowed his eyes. "Don't think you can change my mind because I won't."

"Where does this leave us? Are we buddies? Pals?"

He closed his eyes. "Damn." When he opened his eyes again, she thought she'd never seen him look so sad. "I want to be your friend, but that's all I can be."

"It's absolutely your right to build this wall between us, but put this into your calculation. I love you, Owen." He jerked like he'd been shocked by a live wire. "I've had strong feelings for you for a while. I thought they'd go away, but no such luck."

He opened his mouth, then snapped it shut again.

Squaring her shoulders, she went on. "My feelings are my own and not your responsibility. I'm not sure if I can handle being friends. We'll have to see."

***

After a quiet shift at Easy Money where she tried to minimize contact with Owen, Keeley lay in his beautiful bed between his soft cotton sheets and stared into the darkness. She'd fallen in love with a man whose heart had been shattered. Because of that, he'd closed himself off to whatever had been building between them. She was an optimist by nature, but how could she get past Owen's steadfast refusal to ever love again? Was it possible to grieve for something that never was?

CHAPTER TWENTY

Sitting on the porch with the blanket wrapped around her, Keeley sipped from her coffee mug. She'd had a restless night. She hoped the bright morning sunshine would burn off some of the sadness left over from yesterday's conversation.

She heard the door open and footsteps approach. Owen didn't look like he'd gotten any more sleep than she had.

His hands were jammed in the pockets of sweatpants worn low across his hips. His hooded sweatshirt was unzipped over his bare chest. She deliberately looked away. She had to find a way to smother her feelings so her heart wouldn't ache so badly.

He checked the coffee level in her mug. Wise man. He stared out over the valley, waiting through the appropriate level of caffeine consumption before finally speaking.

"Come with me today."

Her heart gave a hard knock of excitement and she sighed. Damn her stupid heart. "Where to?"

"Tahoe." He held up a hand at her raised brow. "Hear me out. We'll take a road trip. Totally platonic. No hand holding, no kissing. Just friends spending the day together."

"I told you I'm not sure I can be your friend."

His gaze held hers. "I don't want to lose you."

She looked away. She knew it wasn't healthy for her to go with him, but the idea of spending a day together made her yearn. She had absolutely no self-discipline where Owen was concerned.

"What about Easy Money?"

"Jen asked for more hours, so she'll be fine being in charge tonight. You aren't scheduled to work. It'll give us both a break." He frowned. "There's something else. Sawyer texted. Romero made bail this morning."

"I see. A road trip is your way of keeping me safe from Jaxon."

"I don't need a road trip to keep you safe. That's merely a side benefit." Owen sighed. "Look, when I was a detective and a case wasn't coming together, if I could swing it, I'd take a ride on my motorcycle. It helped me clear my head and get a fresh perspective.

"I've got the Bronco now, but you and I can talk through the case and see if we can come up with an explanation about what's been happening. You're the connection, and we need to figure out how and why."

Keeley didn't want to be the connection. She wanted all bad guys to forget she existed and leave her alone. Because she had no willpower, she said, "I'll go with you, but why Tahoe? It's on the other side of the mountains and a long drive."

"It's a little less than an hour and a half one way, so not too bad. I got a text from my cousin Zoey. She and her husband and kids have a cabin on the lake for a couple days and invited me to hang out."

A drive over the Sierras in spring would be beautiful, and meeting Owen's family sounded intriguing. But she was honest enough with herself to acknowledge what she really wanted was time with Owen.

"We'll need to check on Iggy on our way out."

Keeley called her mom and chatted while making sandwiches, letting her know Iggy was doing fine.

Bruce was doing well and having a good visit with his sister. Abby thought they might extend their stay. After an update on what they knew about the attacks on Keeley, they signed off.

Keeley added Fritos and a baggie of sliced strawberries to a tote bag and figured they had lunch covered.

She dressed in jeans and low-heeled boots with a green fleece sweater over a t-shirt, and because mountain weather could change rapidly, she'd grabbed her down coat and tossed it in the backseat of the Bronco.

After leaving Iggy with fresh water, a full food dish, and a good pet and snuggle, they started the drive, taking Highway 50 east out of town.

Keeley relaxed and took in the gorgeous scenery. The winding highway split through stands of tall pines crowding the road then straightened as they flew past wide meadows bordered by tumbling creeks.

The sky was the deep dark blue of high altitude, broken only by crows and an occasional hawk circling overhead. There weren't many other people out today, and occasionally they passed cars coming the opposite direction.

"This is really nice. I haven't been this way in too long. It's easy to forget how much I love this landscape." She smiled at him. "I'm glad you invited me."

Owen's hands tightened on the steering wheel and he nodded.

"Me too." He put on mirrored sunglasses. They looked like a shield. He might want a platonic friendship, but she had a feeling he was struggling with it like she was.

"Tell me about your cousin. Are you close?"

He glanced in the rearview mirror and frowned. "Close enough. We both had challenges growing up, but my grandparents wanted us to know each other. When I spent the summers in Sisters, my grandparents would have Zoey and Charlie, that's her brother, come out for at least a week or so. We all work to stay in touch."

His gaze went to the rearview mirror again. Keeley shifted in her seat so she could see the side mirror. A group of motorcycle riders, she counted at least a dozen headlights, were fast approaching from behind. They stayed there until the road straightened when they passed, open throttles making a loud rumble.

The riders wore matching leather jackets with Ravagers MC stitched in Gothic-style lettering across the back, and black helmets

Keeley thought looked like those worn by the Nazis in World War II.

"Shit," Owen growled.

"Problem?"

"Ravagers are an outlaw motorcycle club out of Sacramento. They're known to cause trouble."

The riders disappeared around the bend and Keeley breathed easier. That is, until Owen steered around the curve and immediately hit the brakes.

The riders blocked the highway, and when Owen swerved into a turnout, they moved as a group and arranged their bikes as a barrier to keep the Bronco blocked in.

"Keep your seatbelt on. This goes sideways I'm flooring it to get us out of here, even if I have to take out some of them. That happens, princess? You get down as low as you can get, and you stay down until I say we're clear." His voice was hard, eyes like flint. "Got it?"

"Yeah, I got it."

He stopped the Bronco, keeping it in drive with his foot on the brake. One of the Ravagers swung off his bike, took his time to remove his helmet and stow it on the bike, then lit a cigarette. He took a drag as he strolled toward them. Owen threw his sunglasses on the dash and pressed the button to lower his window.

Motorcycle guy had a grizzled face with a long beard and gray hair pulled back in a scraggly ponytail. Below the sleeves of his shirt, his hands were tattooed, another design creeping up his neck from under his shirt. "Owen Hardesty. Guess you're wonderin' why I stopped you."

"You know my name. What's yours?"

The older man's eyes were hidden behind dark goggles. He blew out a stream of smoke. "Go by Nero. This ain't what I'd call an adversarial interaction. I got no beef with you. I got no beef with your lady."

"Get to the point," Owen growled.

"I got no beef, but your lady here's got somethin' of ours. We want it back. I get it, you'll be free to go." He tapped the cigarette to knock off some ash.

"You'll need to clarify."

"Talkin' about her former boyfriend who stole something from my club. The former boyfriend says she has it and we're wantin' it back. She gives it to me, we'll be on our way. She don't give it to me, well, that'll be a problem."

"This former boyfriend got a name?"

Nero's forehead wrinkled above his goggles. "We're talkin' about Jaxon Romero with a fuckin' stupid man-bun."

"I know the guy. We agree on the hair. What'd he steal?"

"Information."

"What kind of information? In what form?"

Nero took another pull on the cigarette. "You're askin' a lot of questions."

Owen let the statement hang.

Leaving the cigarette dangling from his lips, Nero tilted his head and sighed like he was in deep contemplation. Finally, he said, "See now, I did a little research. You got background as a cop, and I expect if you're not carrying, you've got a weapon in this vehicle somewhere. This leads me to deduce you're an hombre who don't mess around. Given that, I don't want you too curious about the information fuckin' Romero stole from my club."

Keeley shifted nervously in her seat. Other club members had parked their motorcycles to box in the Bronco. The riders had dismounted and several stood with their hands on their hips.

She didn't think it was an accident that their stance opened their jackets to display the weapons they wore strapped to their bodies. Some had guns in shoulder harnesses, others were in holsters at their waists, while still others had knives in scabbards on their belts.

Keeley's heart was thundering in her ears. Owen rested an arm on the steering wheel. He looked relaxed, but she had no doubt he'd move fast if he decided to. The Bronco engine was still running with the transmission in drive.

"My girlfriend doesn't have anything of Romero's."

Nero dropped the cigarette on the ground and Keeley could hear the scrape of his boot as he stepped on it. "See, thing is, Romero was our accountant."

Keeley could sense Owen's heightened interest. He spoke carefully. "Theoretically, an accountant would have access to illegal activities of a club. If he downloaded that information, he could try his hand at extortion, demanding payment to get the information back. Be stupid, but he might think it worth the risk."

"Let's just say it turns out my accountant's a stupid man. Thought we had an understanding, but he got greedy. Me and Romero recently had us a come-to-Jesus talk." Nero jerked a thumb over his shoulder. "My boys persuaded him extortion isn't a healthy enterprise."

Which explained Jaxon's battered face.

"Romero got chatty and says he gave an encrypted flash drive to someone for safe keeping. Thought it would be to his advantage if we couldn't lay our hands on it."

"How much he want for it?"

"Two million." He shoved his goggles to the top of his head, revealing faded blue eyes. "Look here, Hardesty. I gave you enough so you know what's up. You've given me nothin'." He shifted to focus on Keeley. "No offense, miss, but I'm thinking you're the one he gave the file to. Maybe he didn't let on, but Romero was all about covering his ass, and if he could do that by stowing that flash drive at your place, he'd a done it."

"You're aware Jaxon Romero is out on bail," Owen said.

Nero nodded. "Also know he was at your lady's house demanding she return the flash drive before he got himself arrested."

"Jaxon said I had something of his, but never said it was a flash drive," Keeley told him. Then she added, "I know you, Mr. Paulson. We've met before."

Nero jerked back like he'd been hit, and Owen swung his head around with a startled expression.

"Your granddaughter Destiny was in my class at Vista Middle School. She's a wonderful girl. I'm Miss Montaigne. You came to her IEP meeting in February. How's Destiny doing?"

Nero stared at her hard, then turned his head to address his men. "Stand down."

The other Ravagers' demeanor instantly changed. Some removed their helmets, they started chatting amongst themselves, and a few took out cell phones.

"That one got by me, miss. Didn't recognize you." Nero smiled wide showing stained teeth crowded together. "My granddaughter's doin' good, thanks for asking. Smart as a whip but needs a little extra help, which is what you gave her. Know she's heartbroken the other teacher came back and you had to leave." His attention shifted to Owen, then back again. "You're sure Romero didn't give you anything of mine?"

"I'm sure."

He pulled on his beard. "Flash drive is small. Could be he hid it thinkin' it would be safer with you and he could get it later. Once I get my hands on Romero again, we'll persuade him to clarify what he did with it."

Keeley didn't want to know how his men would persuade Jaxon.

"Meantime," Nero continued, "maybe you can have a look around, see if he hid it anywhere." He paused, then gave a quick nod. "You folks are free to go. We'll be in touch."

"I'll look for it, and thank you, Mr. Paulson."

Nero signaled for a path to be opened.

Ravagers mounted their bikes and moved them out of the way. Owen took his foot off the brake and eased the Bronco onto the highway.

They drove in silence until Owen muttered, "You're something else, you know that?" He glanced at her, then back at the road. "You got the president of the Ravagers to back off and let us go." He shook his head like it would help recent events make sense.

"I find appealing to people on a human level helps to defuse a situation."

"Certainly true in police work."

"It's true in teaching too. If a kid is being disruptive in my class and I can have a minute to talk with them one on one away from their peers, I can almost always defuse the situation."

"The human level."

"Exactly," she agreed.

"Nero thinks you're a good teacher. I'd say he's got that right." He glanced again at the rearview mirror.

"Are they behind us?"

"No, they took off going the other way." Owen put his sunglasses back on, drumming his fingers on the steering wheel.

"They really want that flash drive back. What do you think is on it?" she asked.

"You can bet something high stakes. Accountants deal with cash flow, right? My bet is they hired Romero and paid him well. Ravagers would have been explicit that what Romero learns about their organization stays where he finds it."

"What could he have learned?"

"Evidence of drug dealing, weapons trafficking, prostitution, other criminal activity. It's a business to them, and businesses need to keep records.

"Romero might've seen an opportunity, made copies of sensitive files, and threatened to turn the information over to law enforcement or to a rival criminal organization if he wasn't paid off.

"Something spooked him, and he decided to stash the flash drive with you. You're squeaky clean and nobody'd suspect it. But then you broke up with him, leading to trouble for Romero retrieving it."

"Squeaky clean sounds boring."

He gave her a look that had heat kindling low in her belly. "Looks like squeaky clean does it for me."

She breathed slowly through her nose to calm herself. "You want our relationship to stay platonic, you can't be looking at me like that."

He scrubbed a hand over his face, his beard making a crinkly sound. "Dammit. Sorry."

Keeley leaned back in her seat, thinking of all times she'd spent with Jaxon. "I remember, Jaxon and I went out to dinner once, and a guy came to the table acting kind of creepy. He was a big guy, super muscular with tattoos across his knuckles and neck. He asked Jax how he was doing, and I could tell it unnerved him. Then the guy asked to be introduced to me, which Jaxon did."

"You get his name?"

She shook her head. "Not that I remember. He told Jax to be careful and that eyes were on him, then he left.

"I went to use the restroom and when I got back Jaxon had my purse and was standing by the table. He said we were leaving and practically dragged me out of there. He wouldn't even give me a minute to tell the waiter to cancel our order."

"Would you have noticed if he'd put a flash drive in your purse?"

"Probably not if it was in one of the zippered side pockets. I don't go into them on a regular basis."

They'd been driving uphill and topped a long grade where they were greeted by a sweeping view of the eastern slopes of the Sierras.

Lake Tahoe shimmered like a sapphire gem in the distance.

Owen turned at a sign indicating a day-use picnic area.

CHAPTER TWENTY-ONE

While Keeley used the bathroom, Owen carried the bag with their lunch to a picnic bench in the shade of a giant pine tree. Chipmunks darted around the tables and scurried over rocks, searching for crumbs. The temperature had dropped as they'd climbed in elevation, and with the light wind Keeley was glad she'd brought her coat. A family sat at another picnic table where two toddlers chased each other as their parents unpacked large bags.

Owen uncapped a thermos and filled the cup lid with coffee, handing it to Keeley. She sipped and smiled at him. "You added creamer."

"That's how you like it." He made it sound matter of fact, like of course he added creamer. He didn't use creamer himself, but he'd made the coffee the way she liked it.

She was beginning to realize even while claiming they were nothing more than friends, he did little things for her without making a big deal of it. It made her heart ache.

He pulled open the bag of chips, shaking out a pile on Keeley's napkin before grabbing a handful for himself.

While she munched on her sandwich, she focused on the endless sky where the glint of silver shone from a plane flying overhead. Below, canyons cut into steep mountains, and spindly trees clung to outcroppings of rock.

"It's so beautiful here. The eastern slopes are drier than the western side, and there's a wilder look." She studied him. "You ever think of hiking the John Muir Trail? It's a dream of mine."

"I'd like to, but it's hard to take that much time away from the bar. Some day." He filled the cup with coffee for himself. "You in the considering stage, or the making it happen stage?"

"I'm not in the making it happen stage yet, but I want to explore the backcountry."

He nodded. They ate in silence until Owen remarked, "You think Romero and Demaris were seeing each other after you broke up with him?"

She munched on a Frito. "It's possible. Pam made her interest known at that staff holiday party. Jax was flattered, so maybe."

"I agree. What if he'd hid the drive in your purse and was counting on you not discovering it. You break things off with him so he gets Demaris to go after your purse so he can get it back."

"Why wouldn't he simply ask for it?"

"He didn't want you to know anything about a flash drive. He didn't want you suspicious." Owen sounded like he was thinking out loud as he reasoned through the evidence.

"So first try is with a kid Demaris knows and it goes south and the kid's arrested. He's a juvenile so it's not a big deal. She tries again, and that time is successful. She's killed that night and your purse was found nearby."

"Do you think the Ravagers killed her?" The thought brought a chill to her bones.

Nero had seemed reasonable, almost friendly, but it wasn't much of a stretch for members of outlaw motorcycle gangs engaged in drug trafficking and guns to commit murder.

She didn't like knowing the caring grandfather could also be a cold-blooded killer.

"I don't see the motive for them. I'm not saying it isn't something they would do, but murdering a schoolteacher and leaving her body in a Dumpster? That's going to get a lot of attention."

"What if Nero and his crew confronted Jaxon and he told them the flash drive is in my purse, and by the way, my new girlfriend is stealing it for me tonight. They wait until Pam has my purse and grab her and get what they're after. They kill her so she can't identify them." Whatever Pam had done, she didn't deserve to be killed in cold blood.

"Possible," Owen said, frowning. "But it doesn't fit. Whoever killed her would've taken the flash drive, but it doesn't sound like it was in your purse. If it had been, Romero wouldn't have been at your door, and the Ravagers wouldn't have stopped us today. Romero thinks you found it, and the Ravagers, at least before today, think you'd found it."

She swallowed hard, not liking the direction of his reasoning. "Then who killed Pam?"

Owen's gaze leveled on hers. "Romero. He lets her send the kid for the purse. That's illegal shit, but he's plausibly clear of it. When that doesn't work, he gets Demaris to go after it herself. Her motivation? Residual jealousy, and a desire to please a new boyfriend.

"But there's no flash drive. He's pissed, she's used up her usefulness, and he's afraid she'll be arrested and point the finger at him." He shrugged. "So he kills her."

"But remember she wanted to meet for lunch? That was after Fernando tried his hand at armed robbery. How does pretending to be my friend fit?"

"My guess is she wanted to orchestrate a scenario where she'd have access to you and your purse. She might've thought you'd invite her to your house and she'd have the opportunity to search for the flash drive.

"If Romero told her where he'd stashed it, she'd know exactly where to look. That's easier than tracking you down and assaulting you to get the purse."

"From her end, it might've seemed worth a try." She shook her head. "But I can't see Jaxon murdering Pam."

"That's because you're too sweet and think the best of people. Reality is, you can never tell."

She stared at him as he stuffed the remnants of their picnic lunch into the bag and walked it over to a trash can. She needed to keep reminding herself that he didn't want to be with her.

Back on the road, they descended the eastern slopes, and were soon using the Bronco's GPS to navigate around South Lake Tahoe to the address of the short-term rental Owen's cousin had given him.

They pulled into a driveway next to a hybrid minivan.

A tall, lanky man with dark hair stood in the driveway. He had a little boy perched on his shoulders, and another smaller boy clamped around his leg like a starfish. A short curvy woman with a mass of dark curls turned at the Bronco's approach, a huge smile on her face.

That smile brightened even more when she spotted Owen. They exited the vehicle, and she launched herself at him with a fierce hug.

Keeley smiled at the man. "Hi, I'm Keeley. You look like you have your hands full."

He smiled in return; the two little people attached to him looked at her owlishly.

They had matching dark hair and striking blue eyes that had been handed straight down from their father.

"Hey. I've got a niece named Keeley. Levi Gallagher." He stuck out his hand to shake. After letting her go, he gestured to his shoulder. "Monkey number one is Henry." He pointed down. "Monkey number two is Lucas."

"Nice to meet you, monkeys."

Henry smiled and leaned over to peer at his dad upside down, saying clearly, "Not a monkey," while Lucas only held tighter to his father's leg.

Owen approached with a hand on the woman's shoulder. "Zoey, this is Keeley."

"Happy days, a female. I'm so glad to see you. I'm surrounded by humans with penises and need a break."

Keeley noticed Zoey's rounded belly. "It looks like you're adding another monkey to the circus."

"Circus is right." She rested a hand on her baby bump. "This one's a girl, thank goodness. She'll help even out the testosterone in this family. Come on in. We've got sun tea, and we've got beer. I made my own hummus dip and chopped some veggies for a snack."

"Good thing I picked up Doritos," Levi said cheerfully as he limped to the door with one leg weighted down. "I'll let Keeley choose ranch or original."

"Original," she responded.

Zoey rolled her eyes as she led the way inside the house. They arranged themselves in comfy chairs on a deck that looked out over the stunningly blue lake. Ice tinkled in Keeley's tall glass as she drank the refreshing iced tea and enjoyed carrots and cucumber slices heaped with tasty hummus.

Levi eyed her food choices. "Don't tell me you're crunchy granola like this one." He nodded to his wife.

"Nothing wrong with crunchy granola." Keeley smiled at him as she snagged a chip. "Even so, I'll occasionally indulge in the Dorito."

"Awesome," Levi pronounced.

"How long have you guys been together?" Zoey asked, gaze shifting between Keeley and Owen.

"Oh, we're not together. Owen and I are friends."

Zoey's brows rose to her hairline. "I don't believe that." She pointed an accusatory finger at her cousin. "I'm not blind. There's something going on. Plus, when have you ever introduced me to a woman?" When Owen didn't answer and took a pull from his beer, she went on. "I'll tell you, it's never. Not even the one you married." She turned back to Keeley. "Whatever's going on with you two, it's more than *friends*."

Keeley let the comment pass. What could she say?

Cruising from furniture to people, Lucas toddled his way to Keeley and clambered up. She boosted him onto her lap where he promptly gave her a wet kiss on the cheek and began playing with the ends of her hair.

216

"That one's a lady's man," Levi said. "Watch out for him."

"He's fourteen months and on the verge of walking without holding on to something."

Keeley breathed in the sweet scent of baby powder, her cheeks warming when she caught Owen watching her, his gaze narrowed.

He set his beer on the table to swing Henry onto his lap. The little boy leaned back against Owen's chest and stuck a thumb in his mouth.

Keeley looked away when the yearning for exactly that, except with Owen holding *their* child, slammed into her.

"Since we're changing the subject," Owen said, "what brings you to Tahoe? You live in a mountain town by a lake, so you vacation in a mountain town by a lake? And where's the monster dog?"

Zoey laughed. "Sounds strange, doesn't it? We live in Hangman's Loss, which is a two-hour drive south of Tahoe," she informed Keeley. "We bought a new house because we're tripping over each other as well as the monster dog at our current place, and when baby girl arrives, there'll only be more tripping."

"Mountain dog?" Keeley questioned.

"Lucy is a Bernese Mountain dog. She takes up a lot of room," Zoey replied. "We bought this house and it's really cute and I *love* the windows and the view of the lake, but we wanted to paint the interior before moving in. I can't stand plain white walls.

"Our lease was up in the old place and we needed to be out of there and I didn't want everyone exposed to paint fumes, so the cop arranged for us to come here while the work is being done."

"The cop?"

She tilted her head toward her husband. "Levi is with the Hangman's Loss police department. His brother Brad is police chief. Lucy is hanging out with Uncle Brad and his family while we're gone."

"Added bonus," Levi chimed in. "My brother and brothers-in-law volunteered to move the furniture into the new house. Zoey drew out a plan of where she wants everything, and as soon as the paint crew is done, the furniture gets moved in. Should be done tomorrow and we'll head home the next day."

"Sounds like a win all around." Keeley looked at Zoey curiously. "Owen said you're cousins?"

"We're something. Our mothers were first cousins." Zoey looked at Owen. "That makes Charlie and me your second cousins. Or is it first cousins once removed? I can never remember which."

"It's simpler just to say we're cousins."

"I adored Owen's grandparents, who were my great-aunt and -uncle. They invited me and my brother to visit when Owen was in Sisters. His grandma wanted us to know our family and because of that, Charlie and I got to hang out with Owen, and that way we got to know him. We wouldn't have, otherwise."

"It worked. We're family." Owen's simple statement had Zoey beaming.

Henry's eyes had drooped shut and Levi rose to his feet to gather the boy from Owen's lap. "I'll settle him for his nap." He pointed at Lucas. "He's almost out too. It's a win when they both nap at the same time."

Zoey moved to push up from her seat, but Levi shook his head. "Relax, babe. You're doing the hard work of growing a human. I've got the monkeys." He took Henry and a couple minutes later came back for Lucas. When he returned to the deck, he set a baby monitor on the table.

He dropped a kiss on Zoey's lips. "You need anything?"

"Just you." She pulled him down to sit beside her on the loveseat.

Levi draped an arm behind her and Zoey leaned her head against his shoulder.

Keeley thought there might as well be twirling cupids and hearts over their heads like in cartoons because they so obviously adored each other.

"I can't believe we're adding another to the mix," Zoey sighed. "I feel like we run at borderline chaos as it is."

"You and Levi seem like you have things figured out," Keeley commented. "You've got a good vibe. I'm betting you'll be fine."

"We will. I have a minor freakout every once in a while when I think of managing three kids." Zoey smiled. "We're a good team. We've got four months to get settled in the new house and then baby girl arrives and we'll be back to breast feeding, and we'll have two kids in diapers again. That'll be exciting. But enough about us. Catch us up with what's going on in your life, Owen."

While the little boys slept, Owen filled Zoey and Levi in on the case swirling around Keeley.

Levi sat up, interest in his eyes as he leaned forward in his seat. "Let me get this straight, both the Ravagers and the douche boyfriend think Keeley's hiding the flash drive."

"That's ex-boyfriend," Owen growled. Ignoring the grins from Levi and Zoey, he went on. "Nero's demeanor changed when Keeley recognized him as the grandfather of one of her students. He seemed to believe she didn't know anything about it but asked her to look for it."

Levi turned to Keeley. "You never saw it?"

"If it was in my purse, I—" A thought struck, and she could feel the blood drain from her cheeks. "Oh my god."

Owen's gaze drilled into Keeley. "What's is it, princess?"

"My purse. I can't believe I didn't think of this before. I got a new purse, when was it? Maybe January? Was I still going with Jaxon then?" She wasn't making sense. She stared wide-eyed at Owen. "The purse Pam stole was my new one. I hadn't had it long and the police kept it as evidence."

"Connect the dots for me. You're saying if Romero hid the flash drive, it wasn't in the purse Demaris stole?"

"That's exactly what I'm saying. It could be in my old one. They look similar."

"Where's that purse? Do you still have it?"

"It's here. I've been using it since the other was stolen."

"Here as in Lake Tahoe here?"

"Yeah. I left it on the side table in the entry way."

Levi was across the deck and in the house in a flash, returning a moment later with Keeley's purse dangling from his fingers. He plopped it in her lap. "There you go. Test the hypothesis."

She stood and set her bag on the table. With Owen looking over her shoulder and Zoey and Levi across the table watching with avid interest, she unzipped the main compartment. She found the zipper tab to the inside pocket and pulled it open. Slipping her fingers into the pouch, and with heart pounding, carefully extracted the contents.

"Holy shit," Owen muttered.

Holding it between her thumb and forefinger, Keeley showed the others a flash drive with a shiny aluminum housing.

Levi disappeared, reappearing seconds later with a clear plastic zip baggie. He held the bag open. "Drop it in here, sweetheart. It's possible the forensics guys can get fingerprints."

Keeley dropped the device into the bag, glad to be rid of it. "I've had it with me all along. I feel like such an idiot."

"Cut yourself some slack, princess." Owen cupped her chin and gave her a firm kiss on the lips. "You put it together and figured it out."

"I knew it," Zoey crowed. "There *is* something between you two."

"You're nosy," Owen muttered.

Levi handed the baggie to Owen who slipped it into his pocket.

Keeley stepped back and took a fortifying breath. Zoey might think she and Owen were together, but Keeley knew better. He'd been caught up in the moment, that's all.

"It's hard to believe Pam Demaris might've been murdered because of this," she murmured.

"Makes me wonder what the motorcycle gang was up to if they are so interested in getting it back," Zoey said. "Is it safe to plug in and view the contents?"

Owen shook his head. "Word is it's encrypted. If that's the case, it's password protected."

"If we turn it over to the sheriff's department, would they be able to see the contents?" Keeley wondered.

"Not likely. Even with a warrant it'd be near impossible to access the contents without the password." Owen took out his phone. "I need to call Sawyer and let him know we have it."

Owen leaned against the deck rail as he spoke on the phone.

Keeley helped clear the chips and veggies from the table while Levi grabbed the empty beer bottles. A cry came over the baby monitor now clipped to Levi's pocket.

"That's Lucas." Zoey zipped across the living room.

"She wants to get him before he wakes Henry." Levi stowed chips in a cupboard.

"Henry sleeps longer than the little guy?"

"Yeah, go figure. But Lucas will sleep longer at night. Henry's our morning dude and is up with the sun."

Zoey returned with Lucas in her arms, the boy rubbing his eyes with a chubby fist.

Owen came in. "We need to get going. Sawyer wants the flash drive asap. It was good to see you all." He dropped a kiss on both Zoey's and Lucas's heads.

"Let us know how this turns out," Levi said as the men shook hands.

Zoey pulled Keeley in one-armed. "Don't give up on him," she whispered. "He's had it rough, but I can see you're good for him."

Keeley gave her a searching look. "I'd like to think so," she said in a quiet voice. "But, more importantly, he has to think so."

Zoey gave her another hug, little Lucas staring at Keeley with big blue eyes. "He'll come around. I know he will."

She nodded. "Give Henry a kiss for me. You have a beautiful family. I hope to see you again someday."

CHAPTER TWENTY-TWO

They returned from Tahoe in the early evening, exiting the highway as they drew near the outskirts of Sisters. Owen glanced at Keeley. She'd been dozing for the past half hour. Bringing her to visit Zoey and her family, sharing a picnic lunch, driving up to his home with her beside him—it felt perfect. She was perfect for him, and he'd like to think he could be perfect for her. But he knew better, he knew he'd eventually screw up and hurt her.

He parked in front of his garage and Keeley sat up. He laid a hand on her arm to stop her from opening her door.

"Stay here. I want you inside the car, doors locked, while I take a look around." She gasped when he reached into the glove box and drew out a gun. He paused with his hand on the door release. "It's only a precaution."

"Be careful."

His gaze searched hers, and he said, "I'm always careful."

He exited the vehicle and moved around his house in the dusky twilight, motion-activated security lights coming on. He completed the circuit and unlocked the back door. He searched quickly, but thoroughly. He returned to the Bronco, tapping on the passenger window.

Keeley opened the door.

"We're clear."

She grabbed the bag from their picnic and followed him into the house.

She washed the thermos and a few knives they'd used that morning, setting them on the drainer. She was unusually quiet.

"I have a frozen pizza for dinner." Her hands stilled, and Owen continued to speak. "I can put that in the oven or go into town for some takeout if you prefer."

Not looking at him, she dried her hands. "I'm not really hungry. I think I'll turn in."

And just like that, the kitchen was empty.

Dark, cold, and empty.

Like it would be when she went back to her place.

Realization washed over him. She was wrong. The kitchen wasn't the heart of the home, *she* was the heart of the home. Of his home.

God he was an idiot. An absolute fucking idiot. She'd told him she'd loved him and he'd let it go like it didn't matter. Like she didn't matter.

He pressed his fingers into his eyes.

She loved him. Even knowing how he'd screwed up his marriage, she still loved him. She loved him and was willing to take a chance on him. And he'd been too damned scared to admit he loved her back.

And when she told him she wasn't hungry, she'd looked sad. He felt it like a gut punch.

He had made her sad.

He needed to make it right.

He crossed to the hallway, flipping on lights as he went because he didn't like the darkness closing in. He rapped lightly on the bedroom door. No response, so he cracked open the door and heard the shower running.

She liked long showers. He'd noted that already.

With a plan forming, he pulled out his phone and called Mario, his chef at Easy Money. He texted Keeley that he'd be back in forty minutes, made sure all doors were locked, and hauled ass to the Bronco.

Pulling into his parking space at Easy Money, he knew his priorities had made a giant shift. For the past three years, making his place a success had been his number one goal. Suddenly, being the man Keeley deserved had become his top priority.

He took the stairs to his apartment two at a time. In the kitchen, he searched shelves and drawers, gathering what he needed and throwing everything in a reusable grocery bag.

Down the stairs again, he pushed through the bar's back door and walked into the kitchen as Jen was placing containers in a box. She spotted Owen and grinned.

"Got you covered, boss. Everything you need is here." She held up a bottle and waved it. "Pinot Grigio will pair with the chicken and mushrooms. It's already chilled."

"Thank you for doing this, Jen." He lifted a chin to Mario, who nodded in acknowledgment. He grabbed the box and Jen held open the door for him. "Any problems tonight?"

"We're fine. Go show your girl a good time."

"That's the plan. Thanks again."

He was closing the back hatch of the Bronco when a sheriff's department SUV pulled into the parking lot. Sawyer lowered the window. "You have something for me?"

Owen pulled out the baggie with the flash drive from his pocket.

Sawyer held it up to examine. "Glad you found it." He shot a narrow-eyed look at Owen. "I also heard you fucked up with Keeley."

"How do you—" Owen broke off, shaking his head. "Never mind. Yeah, I fucked up. I'm fixing it though. I hope."

"See that you do. She's one of us."

He made it back to the house in the allotted forty minutes. Barely. The shower was no longer running, but he took a few minutes to set the stage before going to find her.

Nerves jumped when he tapped on her door.

"Come in."

She sat in bed propped against a mound of pillows in the warm glow cast by the lamp on the nightstand. The book in her hand looked thick enough to stop a bullet. She wore loose pants and a zippered sweater. "You got something on your feet?"

She lifted a brow. "I'm wearing socks."

"Good. You might want those fuzzy boots of yours."

"While I'm in bed reading a book?"

"No, while you're having dinner with me on the porch." He stepped into the room.

"I told you I'm not hungry."

"Maybe you're not hungry. More likely, you're pissed at me. You have a right to be. I messed up. Bad."

Carefully, she placed a bookmark in the big-ass book and set it next to the lamp. "You have the right to feel what you feel, Owen. You can't change your feelings because they don't match mine. We're good.

"I called Delaney and I'm going to her place tomorrow morning. I'll be out of your hair. I'll stay with her until whatever danger I might be in is resolved."

He sat next to her on the bed. "I don't want you out of my hair." Gaze steady, he reached for her hand. "I was an idiot and I hurt you. Let me fix this, princess."

She shook her head, drawing her hand away. "You want to be friends. I want that too, but I need time away from you to get past these other feelings." She drew in a wobbly breath. "I can go to Delaney's tonight, if that's better."

"Hell no. I can't fix it if you're not here." He spotted the fuzzy boots under the edge of the bed and bent to retrieve them. "Put these on and come outside. Everything's ready. The only thing that's missing is you."

He felt his future balanced on a razor's edge. If she pulled back, it might kill him.

"Trust me, princess."

He held his breath when she hesitated, but then she nodded. "Okay, Owen." His breath released with a whoosh.

Fuzzy boots on, he pulled her to her feet. He'd left the lights off this time for impact. They crossed to the front room where strings of lights on the porch glowed warmly through the large picture window.

He led her outside.

Her soft sigh as she took in the scene told him he'd hit the mark. He'd grabbed a tablecloth from his apartment, which disguised the raw plywood of his makeshift table.

He'd set it with white plates from Easy Money, along with a vase with spring flowers Jen had snagged from a table in the restaurant.

Wineglasses reflected candlelight from stubby candles, and he'd chosen a mellow blues playlist to stream through his speaker.

"When did you do all this?" she asked. "It's beautiful."

"The string lights have been here, but I haven't used them much. Everything else I arranged this evening." He held out a chair. "Have a seat."

He used the corkscrew to uncork the wine.

"Can I help?"

"I got it." He handed her a wineglass. "Drink your wine and relax. Dinner is being kept warm in the oven. I'll bring it right out."

He needed to give Mario and Jen raises.

He opened the foil containers and plated golden pan-fried chicken with spiral pasta topped with mushroom sauce.

Adding roasted asparagus and soft dinner rolls, he carried the plates to the porch.

He took a seat and raised his wineglass. "To the future."

Her expression turned wary, but she raised her glass, tapping it to his. "To the future, whatever it may bring." Keeley took a bite of pasta drenched in sauce. "Oh, this is so good."

"It's my favorite on our menu. You haven't tried it?"

She shook her head. "You don't charge staff for meals, and I didn't want to cut into your profit by eating the fancy food."

He stared at her in disbelief. "You can eat anything you want. In fact, I rely on staff to give me feedback on the menu."

She shrugged. "I'm glad I haven't because then this wouldn't be such a wonderful indulgence."

He sampled his own dinner and agreed. It was damn good. They ate as the music flowed around them. The view from the porch brought the twinkling lights from Sisters into bright relief, and overhead, stars were strewn across the heavens.

"Did you give Sawyer the flash drive?"

"Yeah, he met me in the parking lot. He's really protective of you."

She paused with her fork halfway to her mouth. "What'd he say?"

"That I fucked up."

"Oh good heavens. Delaney and I talked. She must've told Cam who then told Sawyer."

"Sounds about right."

"Yeah, but Sawyer's your friend. I don't want to get between you. I wish he and Walker wouldn't treat me like I'm sixteen and in need of big brothers."

"I can deal with them. And Sawyer's right, I did fuck up."

She shook her head and the honey streaks in her hair gleamed in the candlelight.

"It's fine, Owen. I appreciate the effort you made tonight to set things right between us." She bit the end of an asparagus spear and chewed thoughtfully. "It's still better for me to stay with Delaney and Walker. I'll go in the morning."

He set down his wineglass. This was it. There was no going back.

"Don't go. I love you, Keeley. I want you to stay."

Her fork clattered onto her plate and her eyes grew wide. "You can't say that. You can't say that if we can't be together. It hurts too much."

"You've got me, Keeley. I don't want to fight it anymore." He gazed into her beautiful hazel eyes and saw his future.

"Everything I am is yours. Protecting myself from pain no longer works because it's painful to be apart from you." He took her hand, turning it over in his, brushing his thumb across her palm. "Do you remember the first time we met?"

She nodded. "It was at Easy Money. Delaney and I'd come in for a girls' night and you were behind the bar."

"You walked in, and I felt like I'd been hit by a bolt of sunlight. You were the most beautiful woman I'd ever seen, and you were so damn sweet."

"Oh please. Anytime we interacted, you seemed irritated."

He gave her a long look that had the color rising in her cheeks. "That was it, Keeley, that moment. From then on, I was always waiting for the next time I'd see you."

"That first time we were there to check you out."

"Yeah?"

She rolled her eyes at his grin. "Yeah. It was a little after you'd bought the place. You'd closed it for a couple weeks and there was a buzz around town about the new owner. Rumor was he was hot, and Delaney wanted to check you out."

"Delaney? Not you?"

"This was before Walker came back and she was trying to move past him emotionally. That plan never worked. But a hot young business owner in town? That's big news."

He scrubbed a hand over his face. "Shit. I thought it was strange so many women came in during the first couple months."

She giggled at his discomfort. "Yep, they were checking you out. I'll admit to doing my own checking," she said primly. "But then you acted nice to everyone else, but were so judge-y with me. That first night you said we were drinking girly drinks."

"You were drinking girly drinks."

"It was a strawberry margarita. That's not a girly drink."

"It's girly if the fruit is used to disguise the alcohol taste."

"No. It means I like strawberries, and that's a sexist attitude. And if that wasn't enough, you carded me."

"I got your name, didn't I? And learned you're four years younger than me."

"I thought you didn't like me."

"I liked you. I more than liked you."

"Seriously? You acted like I was underage, and then said it was probably a fake ID."

"Okay, they were stupid ploys to get you to talk to me."

"You could have tried being nice."

"I'm not known for nice."

He weaved his fingers through hers and pulled her to her feet.

She swayed toward him. "Every time I've come in for the past what, two years? You've been grumpy."

He pulled her closer and they swayed to the music. He dipped his head. "I was already in deep with you. It frustrated the hell out of me. I told myself I wasn't good for you, but that didn't stop me loving you."

She stared at him, her big eyes shadowy.

"Am I too late, princess?"

"Princesses are snooty and snobby."

"Not my princess." His lips drifted along her temple.

She arched her neck, and he took the invitation and nibbled the curve of warm skin. "My princess is beautiful on the inside. She's beautiful on the outside." His lips moved along her jaw and her breath caught. "My princess is good and sweet, and kind."

He nudged her chin up, searching her eyes, and repeated his question. "Am I too late? Can you still love me?"

She draped her arms around his neck. "I love you, Owen. I will never stop loving you."

He felt everything inside him align, and damn if that didn't feel exactly right.

"Good. That's good." He closed his eyes and let the warmth of love seep into his soul.

He felt like he was getting a second chance at life. He'd had to get out of his own way to embrace the future that was waiting right in front of him.

Opening his eyes again, he said, "I told you I was a risk, that I'm likely to destroy everything. You didn't heed the warning. Now I'm yours and you're mine. It's us together, princess."

He brought her hands to his mouth and pressed his lips to her knuckles.

"You won't destroy everything, Owen. We'll build something together."

He spun her around, ending their dance with a kiss full of promise. "Come with me. Let me take you to bed."

"Yes." She glanced at the remnants of their meal. "We need to clear the table first."

"I'll take care of it later."

She was already shaking her head. "You've lived here long enough to know the raccoons will help themselves if we leave this out."

As bad as he wanted her, they cleaned up.

Not that he didn't pull her hair aside to kiss the back of her neck while she was rinsing dishes at the kitchen sink.

Or that she didn't rub her ass against the bulge in his jeans when he stood behind her to reach into a cupboard.

By the time he backed her up to the edge of his bed his need for her was straining his grasp on sanity.

He'd never experienced this level of need scrambled together with feelings of love so intense that all he could see was her.

Her fingers went to his belt, and while his libido said *yes* and demanded he rut like a feral animal, his heart demanded something more.

Grappling for control, he nudged her back on the bed, took her hands in one of his.

"Slow down, princess. I want this to last."

His free hand dipped under the hem of her sweater, and he groaned when he traced bare skin across her rib cage and over a rounded breast to its peak. "No bra."

She tugged her hand free to pull down the front zipper on her sweater and he nudged the material aside. He dipped his nose to nuzzle her breast.

"No panties, either," she whispered.

He groaned. She worked his shirt up to his shoulders. "That doesn't help me go slow. If I'd known you were bare I'd never have made it through dinner."

He pulled his shirt over his head, then tugged off her sweater.

Her breasts were gloriously free before him, and he felt like the luckiest man on earth.

Her fingers returned to his belt, working the buckle loose. "Slow next time." She levered herself up to use her teeth to scrape along his neck. "Fast this time."

Her words broke the dam and he was flooded with a frenzy of need, matched only by her own. He fumbled for his wallet but managed to roll on protection.

Then he was there, poised at her entrance.

Gazes locked together, he plunged. She surged to meet him, wrapping her legs around his hips.

It was a wild ride. He held on to the tattered edges of control to make sure she was there with him.

It felt like they were touching everywhere and wasn't sure where his body stopped and hers began.

They moved together, climbing high and higher, reaching for the summit. Her body tightened around him, and she let out a keening cry met by one of his own, and holding her close, he felt like they were flying to the edge of the universe.

After, they lay together like survivors of a natural disaster. "I think I've gone blind," he murmured the words into her neck. He knew he was heavy but couldn't find the strength to move.

She gripped handfuls of his hair and pulled his head back. "Try opening your eyes."

He blinked. "Oh, that's better."

She grinned and he grinned right back. "Have I told you I love you?"

"Yeah," he murmured. "But you keep right on saying it. It's all I want to hear."

***

Later, they sat cross-legged on the bed, Owen in sweatpants and no shirt, Keeley in an unbuttoned flannel shirt of Owen's and no pants. On her knee, she was balancing a plate with a generous slice of cheesecake.

She fed Owen a bite, then took one herself.

She chewed slowly, eyes closed, making a mmm sound. "Oh my god, lemon meringue cheesecake. This is the best cheesecake ever." Her eyes were glazed over when they opened again. "You get your desserts from Three Sisters Bakery, so why have I never had this before? Rico's been holding out on me." She pointed her fork at him. "*You've* been holding out on me."

"I approached Rico about developing a cheesecake that he'd bake exclusively for Easy Money. We're in the sampling stage. He sent a chocolate option a couple days ago that was pretty good. He says Key lime is next."

"Why haven't I been in on this? I could be your official taste tester. Right now, my vote is for the lemon meringue. It would be a crime against humanity if this cheesecake isn't offered to the public."

"You haven't tried the others." He accepted another bite. She was right. It was damn good.

"Nothing could top lemon meringue cheesecake." Keeley fed them both until she laid a hand on her stomach. "I can't eat another bite." She settled back against the pillows, eyes closed. "I'm in a cheesecake coma."

Since his flannel shirt she was wearing had gaped open, and because there was a blob of lemon cheesecake topping still on the plate, he swiped it up with his finger and rubbed it over the pink tip of her breast.

"What are you—" She broke off when he swirled his tongue over the nipple before pulling it in his mouth and sucking deep. "Oh, good lord in heaven. Owen. You make me feel so much."

He released her and set the plate and fork safely aside.

"That's only fair, princess, because it's the same for me." He let his hand drift over her belly, softly stroking, then lower still. "This time it's slow, remember?"

She sighed and opened for him. "I remember. Love me, Owen."

"Always."

CHAPTER TWENTY-THREE

Keeley stepped onto the porch, a blanket around her shoulders and a steaming mug in her hand. A gusty wind brought the smell of rain. Clouds had moved in overnight, bringing in a spring storm.

She wasn't one to be up with the birds, but a noise had woken her and there was no going back to sleep.

Rolling over had brought her nose to nose with Owen. The half-light coming through the east-facing windows was enough for her to look her fill while he slept.

It wasn't fair that his eyelashes were so long the tips tangled together. The only way hers would ever look like that would be with extensions.

She loved how even in sleep scowl lines formed between his brows. Granted, they were soft scowl lines, but still.

When she had to catch herself before she ran a finger over those lines, she'd forced herself out of bed so he could sleep undisturbed. Lord knew they hadn't gotten much sleep during the night.

Owen Hardesty loved her. The knowledge felt like a warm sunbeam lighting her from within. The future was still murky, and it wasn't clear Owen had changed his stance on marriage and family. For now, they were together, and she would cherish what they had.

The view over the valley showed clouds obscuring the top of Payback Mountain. A flock of birds, ducks, she thought, flew north in a V formation.

She leaned against the rail and sipped from her mug. Then set it on the railing with a clunk. A vehicle was parked on the road in front of the house, all but the rear bumper obscured by a clump of live oak. She thought again about what had awakened her. Had it been a car door closing?

Cars could park on the street. That was perfectly legal. But why on a residential road so early in the morning? And why in front of the address where she was staying?

She chewed her bottom lip. She didn't want to be paranoid, but Jaxon had made bail and was free to be his weird and foreboding self.

The Ravagers had given her a reprieve but could've decided to pay her a visit. She supposed motorcycle gang members might also drive cars. It'd be hard for Mr. Paulson, aka Nero, to take his granddaughter to school on a motorcycle.

She needed Owen. She picked up her mug and turned to the house.

A man stood with his back to the closed door. He must've crept around the porch from the side without her noticing.

In the periphery of her vision, she was aware his shirt was bloody, his face bloodier still. Her focus narrowed so all she saw was the black muzzle of the pistol he held, pointing at her dead center. The mug slipped from her fingers to smash to the floor and the smell of coffee permeated the air.

"Where's the asshole?"

"I don't know what you're talking about."

"It's not a good idea to piss me off, Keeley. Where is he?"

"Owen's still in bed, Jaxon. Asleep."

"Good. We'll keep it that way. Now tell me where the flash drive is. Give it to me and you'll never see me again. I wouldn't be here if you'd handed it over when I first asked."

She clutched the blanket tighter around her like it would shield her from a bullet. She took a step toward the stairs.

"You never asked me for it, Jaxon. You said I had something of yours but not what it was. I didn't know you were looking for a flash drive." Another step. She froze when broken crockery scraped the wooden floor, but Jaxon didn't appear to notice.

He looked haggard, like he hadn't slept in days, and his face had fresh bruises on top of older bruises. He'd always been fastidious about his personal grooming, but the mustache he'd kept carefully waxed was bristly and looked like it'd been smashed into his face.

Half his hair had fallen loose from the bun at the back of his head. Keeley'd bet her next cup of coffee the Ravagers had caught up with him and demonstrated their displeasure with his behavior.

"You know now. I had a flash drive I needed to keep in a safe place. I put it in the inner pocket of your purse." He spoke slowly like he was speaking to a child. She struggled to hear past her heart pounding in her ears.

She took another careful step toward the stairs from the porch. If she could get down the stairs, she could dart away. She'd run to the back of the house and find a way to alert Owen. There were construction materials and the rollaway. Maybe she could find someplace to hide.

Jaxon moved toward her, wagging the muzzle of the gun. "Into the house." He gestured toward the door with the gun. "Don't even think about alerting the asshole. He shows his face? I'll shoot him dead."

His words chilled her to the bone. He waved the gun again. "Pam brought me your purse, but the flash drive wasn't there. You must've found it, and I need it back. It's the only leverage I have over the fucking Ravagers."

"You killed Pam." Keeley no longer felt surprise at the knowledge he was capable of such depravity. "You were using her. She stole my purse, then you killed her when the flash drive wasn't there."

"She wanted me." He smiled and Keeley shuddered in revulsion. "You saw her at that party. She could hardly keep her hands off me. She got herself into trouble."

How could she have ever thought him charming? Keeley couldn't believe she hadn't seen him for what he was. When they'd first met, Jaxon had put on an act of being affable and easygoing, and she'd bought it.

"I would've been forced to kill her even if it had been there. She'd have blabbed to someone." He shrugged. "Whatever. She deserved what she got. Pam failed, and it's caused me nothing but grief. She was supposed to bring the purse with the flash drive, and she failed."

He seemed distracted and Keeley risked another step toward the stairs. Then Jaxon lunged forward and grabbed her arm, taking her elbow in a vise-like grip. He jerked her to the door. "We go in quiet. Get me the flash drive, and you and I will never have to see each other again."

Keeley kept her eyes moving, and her mind racing, looking for a way to escape or something she could use as a weapon.

There were other ways Jaxon could've used the information he'd stolen for his extortion bid beyond storing it on a flash drive. Like everything else, he wasn't good at being a criminal.

She wasn't about to tell him she didn't have the device. He was convinced she'd found it and therefore must still have it. He'd killed Pam so she couldn't identify him. He'd kill Keeley for the same reason. But if he thought she had the flash drive, she was safe. She hoped.

He shoved her at the door. "Open it."

She pushed the door open and stepped across the threshold.

And was yanked loose of Jaxon's hold and shoved behind six foot plus of enraged Owen. The next few moments were a blur of motion.

One second Jaxon was behind her with a gun. The next he'd been slammed against the door frame and Owen had wrenched the gun from his hand. He shoved it at Keeley. "Take it and stay back. He does anything you don't like, shoot him."

He grabbed Jaxon by his shirt and dragged him outside.

She was *not* shooting anyone.

She dropped the blanket onto a stack of lumber and shoved the gun under it before rushing to the open doorway.

Thunder cracked overhead and rain began pelting out of the sky.

Owen hauled Jaxon onto the porch, and holding him one-handed, plowed a fist into his face. Crushing bone made a wet squishing sound and Jaxon's head snapped back. Owen hit him again, a fist to the gut, then one to the jaw.

Jaxon gave an agonized groan, his eyes rolling back, and he went limp. When Owen drew his fist back again, Keeley grabbed his arm.

"Stop, Owen. Stop." His arm felt like coiled steel. "He's unconscious. You have to stop. You'll kill him."

Owen tried to shake her off, but she only tightened her grip. "Let him go. He's no longer a threat."

Owen turned to her, his eyes burning with rage. "He had a gun pointed at you. He wanted to kill you. He hurt you and scared you. He doesn't deserve to live."

"I'm safe, Owen. You saved me, and he's done."

With his gaze still locked on hers, Owen released Jaxon, who dropped to the floor, his head hitting with a thunk.

Owen's fury abated, and in a flash he was pulling Keeley into a desperate embrace, clutching her to him like the world was chaos and only she was keeping him from spinning out of control.

They stayed locked together, her face buried in his neck, his in her hair. Sirens wailed in the distance. He didn't loosen his hold until patrol cars were streaming up his driveway.

***

Keeley sat in a chair on the porch. She was losing count of how many times the police had responded to something involving her. She hoped with all her heart this was the last time. An ambulance crew had taken Jaxon away in restraints. Owen had glowered at her when he'd recovered the gun from where she'd hidden it under the blanket.

He'd been awakened by the shattering mug. Thank god, he'd figured out what was happening and things had turned out the way they had.

She watched him in the driveway talking with Sawyer, who was not on duty but had come when Owen had called.

Keeley took out her phone. Her mom picked up on the second ring.

"Hi, Mom. First thing, we're okay. Owen's safe. I'm safe."

"Tell me what's happened."

"I'm at Owen's. Jaxon showed up with a gun." Keeley shared what happened while her mom peppered questions throughout the story.

"Oh my. I'm so glad Owen was there. I swear that man would throw himself in front of a moving train if he thought it would keep you safe."

"He loves me."

Her mom's smile sounded in her voice. "I know he does. I see it every time he lays eyes on you." She paused. "I don't want to get ahead of anything, but I can't help it. Are there wedding bells in the future?"

"I don't know. It's all new." Keeley moved to the end of the porch where she wouldn't be overheard. "He shared what happened to him, Mom. It was bad. Really bad. It's up to him to tell you about it. But because of that trauma he never wants to get married or have children. He blames himself and doesn't want to risk that kind of pain again. My heart breaks for him."

"He's strong, and now that he has you, he might reconsider."

"I don't know if he will." Owen and Sawyer climbed the stairs to the porch. "I'll talk with you more later. Give my love to Dad and Auntie Carla. Bye, Mom."

***

The days following Jaxon's arrest flew by. The judge ordered him held without bail, and that kept him sitting in a jail cell. Keeley would have to testify, but she was no longer in danger.

With her parents back from visiting Aunt Carla, Keeley moved back to her cottage.

Owen spent his time off with her and she was happy. Giddy happy. Even if marriage wasn't in their future, she wasn't going to worry about it.

For now, living in the present was good enough.

On an afternoon when the sun shone brightly, the storm from earlier in the week having left only mud puddles, the rumble of a motorcycle drew her and Owen's attention. They were sitting at her little patio table enjoying the warm afternoon.

Keeley recognized Nero as he rode up the driveway to stop in front of her garage, another rider holding tight behind him. The passenger let go of Nero and swung off the bike. She took off her helmet and shook out her long black hair. Keeley rushed forward to engulf Destiny in a hug.

"Hi, Miss Montaigne." The pretty girl returned the hug. When she pulled back, she grinned, silver wires glinting on her teeth.

"Oh my, Destiny, you got braces."

"Grampa says he liked my smile just fine, but I'm glad my teeth won't be crooked anymore."

Owen stood at her elbow and Keeley could tell by his watchful expression that he was ready for anything. Keeley had no such qualms. Nero wouldn't cause any trouble with his granddaughter present. He shed his own helmet, and Keeley led her unexpected guests to the patio.

They sat at the table, and Destiny caught up Keeley on what her friends were doing. Abby spotted the surprise guests and waved. She brought out a plate of cookies, and after a short conversation, invited Destiny to the house to meet Iggy.

After encouraging her to take up Abby's offer, Nero watched until his granddaughter was out of earshot before turning to Keeley.

"Got somethin' to share with you both that I'm not ready for my girl to know about." He pulled on his long beard, then proceeded to explain an agreement he'd come to with the district attorney.

Law enforcement hadn't been able to access the encrypted flash drive. Keeley thought Jaxon would be happy to give up the password as part of a plea agreement, but the district attorney had other ideas.

He'd chosen to throw everything he had at Jaxon including the murder charge, and after long discussions with the Ravagers top officers, had proposed an agreement. The sheriff would hold on to the flash drive but would not pursue efforts to access its contents. In return, the Ravagers would give up their criminal activities.

"DA knows our organization has never been involved in human trafficking, and we weren't part of the drugs or gun trade.

"Now, I'm not sayin' what we'd done in the past was exactly legal, but Ravager businesses only skirted the edges of the law. There's evidence of said enterprises on that flash drive, but the DA's always struck me as a principled man. I'm trusting him to keep his word."

"I'm so glad, Nero," Keeley said. "I didn't like Destiny being exposed to that sort of lifestyle."

Nero gave her a long look. "It was talking to you the other day that convinced me to get off the dime and make the changes I'd been considerin' for a while. My son's in prison and I didn't like that my girl might grow up to think criminal behavior was okay. I don't want her to end up in prison." He shrugged. "A lot of us Ravagers are old-timers. We got kids, some of us like me got grandkids. We don't want them caught up in the life."

"So no more Ravagers? That's got to be hard for you."

His blue eyes crinkled at the corners as he smiled. "Not so hard because we're not disbanding. We're still a motorcycle club, but with a new purpose. We're establishing a nonprofit to support our community. We've got some money and connections to get us started. Our focus is helping families in crisis get big things like housing and transportation. But little things too, like diapers and eyeglasses for those who need it."

Keeley studied Nero's weathered face. "That's good work, Mr. Paulson, and Destiny's future is already brighter."

He nodded as Destiny returned and a little later after a last hug good-bye, Keeley and Owen watched the pair ride away. Owen said, "My guess, they probably ran chop shops for stolen cars."

Leaning back against him as he stood with an arm around her, she murmured, "What they're doing now is the best possible outcome. There's such good in the world and it outshines the bad every single time."

She felt his arm tighten and tipped her head back to see his face. "You okay?"

He turned her to face him and caught her in a kiss that warmed her all the way through. "You're the good outshining the bad," he murmured. "I feel like the luckiest man alive."

His body responded in the most delicious of ways. "Yeah? I think you might get even luckier."

CHAPTER TWENTY-FOUR

"Oh man, this is so good," Keeley murmured. She was leaning back on the sofa in the living room of the big house.

Cam and Sawyer had invited their group to the big house at Cider Mill Farm for potluck game night, and Owen's contribution was Rico's latest sample for the exclusive Easy Money cheesecake.

Emery licked her fork. "Who'd have thought Key lime would be so, so delicious. I could live off this." She offered a bite and Shane opened his mouth to accept, his hands busy rubbing her feet.

"No kidding," Cam agreed. "I think Rico's Key lime cheesecake will now be my number one pregnancy craving." She stretched like a cat as Sawyer massaged the ball of her right foot. Willa lay on her back against Cam's leg, four little paws in the air.

After playing team Pictionary, the women were enjoying post-game bliss.

"Looking pretty smug there, princess," Owen murmured.

"Feeling pretty smug. We whooped your butts." Keeley moaned when his thumb delved into her arch. "You can keep doing that. Timer's still going."

"Girls are smarter," Delaney pronounced, sighing when Walker's hands moved up to her shins. "Get used to it."

"Girls cheat, you mean. I ought to arrest every one of you," Sawyer griped.

"For being able to draw more than a stick figure?" Cam shot back.

"I think this one," Shane pointed to his wife, "was doing something tricky with the dice."

"We whooped your butts," Keeley repeated. "Deal with it."

"Foot massages for the winners, and cheesecake for everyone is the best idea ever," Emery pronounced.

Keeley fed Owen a bite, then took another for herself.

Owen leaned forward and whispered, "If the dudes had won, it wouldn't be my feet you'd be massaging."

"Don't disturb my cheesecake coma with your sexy insinuations, Owen Hardesty."

"I thought you said the lemon meringue is the best cheesecake ever."

"I did, but now I'm eating Key lime and it's delicious. I don't know how you'll choose Easy Money's exclusive cheesecake. They're all so good."

The timer went off marking the end of foot massages. Walker leaned forward and laid his head on his wife's belly.

"We heard the baby's heartbeat at the clinic this morning." Delaney ran her fingers through Walker's dark hair. "This guy thinks he should be able to hear it."

"I can't wait until our appointment next week," Cam said. "We're hoping to hear ours."

Keeley laced her fingers with Owen's. He'd been through the expectations of a pregnancy before. It had to be painful for him, but he didn't look upset. He brought up their joined hands to his cheek.

With a sigh she let go of his hand and pushed herself off the couch to gather plates.

Delaney followed her into the kitchen bringing wine glasses and beer bottles.

"Hey, friend," Keeley said, bumping Delaney with her hip.

"Hey back. You okay?"

Startled, Keeley caught Delaney's gaze. "Of course. Why wouldn't I be?

Delaney shrugged. "We're all married. There's lots of talk of babies. You said Owen doesn't want marriage and a family, and I know you do."

Keeley's shoulders slumped. "That's true." She shrugged. "I can't make him want the same things I want. It's okay."

"It's not okay, Keeley. I want you to have everything you've ever wanted."

"Right now, Owen's everything I want. Really. I'm fine."

Delaney pulled her into a brief hug. Stepping back, Keeley caught sight of Owen standing in the doorway, the box with the remnants of the cheesecake in his hands and his brows drawn low over his eyes.

He shoved the box onto the counter and grabbed Keeley's hand. "Come with me."

"Where are we going?"

"Outside." Without breaking stride, he towed her out of the house and down the flagstone path to the pergola. Fairy lights twinkled overhead, and the scent of wisteria perfumed the air. He dropped her hand to stand with his hands on his hips.

"We're getting married."

"What?"

"You told Delaney you're fine. That's girl code for not fine. I don't want you unhappy. We'll get married."

Her heart gave a hard lurch in her chest, then sank. She wanted Owen, and she wanted to marry him. But not like this.

"You'll marry me because I'm unhappy?"

"Yeah. We'll get married, and if you want a couple kids, I'm good with that. Hell, we could have three or four if that's what you want."

This was not how she imagined Owen proposing marriage. Or how they'd have the important discussion on whether to have kids.

He thought he was giving her what she wanted but had left out the heart and soul. She crossed her arms in front of her like she would ward off a chill. "What changed your mind?"

Owen gestured toward the house. "They're all married. They're all having kids. That's what you said you wanted, so that's what we'll do."

Keeley felt a layer of ice forming over her heart. Ice was a good thing. Maybe being frozen would keep her heart from breaking.

"You're saying we should get married and have kids because that's what our friends are doing."

"No." He scrubbed his hands over his face and paced the width of the shelter. "I mean, yes. You want marriage and kids. You've been looking for a man, and you even have a fucking dating app. You went out with the asshole Jaxon, for god's sake. No more. We love each other so you'll marry me."

"No, thank you." She suddenly felt as fragile as ice crystals forming on the surface of a pond. "I need to go."

"What do you mean you need to go? I just asked you to marry me."

"No, Owen, that's not what you did. Tell the others good-bye for me."

She was wrong. Ice wasn't working to keep her heart from shattering. When she would have rushed past him, he grabbed her arm, but she reeled back. "Don't. Don't touch me."

He released her but didn't step back. She hitched a shoulder to wipe the dampness from her cheek.

He looked like he'd been struck on the head by a sledgehammer. "Oh shit, you're crying. I made you cry. I fucked up. I'm sorry."

"Don't worry about it. Not your problem." She tried to edge past him.

"Let me fix it, Keeley. Please don't leave."

She gave a watery laugh. "You can't fix this like a leaky faucet, Owen."

"I've hurt you. I love you more than anything in this world, and I hurt you. I'm sorry."

He looked upset and desperate, and because she loved him, she almost relented.

It would be so easy to simply go along with his non-proposal and make the best of it. But there would be an emptiness in that life that would eventually tear them apart.

She stiffened her backbone, breathed in through her nose, then out through her lips. "I love you, Owen, more than anything in this world, too. I also want a future that includes marriage and family. But right now, I don't want that with you."

"Why the hell not?"

"I'd rather be single than with someone who won't commit. I want marriage because it's the highest expression of our love and commitment to each other, not because our friends are married.

"I want children with a man who loves them, who will cherish them. You want me and because I want kids, you threw them in like a signing bonus."

She laid a hand on his chest. "I don't want children with you if you can't emotionally engage with them. You lost Robby and it broke your heart. You're closing yourself off because you don't want to risk that again." She rose to her toes and kissed him on the cheek. "I understand that, but it's not healthy for you, and I won't have children with a man who can't love them with his whole heart."

When she would have stepped back, he grasped her hands. "Give me a minute, princess." He tipped his head back, eyes closed, clutching her hands tighter. She saw his throat work as he swallowed. A deep breath expanded his lungs and when he looked at her again moisture glinted in his eyes.

"You're right," he said gruffly. "I'm a coward."

"You're not—"

"I am, princess. I thought I could have you and still protect myself from being hurt like I'd been before. It about ended me when Gloria and Robby were killed.

"I didn't love Gloria, didn't seem capable of it. But she was my wife and the mother of my son, and I was committed to our relationship. Robby though," he breathed deep. "He had such a light in him and it absolutely gutted me when he died."

"I know, Owen. I'm so sorry."

In the way he had, he framed her face with his big hands, his eyes shining. "I'll love them, Keeley. I'll love our children. I won't hold back to keep from being hurt. I promise you."

He took another deep shuddering breath. "Let me try this again. Will you marry me, princess? Will you love me as I love you? Will you have a family with me and make the kitchen the heart of our home exactly like you described?"

Love and commitment. Owen was willing to put his heart on the line, to risk having it broken again, to build a life with her.

The love in her heart swelled and she felt like it beamed from her like rays of sunlight.

She turned her face to press her lips to his palm. "You're the strongest man I know. Thank you for trusting me with your love."

She brought her arms up around his neck as his encircled her. Looking into his warm blue eyes, she saw the future unfolding before them, a future of love, family, and friends.

She smiled through her tears. "Yes, I'll marry you and make a family with you. I love you, Owen."

"I love you back, princess. Always."

***Release date Spring '25 for last book in the
Payback Mountain series***

ABOUT THE AUTHOR

USA TODAY Bestselling Author, Diane Benefiel has been an avid reader all her life. She enjoys a wide range of genres, from westerns to fantasy to mysteries, but romance is her favorite. She writes what she loves best to read—emotional, heart-gripping romantic suspense novels. In her stories, she puts the heroes and heroines in all sorts of predicaments that they have to work together to overcome. Her novel, *Solitary Man* was a National Readers' Choice Award winner.

A native Southern Californian, Diane enjoys nothing better than summer. For a high school history teacher, summer means a break from students, and time immersed in her current writing project. With both kids grown and gone, she enjoys her leisure time camping, especially in the Sierras, and gardening, both with her husband.

Diane loves hearing from her readers.

Website: dianebenefiel.com
Twitter: twitter.com/dianebenefiel
Instagram: @diane_benefiel
TikTok: @diane_benefiel_romance
Pinterest: diane_benefiel
Facebook: /DianeBenefielRomance
BookBub: /authors/diane-benefiel
Goodreads: /author/show/8075321.Diane_Benefiel
Newsletter: https://landing.mailerlite.com/webforms/landing/n1i2u8

Sign up for Diane's newsletter for sneak peeks and inside info on her new series.

www.BOROUGHSPUBLISHINGGROUP.com

If you enjoyed this book, please write a review. Our authors appreciate the feedback, and it helps future readers find books they love. We welcome your comments and invite you to send them to info@boroughspublishinggroup.com.

Follow us on TikTok and Instagram, and be sure to sign up for our newsletter for surprises and new releases from your favorite authors.

Are you an aspiring writer? Check out www.boroughspublishinggroup.com/submit and see if we can help you make your dreams come true.
Love podcasts? Enjoy ours at

https://boroughspublishinggroup.com/podcast.

Made in the USA
Middletown, DE
05 November 2024

63615225R00149